Teaching Piano

The Synthesis of Mind, Ear and Body

Teaching Piano

The Synthesis of Mind, Ear and Body

A concise pedagogical approach for prospective and experienced teachers on the development of a pianist's learning and performing skills from the beginning phases of study through intermediate levels.

Max W. Camp

Alfred Publishing Co., Inc., Los Angeles

ISBN: softcover 0-88284-527-6
        hardcover 0-88284-526-8
Item No.: softcover 6032
           hardcover 6518

To all my students, past and present

CONTENTS

PART TWO
THE SIX STAGES OF COMPLEXITY

MUSIC EXAMPLES

xvi

PREFACE

The title, *Teaching Piano: The Synthesis of Mind, Ear and Body*, vividly describes what the book is all about. It examines the all-encompassing role of rhythm and its relationship to mental perception, the ear and the body, and the crucial need to understand this relationship in piano teaching. Using the prodigy as a model, a system for teaching and performing at the piano has been formulated to develop all types of piano students: the very talented, the average student and the slow learner.

The book should be helpful as a text for pedagogy classes as well as for any teachers who are interested in better understanding the teaching and learning process from the beginning stages of a student's development. It also should serve as an important resource for experienced teachers who instruct students at the advanced level. I strongly believe that learning and performing music at the advanced level is not unique; it is only more complex.

The book is divided into two parts. Part One presents the overall pedagogical foundation and discusses the effect that one's beginning years of study has upon all future musical development, regardless of talent. Part Two describes the elementary level of study in terms of six stages of complexity. Key concepts of the six stages are examined and illustrated with recommended literature suggestions for a core curriculum and supplementary materials. Some alternate literature suggestions are included for students who prefer a less classically oriented program of study.

Within the realm of the six stages, the progression of both notational and musical complexities are outlined from the beginning phases of teaching pre-staff notation and intervallic map-reading through the presentation of a variety of musical textures, forms and compositional devices inherent in music from the different style periods. The presentation of the music examples from the baroque, classical, romantic, impressionistic and 20th century styles should be invaluable to teachers in instructing their students on style interpretation.

The effect of notational and musical complexities upon physical coordination and psychomotor development is examined as well as the many aspects of learning to be an excellent teacher who is a "super diagnostician." Suggestions are given to help the teacher avoid the pitfalls of making poor literature choices that result in the student experiencing physical coordination problems.

The outlined stages should help teachers assess the advancement of their students regardless of what method books are being used. Relating that Justin is in the Level 2 books of series X or that Jonathan is in Book 3 of series Y only relates those facts. This is because the leveling system differs so widely from one method series to another.

Describing a student's level of achievement in terms of length of study is also problematic. Wynn may have advanced more in one year than Ann did in three years of study. The presentation of complexities within each stage will give teachers an established point of reference in identifying their students' progress as well as offering guidelines for verifying the advancement level of transfer students.

The stages are not self-contained units nor do they represent any prescribed length of study. The stages only describe the rise in the overall complexity of music, both notational and musical. Within the descriptions, the complexities have been discussed in terms of how the rise affects the student's mental, rhythmic, aural and technical controls. The result is a comprehensive presentation of how music becomes more challenging not only to read but xx

also to perform as different types of textures and styles emerge. The synthesis of the six stages should help teachers make better literature choices for all of their students whether they are normal learners, musically gifted or those who encounter more problems with learning than the average student.

The prescribed philosophy represents the knowledge and experience that I have gained from over 25 years of teaching piano to young students, college undergraduate and graduate students, and from conducting pedagogy classes for 20 years. I believe the combination of experiences has offered me the exciting opportunity to understand the teaching process from the beginning phases of learning and performing through the advanced level of study.

ACKNOWLEDGMENTS

I am very grateful to the many people who have assisted me in the formulation and writing of this book. First, I must thank the numerous piano students who have passed through my studio bringing to me many exciting aspects of learning and performing at the piano. At times, perhaps my most advanced students have presented me with wonderful insights into the total learning and performing process. At other times, it has been the young child who has "shown me the way" to solving problems with the advanced student. Perhaps I have learned the most from students who presented me with the most problems as this provided me with the need to do more soul-searching. How wonderful it has been to have experienced the wonders of learning and performing with so many different types of students. I owe all of these people enormous gratitude for letting me share in their development.

I am very grateful to many former and present students who assisted me with ideas, criticism, editorial suggestions and encouragement. I owe special gratitude to Stephen Cook, Betty Blevins and Carolyn Arnold Karpinos for their critical guidance in editorial matters and thoughts for improving the pedagogical coherence of the book. Other present and former students who willingly gave valuable criticism and assisted in proofreading include: Louella Gibson, Jeanine Skinner, Deanna Young, Stephen Taylor, Ann Wilson and Jane Bader. I would like to cite Georgia Cowart for her helpful editorial comments and give special thanks to Willard A. Palmer and E. L. Lancaster for their advice on the coherence of the book.

I am especially grateful to the person who originally believed in my talents as a young teacher and was instrumental in bringing me to the University of South Carolina: Dr. Arthur Fraser, deceased, a former head of the Department of Music. I am also indebted to Dr. William Moody, past Director of the School of Music at the University of South Carolina and the present director, Dr. Manuel Alvarez, for their support and encouragement in the project.

An acknowledgment is made to the publishers who kindly granted me permission to reprint copyrighted music examples. Although these acknowledgments are stated in citations in the text, I would like to express my special thanks to them: Alfred Publishing Co. Inc., Boston Music Co., The Willis Music Co., Carl Fischer, Neil A. Kjos Music Co., E. C. Schirmer-Boston, Chester Music Ltd., G. Schirmer, Inc., CPP/Belwin, Inc., Hal Leonard Publishing Corp. and Betsy Barrett, composer.

Special gratitude goes to Morton and Iris Manus and all the staff members at Alfred Publishing Co. who have been so very helpful in assisting me in the many phases of the publication, especially with editorial and production matters. They have been most encouraging throughout the entire publishing project.

PART ONE

A Pedagogical Synthesis

INTRODUCTION

A large portion of a child's musical experience, in the past few decades, has centered on the concept of "learn the piece and win the prize!" To a large extent, this has been true for both private lessons and public school music programs. Less effort has gone into developing students so that they can function musically after lessons have ceased. Preparing for musical competitions can be a great incentive for studying music, but many times it fails to provide children with an understanding of how to learn and interpret music well enough to continue music-making independently of a teacher.

Music competitions definitely have a place in the American music scene, but perhaps we have made them the raison d'être of children's musical experience. Many piano students spend a complete year learning a few "hard" pieces, hoping for a superior rating at the next piano festival. Band students concentrate on football shows or marching band competitions, and choral groups direct their efforts toward the next state choral festival. The most gifted children survive and many others experience excellent musical training. Yet across the board, thousands of students will stop making music when lessons cease. The reason: too many students are unable to understand "how the music goes," or in some cases, to comprehend what the symbols on the page represent. People continue to read newspapers and magazines after formal schooling ends. With music, however, many music students are finding it easier to listen to a cassette player or to watch MTV.

Piano teachers continue to search for better approaches to teaching piano to children, especially at the elementary level. The search brings up a number of important questions. How can teachers keep their students interested? Which method series books are most effective? What is the best approach to teaching musical interpretation? Many teachers may feel that they have found satisfactory answers to the first two questions but continue to search for a more conclusive answer to the third. Are teachers still influenced by the old 19th-century ideas on teaching musical interpretation? Has there been any change during the past few decades? Most definitely there has been a change, but many teachers continue to depend on the old 19th-century imitative approach, thus ignoring many of the 20th-century ideas on developing a musician.

From the beginning of the 20th century, most teachers attempted to hand down "interpretive secrets" from the old European masters. Students learned interpretations of works by imitating their teachers who, in turn, learned from their teachers in a kind of apostolic succession. But as a means of developing a child musically, this method is now regarded as being very limited because the underlying principles of musical understanding and rhythmic control are neglected. Instead of promoting musical independence, this approach actually retards or precludes it. Rather than strictly imitating another person's interpretation, the phenomenon of learning how to make music should occur within the child. We now know that the task of learning and performing music should be experienced cognitively, emotionally and physically. Irwin Freundlich, the esteemed Juilliard piano teacher, thought that:

> *In order to communicate to a young person the essence of the problem of performance, of projecting a musical work, it is not sufficient simply to say to the young person, this is the way it goes. Do likewise. Imitation is an obsolete method of teaching.* [1]

A child or an adult is unable to respond emotionally to a teacher's aural image of a musical idea. The same is true for the aspect of physical response. Physical response to rhythmic patterns cannot be based upon another person's rhythmic understanding. Tonal relation-

4

ships are impossible to judge through another person's auditory system. Rather than just learning to imitate their teachers, the musical experiences of children should be based upon a developmental system for learning that will foster the many aspects of musical performance, including aural, rhythmic and physical controls.

Rhythm continues to baffle students and teachers alike. Although it is difficult to teach, we certainly know when it's lacking. Rhythm is like electricity—we can't see it, but we definitely know when it is not there. Piano teachers constantly are pointing out that "the rhythm is wrong." Musicians have trouble explaining it. All during the 20th century, piano teachers and critics have called for the development of rhythm. Some very young children show a natural sense of rhythm, yet many professional musicians continue to struggle with it.

Sometimes a music score calls for the rhythm to be unrelenting. Other times the score suggests that it should be very expressive. The word *rhythm* means different things to different people. To some musicians, the word refers only to note values or to the mathematical bookkeeping in music. To others, especially those who have an innate sense of it, rhythm refers to the recurring swing in music that encompasses all aspects of learning and performing. By becoming aware of the relationship between the rhythmic organization of music and the perceiving, learning and performing of rhythm, one begins to understand the essence of developing a child rhythmically. Since most music generally is organized metrically by composers, except the liturgical chant of the Middle Ages and aleatoric music of the 20th century, the study of the metrical organization of musical ideas is the most obvious and practical way to foster learning, interpretation and performance even from the beginning years of a child's musical training.

Music teachers have long recognized that children who have an intuitive sense for feeling rhythm tend to learn music more easily and perform more successfully. This intuition implies that a person has a natural instinct toward hearing and feeling tempo and rhythm or pulse without going through a set of intellectual processes. *Pulse,* used more and more interchangeably with the word *rhythm,* is the rhythmic swing or beat in music that makes us "nod our heads" and "tap our feet." Pulse is the element in music that organizes our listening. In rock music, it's what "rattles the rafters" though in slow lyrical music, the pulse is of a more subtle nature. Pulse is the aspect of music that makes the notes on the page come alive. Dancers organize their movements to it. Jazz players "feel it in their bones." Although the pulse is sometimes more difficult to perceive in classical music, child prodigies tend to sense and feel it intuitively.

The pulse or rhythmic beat in music must be understood, heard and felt before a tempo can be determined, because that's the unit that sets up the tempo of a piece. Pulse is also the rhythmic unit which guides the continuity of physical motions at the piano and fosters the understanding of phrase shapes, sections and complete compositions. For example, as students understand and grasp a feeling for what is a small-unit grouping, such as the pulse, these groupings can be understood at higher architectonic levels. This is when smaller ideas combine to form larger ideas in a musical setting, such as the phrase, section or complete composition. This is needed because music is like our language: letters group to form words, words group to form sentences and sentences group to form paragraphs and so forth. Both music and language are basically architectonic in nature. Children learn to read letters or words, then phrases and complete stories. The same should be true for reading music. After note values are understood and sensed aurally, the pulse-unit should serve as a "beginning whole" which leads one to grasp phrases, the relationship of phrases and ultimately the complete piece.

An understanding and feeling for pulse helps promote the holistic perception of music symbols, the emotional reaction to the symbols, the shape of the aural image and the organization of the motor skills needed to produce the image. There is mounting evidence of a strong relationship between success in learning and performing music and one's natural instinct toward perceiving music in metrically grouped pulse patterns. This instinct implies that a person has the ability to perceive pitches and their rhythmic values in definite strong-weak or weak-strong relationships as they occur within a meter, such as 2/4 or 3/4. For example, note values within a 3/4 meter would group to form a strong-weak-weak pattern, which is delineated by a strong or natural metric accent occurring on the downbeat of the measure. Natural accents on downbeats refer to the relative strength of the downbeat or to the relative strength of the primary and secondary accents in 4/4 meter, not necessarily to the dynamics of that beat.

Performers and listeners may react with some bodily response to downbeats, and they may strongly hear it coming, but that doesn't necessarily mean that downbeats are dynamically loud. Pulse is like one's heartbeat. We hope that it keeps recurring, and it certainly is crucial, but we don't want to be jolted every time it happens. Music is similar. We don't want to be jolted dynamically every time a downbeat occurs, but we do need to sense inwardly when it happens because it helps organize our listening as it signifies the beginning of a new circle of musical motion. Natural metric accents are rallying points for further musical motion. After one natural accent occurs, both the performer and listener feel the pull to the next one.

Musical motion doesn't stop at the rallying point; it continues through and on to the next one. It is this aspect of music that makes it continuous. Even young students should learn to feel the strength and pull of it, yet it must not be considered as always loud. Accentual treatment, first suggested during the 19th century, is advocated by some pedagogues as a means of promoting a student's consciousness of pulse or rhythmic grouping. This treatment entails dynamically accenting the pitches occurring on the first beat of a pulse grouping— Loud-soft-soft as a means of fostering the student's awareness of how notes group to form strong-weak rhythmic units. The LOUD-soft-soft treatment gradually will evolve into an inner feeling for sensing the grouping. The loud should serve as a mental–aural reminder only of the beginning strength of a pulse grouping, not the dynamics of the beginning. The dynamic accent must gradually be de-emphasized and later replaced by only an internalization of its feeling. The student must understand not only the concept, but the need for perceiving the concept aurally. Without any aural consideration, the concept of loud on each downbeat is difficult to de-emphasize and internalize. The key to successful implementation of accentual treatment, as a means of getting students to feel grouping, lies within the aural conception of the accent. The concept should never be practiced mechanically.

Sensing or feeling how notes group into strong-weak patterns is not something that is written out on the score, but is the result of the interaction of melody, harmony, rhythm and texture. The student has to sense grouping intuitively or grasp it through understanding the relationships of all musical elements present. Here lies the problem: many people are not able to sense grouping intuitively and many others have not experienced instruction that provides the basic tools for understanding grouping and feeling it. As a result, we have a large number of students who find learning and performing music an unorganized and frustrating experience.

All rhythmic grouping affects motor skill development because physical motions are reactions to mental commands. How students perceive a music score controls their physical responses. That is to say if students perceive music from an unorganized metrical standpoint, e.g., by separate note values or by motives, then those students are training their psychomotor activity to function outside a basic metered-pulse organization. This results in students having one set of actions for learning music and another set for performing it. The student "learns the notes" and then the teacher teaches him "how it goes." Having two separate "tracks" affects a child's development of motor skills in piano playing and decreases the chances of developing his or her full musical potential. The system for developing motor skills in learning music should be related directly to how the system needs to function in performing music.

Motor skill development is dependent upon sensing and understanding many rhythmic variables. These variables may be grouped basically into two categories:

1. Metered rhythms—those implied by patterns of strong and weak beats
2. Motivic rhythms—those consisting of various durational patterns that can be seen on the score[2]

These durational patterns may begin or end at any point within the strong-weak grouping of a measure or groups of measures. Thus, measures and groups of measures can have a strong-weak relationship analogous to the strong-weak relationship that beats have within a measure.

When a child learns to read music, the motivic rhythm can easily dominate that child's perception of the symbols, because the motivic rhythm is what one actually sees on the page. The metered rhythm is rhythm that is sensed intuitively or understood and felt after studying the interaction of the elements and the general musical texture. Children who intuitively perceive music in metered rhythm learn more quickly because they have not had to go through so many stages of trial and error. The organization is there from the beginning: the timed perceptions, aural images and all physical motions. The mind, ear, emotions and body are involved in the "thinking and doing" of music-making right from the start. This frees the mind and ear to concentrate on gauging tonal and rhythmic relationships at higher architectonic levels, such as at the phrase and section level. No longer is the student so keenly involved at the individual pitch level. The process becomes one of making music, not one of "just finding the notes."

Recent research concerning the relationship between the perception of rhythmic grouping and motor performance in piano playing vividly points out how one's mental organization of music notation directly affects the formation of motor patterns, i.e., the physical motions used in piano playing. For instance, when a pianist perceives music by individual pitches, this programs the wrists to "pump out" the notes accordingly. The same is true by the arrangement of the articulation: the wrists are programmed to make separate "pumping" motions at the beginnings and endings of motives as the articulation changes from legato to staccato (a phenomenon Abby Whiteside referred to many times as "rhythm of articulation"). This sets up a motor program of physical motions organized around the articulation or motivic aspects of the composition as opposed to a physical organization reflecting the metric or structural rhythm. This would make the physical motions used in learning a piece not applicable to those used in the performance of that same piece, for motor skills in performance must be organized around the metric or structural rhythm of a piece.

Because of the relationship between rhythm and the development of motor skills, a student's rhythmic understanding surfaces very early as a major factor in making music. Teaching students to understand rhythm, however, as well as many other facets of making music involves a number of tangible and intangible aspects of the process. Recognizing intervallic relationships and meter signatures is tangible, but most of the complex aspects of rhythm are intangible, such as sensing rhythmic grouping, keeping a steady tempo and gauging ritardandos and accelerandos. The tangibles in music are definitely easier to teach, but the intangibles must not be neglected.

Teaching young children on a one-to-one basis until late in the evening, nevertheless, can make tangibles or intangibles the farthest thing from a teacher's mind. By 7:30 p.m., and after a string of bad lessons, a teacher may be positive that he or she is the only living adult on the face of the earth who is still at work! At that point, all patience may be exhausted. A teacher may find it more appropriate, and justly so, to say, "Just learn your notes correctly for the next lesson, and for goodness sake, use that metronome!"

Perhaps those doing research on how we learn and develop musically also tend to study the more tangible concepts. We are now to the point, nevertheless, where some psychologists, neurologists and musicians are beginning to delve into that intriguing arena of timing and how it affects musical competence.[3] A recent issue of the *Journal of the Society for Music Theory* devoted an entire issue to "Time and Rhythm in Music."[4] Also a number of psychologists and others in the cognitive sciences are becoming more interested in human rhythmic behavior. The experimental studies of skilled performances, done by Eric Clarke, have illustrated that an inner sense of rhythm helps promote performances that communicate in a more aesthetically expressive way.[5] Clarke's studies substantiate two rhythmic concepts concerning musical performance:

1. Rhythmic control in musical performance depends upon the ability to feel pulse within a metered organization.
2. Musical performance is composed of expressive rhythm, sometimes called musical rhythm, as well as exact durational values which transform into more complex groupings.[6]

Clarke's studies add support to the idea that children should be taught a system for learning to read and perform music that has rhythm as its guiding force. Lack of guidance in this area allows too many children to create a "random-like approach" to learning music, resulting in disorganized physical motions and unorganized sounds.

Notes

[1] Irwin Freundlich, "Observations," ed. Dean Elder, *Clavier* 16 (September 1977), 18.

[2] Jonathan D. Ensminger, "An Approach for Understanding the Rhythmic Structure of Piano Compositions" (D.M.A. diss., University of South Carolina, 1986), 2.

[3] Frank R. Wilson, *Tone Deaf and All Thumbs?* (New York: Viking Penguin, 1986), 115-134.

[4] "Music Theory Spectrum," *Journal of the Society for Music Theory* 7 (1985).

[5] Eric Clarke, "Some Aspects of Rhythm and Expression in Performances of Erik Satie's Gnossienne No. 5," *Music Perception* 2 (Spring 1985), 229, 312, 324.

[6] Clarke, 299-328; see also L. H. Shaffer, "Performances of Chopin, Bach, and Bartók: Studies in Motor Programming," *Cognitive Psychology* 13 (1981), 326-376.

Chapter I

A TEACHING AND LEARNING PERSPECTIVE

Model Learners

Child prodigies, jazz players, talented dancers, top-notch conductors and first-chair performers of major orchestras could all very easily serve as model learners, for most usually have a natural sense of pulse, tempo, rhythm and in turn, a natural unity of mind and body processes. Upon hearing a very gifted child perform, listeners often comment: "My, what a talent! I just love watching her perform because her body moves so perfectly with the music." Although one thinks of a musical performance as being an aural experience, listeners usually describe the experience in both aural and visual terms. "People only half listen to you when you play," says violinist Itzhak Perlman, "The other half is watching." The listening and watching become intertwined. This idea suggests that audiences not only like experiencing a performer's emotional response to the music through the sound, but they also enjoy seeing the performer's physical response to the rhythm. Thus convincing performances display a marriage between the performer's emotional response to the musical phenomena and the performer's physical response to the basic rhythmic swing of the music. Super-talented students are able to create this rare marriage intuitively. They have the innate ability to order the psychomotor processes—the cognitive and the motor—into a rhythmic synthesis or gestalt which promotes the establishment of an excellent system for learning music in addition to superior performances.

The prodigy may be considered as an individual who moves very rapidly through a series of learning stages, "exhibiting a speed of learning that seems to render him qualitatively different from other individuals." Observing the advancement of a prodigy is like watching a series of "fast-forward" pictures of musical development.[1] Although only a few children are musical prodigies, their system for approaching a musical task can be considered as a model for all other learners. The most salient feature of the prodigy's process appears to be the innate ability to *see* and *hear* music symbols in logical rhythmic proportions and tonal relationships without conscious reasoning. "They just see it and do it." For many others, the trial and error approach dominates. The same type of errors may plague a student throughout his musical experiences. This is true especially in reference to rhythmic accuracy. Rhythmic habits, good or bad, tend to remain in the memory bank, thus, establishing rhythmic accuracy is of major importance even from a child's beginning lessons.

Learning to Play

Learning to play the piano involves the mind, body, emotions and the senses of sight, hearing and touch. Within these involvements, a child must develop an approach to reading, rhythm, musical understanding, a technique of playing the keyboard, artistry and style interpretation in order to learn, interpret and perform music. As a result, it is easy to understand how the complete process can become very separated and inundated with corrections. This makes it difficult to decide how to approach the process with a beginning student. What should be the primary concerns? Which piano method books should be used? How should reading be approached? How should the responsibilities be divided? Should they be divided among the student, the teacher and what is outlined in the method books? The overall answer is to approach the process from a *holistic point of view* because success in teaching and learning is very minimal if each component is considered separately. Although the complete process may be crudely planned, it should be considered from the beginning lessons. Each component is important but only as each component relates to the whole concept of learning, interpreting and performing. For example, a teacher can easily become engrossed in whether a child should be taught from the Middle-C approach, the Multiple Key approach or from a combination of reading approaches—an Eclectic approach. This sometimes happens without any concern for how the mind and body are responding to metered rhythm. Lack of any aural or emotional involvement may also go unnoticed. Sometimes during the beginning stages of piano study, there is so much emphasis placed upon the correct hand position, definitions of tempo suggestions, and the memorization of note names that the aural and rhythmic aspects are almost ignored. *However, when a child's aural and rhythmic development is ignored during the early years of study, that child's performances continually will show a lack of musical rhythm and tempo control, an insensitivity to pitch accuracy and an inconsistency in mind-body coordination.*

Musical interpretations also are usually not convincing when a student's aural awareness and rhythmic awareness are both weak. Early learning skills, therefore, should involve the *whole process* of learning and performing; not just the technical skills of learning pitch names, rhythmic values and finger numbers. There must be a total process, from the beginning, involving the mind and body developing a system for learning which will enable the student to take the symbols off the page and turn them into sound in a rhythm.

A Holistic Approach

Since making music involves an understanding of melody, harmony, rhythm, tempo, meter, dynamics, tonal quality and quantity, phrasing, balance, clarity and style, it is obvious that any approach to learning music must be all encompassing in nature. All of the understandings have to work in a synthesis for the mind and body to direct the process like a conductor. This relates directly to how developmental learning theorists believe that individuals learn. They contend that humans transfer whole learning structures from one situation to another in a synthesis rather than in separate parts. That is why learning music and playing the piano should be approached from a holistic approach right from the first lessons and fostered throughout all levels of advancement. For instance, developing a vocabulary for reading music should be approached in the context of a learning and performing synthesis of mind, body, ear, rhythm and tempo as opposed to just learning pitch names.

Holistic thinking is derived from principles of Gestalt psychology. Gestalt psychologists believe that the whole differs from the sum of its parts. "The whole of something is not at once perceived, but what is perceived is perceived as a whole, a unit of ideas."[2] For example, in reading from a score, a child—as soon as the beginning rudiments of reading are conquered—should learn to perceive music symbols in a pulse grouping, including the pitches, note values, fingering and articulation as a whole entity. Teaching and learning from a holistic approach also implies that the process will include considerations for:

1. The individual student
2. The teaching material selections
3. The approach used for teaching the materials
4. The student's mind, body, ears and emotions
5. The student's development of a system for learning the tasks

Although there are many separate parts to consider, all of the parts must be melded into an overall teaching and learning whole or gestalt.

There are many theories concerning how we learn that have been set forth by developmental psychologists and musicians, including ideas on the relationship between human development and cognition.[3] Most of the theories agree that human development occurs in sequential patterns of growth-phases or stages—from infancy to young adulthood. This implies that there are times that are more conducive for acquiring knowledge or skills than other times. "For instruction to be effective, the child must be at a level of maturity that allows her to assimilate it."[4] Other theories suggest that "it should be possible to identify an individual's intellectual profile at an early age and then draw upon this knowledge to enhance that person's educational opportunities and options."[5] In other words, children who are identified as having a strong intuition toward music should be given special educational opportunities at a young age. Those with unusual talents in a specific area like music could be channeled toward developing their full potential, with this channeling beginning as soon as the aptitude is discovered.[6]

Presently, more emphasis is given to intelligence tests involving verbal and quantitative ability, thus ignoring the theory that humans may be born with multiple intelligences. Howard Gardner believes that, normally, we are born with several intelligences and that these "intelligences actually interact with, and build upon, one another from the beginning of life."[7] He contends:

> In its strong form, multiple intelligence theory posits a small set of human intellectual potentials, perhaps as few as seven in number, of which all individuals are capable by virtue of their membership in the human species. Owing to heredity, early training or, in all probability, a constant interaction between these factors, some individuals will develop certain intelligences far more than others; but every normal individual should develop each intelligence to some extent, given but a modest opportunity to do so.[8]

Thus, what musical intelligence or ability is there, a child should be given the chance to develop it and do so in a manner that does not isolate the individual components of learning and making music. The whole process must be developed, not just the technical/physical or the skill of learning "to read notes and rhythm." If humans tend to perceive, recall and assimilate experiences as a whole rather than in separate components as stated before, then "mental development begins with the perception of a whole, which tends to become more clearly articulated and defined with increasing experience."[9] In applying these theories to music, rhythm serves as the all-encompassing force in the whole or overall structure of a composition:

> There are in music three types of rhythmic Gestalten, three forms of rhythmic patterning, capable of immediate apprehension as such: (a) "pulse" or intensity patterning; (b) duration patterning and (c) "form," which includes phrasing. . . . It is self-evident that unless a rhythmic pattern is perceived as a Gestalt, it is not perceived at all. [10]

Teaching from the holistic approach strongly encourages children to perceive music symbols in a pulse or measure units. From the long-term standpoint, it encourages the continuation of reading music from the whole as opposed to reading note-by-note. The pulse unit serves as the beginning whole or the beginning building block for learning to read and perform music. Recognition of pitches, note values, articulation, voicing and dynamic considerations all should be done from the concept of the whole. Although the concepts may be exaggerated or imperfect at the beginning, they can be refined gradually as the student undergoes more musical experiences in different contexts and in more complex musical settings. This allows for the student's learning to be enhanced by the integration of successive learning procedures, which build continually upon what previously has been experienced.

The Role of Perception

Perception of a music score, how a person "sees" the symbols, is a major factor in how that individual's learning process functions because *perception leads to the formation of concepts.* How a young student learns to perceive a music score has an enormous effect upon how that student forms concepts about music, which is the basis for musical learning. For instance, if a young child learns to perceive upbeats as downbeats, that child will always have a tendency to read and play phrases starting on an upbeat as phrases beginning on downbeats. This will make the tonal relationships incorrect right from the start because "the downbeat-sound" would be played at the wrong place in the measure. The child would be "putting in his ear" the wrong sound while he is learning the notes. Later the teacher would have to place the correct sound upon the notes after the notes already have been learned, producing two sets of concepts: one set without any aural image or idea of sound relationships and another set, instigated by the teacher, with logical upbeat–downbeat tonal relationships. The error: the child failed to *perceive* the symbols correctly in relationship to where they are placed in the rhythmic structure, in the measure, on the score. Wrong perceptions set up an incorrect chain of concept formation affecting the whole musical operation: the aural, rhythmic and physical. Concepts do give students a chance to categorize their musical experiences, but the musical experiences are only helpful if the concepts are formed from correct perceptions.

The more correct concepts students have at their disposal, the easier it will be to sight-read and learn music of greater complexity. The process is like taking a new job with a company. As beginning duties become second nature, more complex ones can be assigned. The new duties gradually are understood and absorbed as second nature. There is an integration of the old and new duties as a whole. Learning music should follow the same procedure. After a child gains ownership of concepts in simple notational textures, these same concepts can be presented again and again gradually in more complex music.

Learning to Read Music and Its Effect Upon Psychomotor Development

Many pianists display a natural sense of timing when playing by ear or improvising. When they begin to read and play from a music score, however, their natural sense of timing dissipates along with their mind and body coordination. What causes the change? It is like one set of mental and physical switches turns off and another unrelated set turns on. How is this possible? Does an individual's sense of rhythm direct mind and body synchronization more easily when the eyes are not involved with reading from a score? Is it an eye–hand coordination problem? The more the problem is observed, the more the path leads back to *how an individual sets up patterns of learning to read music as a child.* A child who learns to read music in an unorganized, visual fashion, regardless of his or her natural sense of rhythm, will tend to continue as an adult to approach a score first from how it looks rather than from how it should sound.

Bringing the score into the process of making music obviously changes some students from aural learners to visual learners. Although with the super-talents, bringing the score into the process usually doesn't alter the situation. Their psychomotor responses organize and play melodies and harmonies in a metered rhythm and at logical tempos. It is as if their minds and bodies intuitively know what to do and when to do it. The music symbols are perceived and turned into aural images, rhythmically organized, and their pre-hearing (the aural image) and post-hearing (the "sound" results) go into operation as a matter of course.

When poor reading habits are allowed to continue year after year, the student becomes a "piecemeal" learner. *The correct reading process may be understood, but the incorrect process may continue to dominate.* The teacher continually has to correct notational minutiae, one by one, until each new piece is ready to be worked on musically. This approach to learning music results in so many faulty versions of a piece that the student is ready to throw up his hands and say, "Just tell me what to do and I'll do it." The student becomes completely dependent upon the teacher. This indicates that the student has no process by which to learn on his own. Any transfer of training becomes impossible because nothing is understood or psychologically owned by the student. Poor reading habits produce a succession of conflicting commands from the mind to the body. Numerous errors occur in every piece that is played. Lessons begin and end with, "Sam, when are you ever going to remember that the key of G Major has an F#?" The saga continues with, "I have already told you twice that D is wrong, plus that is a half note instead of a quarter note, and remember now, you must use the second finger there instead of the third finger. Honestly, you are going to be on this piece forever." In this situation, corrections are dominating the lesson. Progress has ceased to exist.

These problems can be traced directly to poor reading habits. The slower a child learns to read music correctly, the slower musical understanding and rhythmic control develop. Consider what would happen to a child's reading in school if the child haphazardly learned the alphabet in grade school, recognized words in middle school and finally learned to recognize and write sentences in high school. The child would never learn to perceive, think or write in sentences as an adult. Accordingly, the same would be true in learning music. How a child approaches reading music during the early years of study has a tremendous effect upon all future musical development.

Whether a student learns to read from a Middle-C or G position is not necessarily the problem with poor readers. If it were, the wonderful array of new teaching materials published during the past few years would have solved all the problems of teaching students to read music. The teaching material itself does not fail, neither does the material necessarily teach students bad habits. *What fails is the system or pattern that the student develops for learning to read the material.* Those students who are super-talented succeed under all kinds of conditions, materials and approaches. Students who are normal or slow learners, nonetheless, will succeed more easily with teaching materials that present a more logical system for learning to read.

Physical Coordination

Even during the beginning stages of piano study, there must be some concern for physical coordination or technique for playing the keyboard. Much of the concern, though, should be centered on rhythmic and aural concepts, not technical ones. When too much emphasis is placed upon the actual striking of the keys, young students begin to zero in on the visual and tactile aspects of playing. The ears appear to shut down. The child thinks: eye–page–finger–strike, omitting any aural involvement. The ears forget to function. Subsequently, the design of beginner books affects physical coordination in addition to how one learns to read. For example, some of the method series begin with pre-reading experiences, using the second, third and fourth fingers one at a time–or the third finger only–on the black keys. This experience produces many benefits because it allows the student to begin playing with fingers which are balanced more easily than the thumb and fifth finger. From that point, pieces are presented which gradually use all fingers on the black and white keys in different positions.

When notational textures demand finger patterns that are too complex, the result is poor coordination as opposed to fostering it. The teacher should be constantly aware of notational textures that tend to disrupt whatever physical coordination that has developed. Sometimes a particular type of notational pattern will make a student's mind simply block. On the other hand, the student may play the same pattern quite easily once the pattern is heard rather than just being seen. For instance, a child usually will become uncomfortable physically if harmonic intervals appear in the music soon after lessons have begun. This is evident when the fingers show a reluctance to become "unglued" when moving from one harmonic interval to another. Once the harmonic intervals are approached in a simpler setting and more from an aural standpoint, the physical problem tends to disappear.

Sometimes a teacher will consider a problem with physical coordination as being purely physical, while on the contrary, it may be a problem caused by poorly sequenced notational textures. The series of notational symbols may be too diverse for the student to grasp holistically. The mind may block or refuse to take in what is on the page. On the other hand, when a student sees and hears immediately what the symbols indicate, physical coordination tends to occur intuitively. Physical exercises and the transposition of warm-up exercises are advocated sometimes in children's books as the answer to any physical problems. The sheer effect of these will be marginal unless the exercises are considered in a mental, aural and rhythmic context in addition to a physical one. *The practicing of exercise-type pieces always should be done in the context of producing sound in a rhythm.*

So often one is lead to believe that a young student will become well-grounded technically by just "experiencing" a series of physical exercises, such as the playing of:

1. Five-finger patterns, 5-1 or 1-5
2. Numerous pieces containing all legato or staccato touches
3. Harmonic intervals
4. Contrapuntal passages
5. Different rhythmic patterns
6. Handcrossings
7. Transposition of five-finger patterns as well as an extended version to an interval of a sixth in parallel and contrary motion

Success doesn't automatically materialize unless these experiences have been ordered sequentially in a way that fosters continued learning and performing control. In other words, all of these notational patterns would need to be sequenced properly into a student's overall literature curriculum.

Influence of Personality

Personality appears to dictate how one's learning process develops. In extremely detail-oriented personalities, there is a common need to click off each note value or chord individually when playing from a score. This is similar to a child having the need to line up toys before agreeing to go to bed at night or an adult who constantly has the need to arrange everything visually in a definite spot. For example, after a table is dusted, an individual may have the need to see that each item is placed back on the table in exactly the same spot. Another example would be a person who labels a container on a desk, *gem clips* or *rubber bands*, even though the container is made of clear plastic. This is similar to having an overpowering obsession for keeping items visually organized. This same kind of personality usually has difficulty grouping notational patterns into pulse-units as well as grouping their physical motions. The individual may understand intellectually what to do, but psychologically there is a reluctance to let it happen. With this type of individual, the mind, wrists and fingers approach each chord or set of pitches individually. Repeated head motions and the "pumping" of the wrists will reflect that student's perceptions. This implies that there must be a correlation between how a person views the world—from a holistic viewpoint or by separate details—and how that same person views a music score. Whether this aspect of the personality is innate or learned, all young students can adapt to perceiving symbols holistically in metered-pulse patterns more easily and much more quickly than adults who already have developed detail-oriented patterns of perception.

Teaching a student to perceive symbols in metered-pulse patterns is similar to teaching an individual to read words from the grouping approach, referred to by many learning psychologists as "chunking." This prevents a child from reading by letters first, such as seeing the word individual as i - n - d - i - v - i - d - u - a - l. The chunking approach fosters learning to read a page in larger cognitive units. The same is true for learning to read music. As soon as note values and intervallic reading are understood, all newly assigned pieces should be approached gradually from the pulse-unit standpoint.

In regard to the aural aspect of piano playing, some personalities may have the psychological need to hear a set of vertical pitches (chords) longer than is notated on the score. This has been observed in a number of students, especially those with perfect pitch. There may be a psychological need in some students to resolve one set of pitches, e.g., a melodic note and a harmony, into the next set of pitches without any regard for length of note values, pulse, meter or tempo. This same need, however, may not occur when the individual is listening to music produced by someone else. The problem only occurs when the person is actually producing the sounds. The question arises, do musical stimuli affect a person differently when making the sounds as opposed to being involved only as a listener? In observing the situation, one recognizes very quickly that some individuals most definitely are affected differently without realizing it. This denotes the need for teachers to recognize that individuals respond not only emotionally to musical stimuli, but psychologically as well.

The Effects of Eurhythmics

When children respond bodily to music as listeners, the auditory system may be more inclined to direct the responses. Whereas, when these same children are involved in playing from a score, the visual aspect may block out the auditory system's ability to monitor. Perhaps with some students, the motor learning (the body responses of large muscles when listening to music) does not transfer easily to the motor activity required of the small muscles in playing the piano from a score. Bodily responses made when listening to music offer experiences which are helpful in fostering rhythmic feeling but do not automatically transfer to playing the piano from a music score. This brings up the question: is rhythm mental, aural, psychological and/or physical? Not only Jaques-Dalcroze, but James L. Mursell and many others have advocated the teaching of rhythm through physiological approaches, such as clapping, walking and other movements involving the large muscles.

Children normally are receptive to these experiences, but many fail to make the transfer—the internal or outward physical response to the rhythmic grouping—when only the smaller muscles are involved with playing the piano. Some musicians, including Artur Schnabel, have questioned whether or not there is any transfer. Many musicians believe there can be a transfer, but in a majority of cases the transfer has to be fostered by the teacher. *Piano students are all individuals, and their ability to automatically transfer concepts varies widely, especially in regard to rhythm.*

Habits of Learning

Human beings are, by nature, creatures of habits. Even from the first time a child learns to do a task, habits begin forming. Learning to play the piano involves forming many different kinds of habits, such as:

1. Mental Perception
2. Concentration
3. Rhythmic
4. Aural
5. Emotional
6. Physical/Tactile
7. Pedaling

These and many other habits are interrelated in the process of transforming the music symbols from the score into sound. These habits can be correct or incorrect. Some of the incorrect habits result from approaching the process:

1. Mentally without any regard for rhythm
2. Physically without consideration for how rhythmic perception affects bodily response
3. Mentally without any emotional consideration
4. Rhythmically without any regard for where rhythmic patterns or motives occur upon the metric structure, e.g., upbeat-to-downbeat versus downbeat-to-upbeat
5. Dynamically without any consideration for the rhythmic placement of syncopation or dynamic stress accents
6. Visually as opposed to aurally

Most children approach new learning situations with a positive attitude, therefore entering into the process with a feeling of excitement and a sense of confidence. Children are receptive to directions even if they do not always follow them carefully. They are commonly optimistic and willing to take risks with any new learning situation. This optimism allows them to approach a task from a more natural state of being, as opposed to what happens with the adult learner. With children, there are no mental habits that have to be reprogrammed or incorrect physical habits that need changing, because usually they had not been previously programmed as is the case with most adults. In other words, children come to a new learning situation free of preconceived ideas of how to approach the task.

The majority of children quickly develop habits or a system for learning music and playing the piano. Consequently, many of the bad habits formed with the young student can be modified instantaneously. With the older student, however, it is much more difficult to make the change. Attention, therefore, should be given during the early years of study to teaching children *a model process* of learning music rather than emphasizing the "learning of pieces" for competitions. The process of learning music, whether it is good or bad, develops very early in every student's background. The model process far outweighs the learning of a few select compositions. Through stressing this process while learning specific pieces, long-term goals of learning can be realized. This will allow a student to continue learning throughout his or her lifetime.

As a student progresses into the intermediate and advanced levels of performance, the approach to reading music that had developed during the early years of study continues to operate, especially during the beginning stages of learning a composition. If the old "stopping and starting" approach was the norm with the student as a child, the same usually continues during adulthood. Those students who were dominated by a rhythmically unorganized visual aspect of the score tend to read music the same way after they become adults, thus remaining poor readers. On the other hand, students who were dominated by metrically perceived aural images become excellent readers as adults. Their correct habits of learning music are already in place. Consequently, there is little that has to be repro-grammed. Poor readers find learning music puzzling throughout their lives. Their lessons continue, week after week, to involve more corrections than instructions. Lessons commonly become intolerable by age 12. After weeks of struggling with learning to sight-read new pieces, Heather may announce to the teacher, "I hate music and never want to take an-other lesson." It may be that she does not hate music; she is just frustrated with the struggle of learning the notes and trying to decide "how the music goes."

Selecting and Evaluating Piano Method Books

Selecting an elementary piano method for a student's first few years of instruction is one of the most important decisions a teacher makes. Within the realm of choices, many teachers follow the suggested sequencing of events advocated by the piano method book authors, while other teachers use books from a variety of elementary piano courses and organize their own sequencing. The sequencing suggested in the method books is perhaps the best choice for a core literature curriculum with supplementary materials being added for specific needs and purposes. Teachers, therefore, must carefully evaluate their method book choices. The sequential process advocated in Chapters IV through IX, outlining the six stages of complexity of the elementary level of study, may be used as a guideline for making these choices. Although many teachers are capable of organizing a literature curriculum for their own students, it is often difficult to design a core curriculum for elementary level students without omitting some very significant concepts of an overall program for pianistic development.

The music selections that a student experiences should display proper sequencing of the majority of notational complexities, including intervals, note values, articulation, voicing, scalar and arpeggiated passages, chords and inversions, keys, phrasing and pedaling. These complexities need to be properly sequenced as well as *all of the physical demands of executing these complexities*. In all aspects of the process, sequencing is the key! Proper sequencing is a monumental task for the teacher, but one that can be accomplished with the help of litera-ture that presents concepts in a sequential order. Specific piano books "won't make the student," but poorly organized books certainly can stand in the way of successfully building a student's all important reading foundation. When a child is struggling with a series of reading pieces compiled with little concern for the effects of sequencing, making music becomes the furthermost thing from that child's mind. The struggle dominates. The desire to study piano gets lost in the process. The teacher, therefore, must learn to make the best possible choices when selecting music, because the better the selections are, the greater the possibility will be for success. The teacher will not always be successful with every student, but optimal conditions can be created for setting the process in motion.

18

Notes

[1] Howard Gardner, *Frames of Mind* (New York: Basic Books, 1983), 27.

[2] James Mainwaring, "Gestalt Psychology," *Grove's Dictionary of Music and Musicians,* Vol. 3 (1966), 612.

[3] Marilyn P. Zimmerman, "Child Development and Music Education," oral report presented at the National Symposium on the Applications of Psychology to the Teaching and Learning of Music, Ann Arbor, Michigan, July 30-August 2, 1979.

[4] Zimmerman, "Child Development and Music Education."

[5] Gardner, *Frames of Mind,* 10.

[6] Gardner, *Frames of Mind,* 10.

[7] Gardner, *Frames of Mind,* 278.

[8] Gardner, *Frames of Mind,* 278.

[9] Mainwaring, "Gestalt Psychology," 612.

[10] Mainwaring, "Gestalt Psychology," 612.

Chapter II

TEACHING STUDENTS TO READ MUSIC

Today's child is growing up in a visually oriented society with televisions and computers being commonly found in homes and schools. Consequently, special emphasis must be placed upon reminding each beginner that music is an aural endeavor as opposed to a visual/mental one. Visually oriented students can easily regard a music score as a diagram where you read the symbols and strike the keys without any consideration for how the symbols sound. Approaching a score from the visual standpoint results in learning to read note-by-note or learning to read motivic patterns without being concerned with where these patterns occur within a strong-weak metric grouping, and how the patterns turn into musical sound. If a child grows up directing an enormous amount of mental energy towards deciphering what the notational symbols mean, very little energy is left for any emotional or aural considerations. The child plods on week after week with reading problems. There is a tendency to blame the problems on the method books that are being used, when in reality, the blame may be shared among the teacher's approach to presenting the materials, the student's approach to perceiving the materials, and in some cases, the level of difficulty of the materials. Since learning to read has such a dramatic effect upon how a student develops as a musician and performer, special emphasis must be placed upon the selection of literature for each individual.

Understanding What is Read

The teacher should examine how well the student is understanding the concepts that are being presented in the literature. In other words, is the child saying, "Yes, I understand," because she knows what the teacher is talking about, or is the "yes" given to the teacher in order to avoid the confrontation of not knowing? Is the "Yes, I understand," simply a courtesy to the teacher? The true answer can be discovered best by:

1. Asking the student questions
2. Demonstrating versions—correct and incorrect—of the concepts
3. Using imagery and analogies

For example, recently I said to a young student, "Anna, did you hear that your eighth notes were very uneven in the piece you just played?" She replied, "Yes, they were all bunched up in uneven patterns. They were like a group of mice going after a large hunk of cheese: some of the mice got little chunks and others got big chunks." She continued on, "That's just like my eighth notes: some were long and some were short." By the analogy, Anna let me know in her own words that she did hear and understand the error.

Another analogy given by the same student was this reply, "Oh yes, I understand what you are talking about. Playing a phrase in a bowed or rounded shape reminds me of a boiled egg. The outsides are white, the next layer is 'kind of yellow' and the kind of yellow blends into the real yellow in the center." Continuing on, she said, "But all of it kind of blends together to make up the rounded shape of the egg because the colors don't have sharp edges." That let me know she knew that the phrase needed to start softly, dynamically rise in the center and taper off at the end, and that the dynamic changes should be gradual rather than abrupt.

Aural concepts are hard for some children to grasp. Nevertheless, children can begin to grasp them more easily if the concepts are also presented verbally. That is where imagery or an analogy can help. When students are able to give an analogy of an aural concept, that assures the teacher that the student is beginning to grasp the concept. In Anna's case, the analogies that she gave indicated that she has the ability to think holistically concerning a concept. Her playing of the phrase, dynamically shaped, verified that she understood, reacted emotionally to the understanding and created an aural image of it before playing it. Obtaining psychological ownership of concepts is imperative if the concepts are going to be transferable to other music. Many times what happens in a studio is that the student sits back and just continually says, "Oh yes, I understand," when in reality the student has no mental or aural understanding at all. The student is just agreeing with the teacher in order to progress on to the next piece. After several years of studying, these false understandings can add up to a large accumulation of concepts which baffle the student. Eventually, lessons follow a pattern of constant corrections in response to everything that is played. This can be very misleading because literature selections usually are based upon what the teacher believes the student understands.

There is no way that individual books can be designed for each specific learner. Instead, they have to be designed for hypothetical learners. The teacher has to make decisions on what book or combination of books is best for a specific individual. The better the choices are, the more outstanding the results will be. Making decisions concerning beginning books is crucial because these are the books that will or will not foster the reading and music-making process. The results from a beginner's interview and audition must be evaluated. This evaluation should include the beginner's responses to directions, questions, aural concepts, rhythmic concepts and to the beginner's overall reaction to starting lessons. As a result, book selections can be based upon the student's actions and responses to the whole evaluative process.

Pre-Reading

Most beginners' books include pre-reading experiences. Sometimes these experiences are looked upon by the teacher as a magical way to begin reading. Although pre-reading experiences do enhance the beginning process of reading, they should be looked upon also as experiences in getting the mind and body processes to work in a rhythm. This is as important as reading itself. Teaching a student how to read is a significant part of the beginning process, yet getting the mind accustomed to directing the ear, emotions and body in a rhythm is equally important. The pre-reading stage of learning is where all of this must begin. The beginner should be taught that she should be just as concerned with making music as she is with understanding the notation. If playing the piano starts only with deciphering the notation, taking lessons may not be as rewarding to a student as was expected. Pre-reading helps bridge the gap because it offers experience in making music even at the first lesson. The use of duets and rote tunes also enhances these first efforts. The child obviously wants to make music. That is why she is taking lessons. Experiencing lessons that dwell only on learning to read notation may not satisfy that desire. More likely, working on a few pre-staff pieces, some compositions from the Grand Staff, a few rote tunes and some harmonized scale-duet arrangements (with the teacher) will be much more satisfying to the student. Playing duets is rewarding because it allows the student to begin making music with both thin-textured melodies and melodies with harmony in a rhythm. This will sound like "big music" to the beginner, especially if the teacher has added pedaling to the already wonderful world of piano sounds.

Approaches to Reading

Method books present a number of different reading approaches: Middle C, Multiple Key, Intervallic, modified versions of each and Eclectic. More recently, the Eclectic approach—using the best of all the approaches—has become the favored one. With all of the approaches, nevertheless, a teacher must learn to fill in the gaps. What one student considers as easy to understand, another student might think of as being confusing. Although one student may struggle with the basic concepts presented on each page, other students may welcome additional assignments, such as transposing the pieces to other keys. *What is to be accomplished with the first set of beginner books has to be examined on an individual basis because students react very differently to understanding how to read music.*

Most method books include guidelines for understanding the staff, including hand positions or landmarks, e.g., C position, G position or Landmark F. Each concept usually is presented (later on in the book) at several different octaves. This acquaints the student with a wider range of the keyboard. It is imperative, however, that each concept be thoroughly understood by the student before introducing the concept at other octaves. Some students may continue to have trouble grasping ownership of a position or landmark even after they have experienced it in several pieces. Therefore, when a student has to be reminded constantly where a position is on the keyboard, the student has failed to gain any insight into what kind of reading approach is being taught. None of the approaches works effectively unless the student acquires a sense or feeling for the location of the starting keys. The student needs to have something on the page that is familiar, thus something to set the reading process into motion.

How long should the neighbor-skip (2nds and 3rds) concept or intervallic reading be stressed before note names are emphasized? At least for a short period of time, because most leading pedagogues believe it is definitely better to acquaint the student with reading from the neighbor-skip, intervallic concept before note names are emphasized. At the beginning, though, some note names—connected to the position or landmark names—do need to be learned. Teaching beginners to read strictly by note names, to a large extent, fosters isolated reading of pitches and rhythm. Note names can be introduced on a gradual basis, as the names will help clarify the intervallic system of reading and key areas. At the beginning, nevertheless, the note names should not be the main focus of the reading approach. The starting position of melodies, a directional sense and an intervallic understanding are more important. Note names definitely will have to be learned by the time the student experiences key signatures, but they should not be emphasized at the beginning. With some students, it will be intuitive, but others will struggle with it because note names further complicate an already complex situation. The child is having to remember the direction of the pitch pattern, the rhythmic pattern, fingering, the clef and keeping eyes on the page! This is similar to having to read a difficult passage in a foreign language without any previous knowledge of that language.

A teacher should examine the pages of a beginner book very carefully with definite considerations:

1. Are the presentations sequentially ordered?
2. Are the pitch and rhythmic patterns reiterated several times or do the patterns constantly change with each piece?
3. Is there a logical sequence to the progression of types of motion on the score—parallel, oblique and contrary?
4. When do the pieces begin to combine parallel and contrary motion with contrasting intervallic patterns? Does it occur much too soon?
5. Do the beginning books look enticing or do they look forbidding?

The progression and sequencing of these aspects are more important for the normal and slow learners than for the very talented. The normal and slow learners, however, make up the majority of the people we teach. Very talented students and prodigies represent only a small fraction of the students who study piano. To them, the sequential order is less important because they appear to grasp ideas so intuitively regardless of the sequencing. Prodigies sometimes can be introduced to a mixture of intervallic combinations and rhythms and find it to be just as easy as patterns that are much simpler.

Intervallic Map-Reading

When reading is approached from the concept of intervallic map-reading, there is less of a chance that isolated reading habits will develop. Starting from the neighbor and skip concept (2nds and 3rds) and proceeding into intervallic reading helps a student to understand that the new world of reading music is like reading a road map. Neighbor and skip notes can be translated easily into intervallic terms. Interval recognition needs to be coupled with the sound of the intervals, making it possible for students to hear when they have made a mistake. Visual recognition without the aural recognition is limited. Students can be playing a number of incorrect intervals between lessons without knowing it unless they can detect the errors aurally. Consequently, from the beginning, the aural aspect of intervallic reading should be fostered both at the lessons and during group musicianship classes. This can be accomplished by singing interval tunes, singing the words to some of the beginner pieces or by other means. The notational arrangement of pitches in the beginner books can also help. For example, neighbor notes should be presented in several pieces before the student has to experience skip notes. Simple note values should be presented, one at a time, before there is a general mixture of quarter, half, dotted-half, whole and eighth notes. Similarly, the pitch patterns should follow one direction for more than two or three notes before going in the opposite direction. Also, the pitch patterns should remain in one hand for two or three measures. When there are many directional changes and changes in pitch patterns from hand-to-hand, the student quickly becomes confused. Although a very bright child may perceive the changes very easily, most normal and slow learners will have problems because at this point, they do not have mastery of a mixture of directional changes and constant hand alternation.

As a child recognizes line and space notes and how these notes relate to the intervallic concept, the idea of reading a map—direction and distance—enables the child to cope gradually with more complex notational settings, such as:

1. Notes divided between the hands
2. Notes arranged in a mixture of parallel and contrary motion
3. Notes in a melodic/harmonic setting
4. Notes occurring in a more complex rhythmic pattern

The Relationship Among the Score, Keyboard Topography and Sound

For many students the logistics of up and down the music score, up and down the keyboard topography and how this relates to sound are all very logical. To others, the relationship may appear very complex. It is up to the teacher to discover whether the student is grasping the correlation among the three. When reading is approached one note at a time, the correlation is more difficult to comprehend, especially for a young child. Since music is made up of a series of tonal relationships and rhythmic proportions, reading should be approached from the relationship and proportion standpoint: pitch relationships, sound relationships and rhythmic proportions. The student must know where the hands begin, which direction the notational pattern is moving, the distance to the next note and the rhythmic proportions.

Textural Considerations

A teacher must examine every aspect of the texture in the pieces of books used, including the arrangement and sequencing of all aspects of the notation, such as pitch patterns, rhythmic patterns, rests, articulation, dynamics and tonality. The arrangement affects how the student perceives the score, particularly in the area of intervallic arrangement (melodic and harmonic), frequency of repetition or contrast, range, rhythm and sequential order. Textural arrangements affect students in different ways. A mixture of intervallic relationships and motion changes, e.g., parallel and contrary, will baffle one student whereas another student may say, "Oh, I see what is happening. The notes now are moving in contrary motion with the left hand moving up a fourth while the right hand moves down a third." Others get that confused look as if they have lost their grounding and are thinking, "Where do my fingers go next?"

Aural Aspects of Reading

As a child works with the music page and learns to read, a reading synthesis needs to develop. This synthesis should include the pitch pattern, the rhythmic pattern, the sound of the pattern and the articulation. Too often learning to read is explained as a skill involving only the recognition and execution of the pitches and rhythm. The aural aspect is never mentioned. Yet the sound that these pitches and rhythmic symbols produce is a vital part of the complete process. The concept of neighbor and skip notes, up and down the keyboard and the relationship of keyboard direction to pitch direction should all be placed in an aural context. Leading the child in singing neighbor and skip notes greatly enhances the prospects of that child tying sound to the task of reading.

How the eye and ear collaborate in reading music has always been a puzzle. Even students who have an excellent aural sense when playing by ear or listening to music sometimes have problems with this coordination. Teachers will ask, "Why do some people have problems with getting their aural sense to function when the eyes become involved in perceiving the score?" With some, it is only a matter of course. The inner hearing just develops naturally. Many, many others have great problems connecting inner hearing with learning to read. Yet developing a child's own inner sense of hearing symbols in a rhythm is the keystone of the total reading and music-making process, because the ear directs the complete operation.

Teachers may attempt to force this inner hearing to develop by "beating out the rhythm" of a piece and singing the idea at the top of their lungs. Students do play better, temporarily, and seem to pre-hear what they are playing. When they return for their next lesson, though, that inner sense of hearing seems to have evaporated. The pre- and post-hearing must develop within the student. If young students develop an inner sense of hearing, they can more easily detect errors because they have an aural idea in mind before they depress the keys. The ability to pre-hear musical ideas should come early in a child's training because it directs the physical motions, and hopefully, guides the memory work. When young students learn to develop their own inner hearing, their reading, physical motions and memory work are less problematic. Perceiving and playing the score as well as memorizing are more integrated. Mechanical or tactile memory work alone is less dependable in performance.

Memorizing should be the result of proper learning habits as opposed to being a separate task that must be "tacked on" after a piece has been learned. Examine how your students memorize. Sometimes you may say, "Susan, why don't you memorize or play this piece by heart?" Susan, and many others who have already developed an inner sense of pre-hearing in combination with their learning to read, will reply: "I believe I can already play this piece without the music." This means that the student is integrating music reading and memory while the beginning stages of learning are taking place. The degree of accuracy will vary with different individuals, but the correct process is obviously developing. Yet with others who haven't had the ear involved, playing from memory will be like beginning the piece anew. When this occurs, there is definitely a problem with the student's process of learning, because memory work should be an integral part of the total "learning/performing operation."

Reading and Playing in a Rhythm

Perhaps understanding the many faces of rhythm is one of the most complex set of concepts the young student will encounter. After receiving a correction concerning a quarter note, the student may reply, "Well, if my quarter note was too short, just how long is a quarter note?" How note values relate to each other is very difficult for some students to grasp. Note value concepts must be understood thoroughly before a sense of rhythmic grouping can be attained. After gaining ownership of simple note values, the student is ready to attempt grouping notes into strong-weak patterns. This not only has to be understood, but also heard and felt. Musical intuition will play a part in this process. The student may begin the grouping process soon after lessons begin. To Billy, it may be just something he feels. He may say, "That is just how the music goes." To Darlene, it may be a concept that makes no sense at all.

Which system of teaching rhythm is the best? This may differ with specific individuals. Saying note values out loud? Using the tah-tah-ti's? Counting 1-and-uh-2-and-uh? How about eurhythmics? "Should I have students swinging, stepping and conducting to music before we try doing rhythmic grouping from the score?" There are no simple answers because individuals perceive rhythm so many different ways. Some students have a wonderful intuitive sense of rhythm while others find it to be very problematic. As an introduction to understanding the length of note values, saying the note values out loud—Quar-ter, Quar-ter, Half-note—is the most successful system for the majority of students. The teacher must be sure, however, that the student understands that the saying of "half note" must equal the rhythmic duration of saying "quar-ter, quar-ter."

The rhythmic bookkeeping type of counting—1 and 2 and 3 and—is too complex for most children because confusion often occurs with the different sets of numbers: how their fingers are numbered; the fingering suggestions on the page; and the numbers used to count the rhythm. Using the tah-tah-ti system is also confusing for children who have not experienced it in general music classes in the schools.

Young children who are not quite ready to comprehend the bookkeeping side of counting often can relate to the syllables of words, such as quar-ter, quar-ter, half-note. Saying syllables of words can also be very successful in teaching students to group or feel pulse. Using words with three syllables, such as "Cho-co-late," can promote understanding and feeling for the rhythmic pulse in a 3/4 meter piece. Some children will be ready to go into the grouping concept soon after beginning lessons, but these will be children who already have a natural feel for rhythmic grouping.

Understanding, hearing and feeling note length is an important link in understanding, hearing and feeling rhythmic grouping. There will be some rare instances, though, where a child may struggle with note values, yet sense grouping quite easily. The whole complex system of rhythm depends upon these two fundamental aspects: note value and pulse. Upon mastery of these, other more complex rhythmic concepts can be understood, heard and felt, such as:

1. Strong-weak groupings at the mensural (measure) and intermensural (groups of measures) levels
2. Placement within the measure of the fluctuating tensions and resolutions in music
3. Rhythmic incongruities (lack of conformity) among the basic three rhythms—the melodic, harmonic and metric
4. Incongruities between the musical (dynamic) and metric (natural) accents. (For further study on complex rhythmic concepts, see Camp, *Developing Piano Performance: A Teaching Philosophy*, Alfred Publishing Co.)

There are many different kinds of problems which can arise in teaching rhythm, therefore the teacher must constantly be on guard for what may or may not be happening. Is the student's perception of note values correct? Is the student perceiving the symbols in a pulse? Is the student ignoring the rhythmic aspects of practice? Am I, the teacher, presenting the rhythmic concepts clearly? If there are problems, they may be due to the lack of concentration and/or lack of desire to play in rhythm. Lack of concentration usually goes along with a lack of any aural involvement with the rhythm. Without any aural sense of what has been played, error detection on the student's part is very minimal. Aural detection of rhythmic errors requires a sense of pre-hearing. Judging the results, (post-hearing) always demands pre-hearing.

Eurhythmics sometimes can be a valuable aid to teaching rhythm since it allows the student to respond physically to what has been heard and felt. There must be a concentrated effort, though, to get students to make the connection between sensing and feeling rhythm when listening to music, as opposed to playing music, from a score. The issue, as mentioned previously, that keeps raising its head is, why is aural control or critical self-listening such a problem when playing from a score? Is it because the student is approaching the task from the visual standpoint only? Musicians do not have an easy answer other than it is like learning itself: we know when it happens, but we are not sure how it happens.

In the early stages of teaching how note values group to form strong-weak pulse groupings, the concepts of both bodily and aural response to rhythm must be explored. Eurhythmics can be of assistance in that exploration, regardless of whether it is the tapping of feet, clapping, conducting and/or moving the whole body to rhythm. Younger students usually respond well to the concept of swinging to music. Do rhythmic drills help? This is questionable because isolated drills, such as the use of rhythmic patterns on flash cards, can become a mechanical process, which has no transfer value. Many teachers find the use of the pie-system of rhythm, outlined in the Hazel Cobb books on rhythm, the best concept to use in teaching rhythmic grouping. The association of words, with which children are familiar, such as *Huck-le-ber-ry* for ♫♫ ; *Ap-ple* for ♫ ; *Black-ber-ry* for ♩♫ ; and *Cho-co-late* for ♫♩ . This promotes an understanding and feeling for the sound of those note values. [3]

Literature: The Vehicle for Teaching Reading

Selecting books for teaching students to read is crucial, because a teacher must make the best possible choices for each individual student. A teacher may choose all beginning books from one piano method or select a combination of books from different method series. If a teacher is familiar with most of the series, the choices are somewhat easier. New series, though, continue to be published each year; therefore, a teacher must continue to evaluate the choices that are available. In examining the books from the different piano methods, the following questions should be considered in addition to those mentioned earlier in the discussion of the beginning books:

1. How does the method series approach reading, rhythm, range of keyboard, physical coordination, creativity, musical understanding and theory?
2. Are the concepts in the method series books presented in a sequential order and reiterated in other pieces before going on to new concepts?
3. Are the books based on a sound pedagogical foundation and psychological theories of learning, including principles of holistic thinking?
4. Will the overall design of the books appeal to the child?
5. Will the sequence of concepts foster rhythmic organization, holistic perception and physical coordination?
6. Will the sequence promote the development of a child's inner sense of rhythmic perception and understanding?

These and many other questions should be examined before making literature choices. Many times literature is selected only on the basis of being fun to play. The fun or enjoyment issue is certainly noteworthy, but selecting pieces and books that can be used as a vehicle for learning to read and perform is most critical. Beginner pieces should be selected that will present the concepts a particular student needs in order to develop a foundation for reading and making music. As the student advances from the beginning stages of reading on to more advanced music, there are many other types of literature to consider, such as:

1. Variety of notational and textural patterns
2. Use of full range of keyboard
3. Music that displays characteristics of the different style periods
4. Music utilizing a variety of moods
5. Music that is easy to read and play, but sounds difficult
6. A wide variety of compositions, including those utilizing chords—both blocked and arpeggiated—and scalar passages
7. Numerous selections of embryonic versions of compositions by the master composers

For the majority of the time, there should be *sound pedagogical reasons* for making literature choices, particularly during the early years of study. This is because the music chosen serves as the vehicle for fostering the student's perception, and the formation of concepts, for the development of a musical understanding or "language" needed to direct the physical coordination required to communicate that understanding. This includes the development of a student's aural, rhythmic and physical controls. The better the choices of books, the more easily musical understanding can foster the development of these controls. In making elementary level literature selections, the presentation, sequencing and frequency of occurrence of the following notational aspects need to be evaluated:

1. General concepts
2. Pre-staff notation
3. Grand Staff
4. Keyboard positions or landmarks
5. Intervallic reading
6. Rhythmic reading
7. Melodic intervals
8. Rhythmic patterns

9. General notational textures
10. Five-finger patterns and extensions
11. Accidentals
12. Motions—parallel, contrary and oblique
13. Harmonic intervals
14. Articulation
15. Creativity
16. Physical coordination
17. Ensemble (optional duet parts)
18. 8va's
19. Words to promote a sense of rhythm
20. Triads
21. Pedaling
22. Melodies with chord accompaniments
23. Aural and physical presentations of pedaling
24. Frequency of pedal changes
25. Physical demands involving the sequential ordering of intervals, the mixture of melodic and harmonic intervals, triads, crossings and scalar patterns involving smaller note values

Reading Problems

Although a teacher cannot force a student to read correctly, the teacher can create optimal conditions for learning to read and perhaps prevent the student from encountering some of the following problems:

1. Perceiving music symbols as individual entities long after reading by pulse groupings has been initiated
2. Reading by motivic patterns, without regarding how these patterns are arranged upon the metric structure
3. Perceiving wide leaps, chords with unusual mixtures of pitches, long note values and textural changes always as downbeats without any regard for where they appear in the measure or metric structure
4. Reading at a tempo that automatically will cause "stopping and starting"
5. Reading without any regard for note values or fingering
6. Guessing the meaning of each symbol, forcing the teacher to make constant corrections
7. Stopping rhythmically each time the notational pattern changes clefs

Chapter III

THE TEACHING AND LEARNING PROCESS

Guiding Perception

Even with proper sequencing, students may progress slowly because of improper perception of the page. As mentioned, (see The Role of Perception, Chapter I) how one perceives the page affects all the other processes of turning the symbols into sound: rhythmic, aural, emotional and physical. Since these are all integrated in performance, the original perception that is put into action during the learning process automatically affects the end result, the performance. As the eyes perceive the symbols, many errors can occur in pitch, rhythm, articulation and voicing. Although the mind/eye, ear/body processes work in quick succession, the "total package" may omit part of what must be perceived holistically. One student may be drawn mainly to the pitch, especially if that student has an excellent sense of pitch. Another student may perceive the pitches and note values, but ignore the accidentals. Often a student will play in perfect rhythm in the sections where the symbols are easy to read. Yet the same student's strong rhythmic sense may "go down the drain" once the pitches become difficult to read. As familiar notes reappear, the student's strong rhythmic sense returns. The rhythmic discrepancy is not noticed during practice sessions, because the student is accustomed to hearing the wrong rhythm. To discover the problem, the teacher has to become a diagnostician, a detective looking for the root of the problem. Is the student failing to notice the accidentals or the articulation? Is the student ignoring the note values or pulse patterns?

The Teacher as Diagnostician

What is the problem? Why does a student suddenly start reading out of rhythm? Why can't the student see the accidentals or recognize the mixture of articulation? In being a diagnostician, the teacher has to discover the root of those errors whether it be concentration, rhythmic, aural or a perceptual problem. Just correcting the error, the *portato* notes or the quarter-dot-eighth, will not solve the problem, because the student will continue to repeat the error. **What is causing the repetition of the error must be found**. Once a teacher becomes accustomed to working from the diagnostic standpoint, the procedure becomes easier. Often the tangible errors are spotted first. For instance, if the sound doesn't agree with the pitch symbol, that can be detected easily as an error. Yet deciding why a student continually speeds is more intangible. Attempting to detect why a student is perceiving a score incorrectly is like "getting inside the student's thinking." Sometimes a teacher can best discover the problem from the student's sound, because sound that is produced by hitting the keys usually is made without any aural judgment or emotional involvement. The student strikes the keys as if he were strumming on a table. Lack of tempo control indicates the student plays with no conscious control during practice or perhaps confuses dynamic change with rhythmic change. Errors become syndromes. They can occur individually or several at one time. When they occur collectively, it indicates total lack of concentration during practice and lessons. Most errors become symbolic of syndromes—signs or symptoms of something malfunctioning within the total process from perception to execution.

Errors indicate the existence of a "short-circuit" occurring within the learning process. The teacher has to diagnose what is happening. Does the ear stop functioning when perception of the symbols begin? How does the student perceive the score? By note values, motives or in a holistic metered-pulse pattern? Young children tend to continue individual note-reading as long as the teacher permits. More advanced students tend to

30

perceive music as motives. Many students automatically make a downbeat sound where a motive begins and another downbeat sound where it ends, regardless of the placement of the motive in the measure. The teacher should attempt to discover why these common errors are happening. If the teacher checks closely, she may discover that Steve always plays new pieces faster than he can read them, stopping and starting when necessary. This indicates that Steve loves to practice pieces up-to-tempo with full excitement, regardless of the errors that are committed. This continues week after week. Obviously, the effect of the corrections made by the teacher will be limited because changes in the perception—mental, rhythmic, aural, emotional and physical—are nearly impossible to make as long as Steve practices full speed ahead! Does Heather always play wide leaps as downbeats or difficult-to-read sections out of rhythm? Examine Johnny's practice habits with new pieces. Do you find similar errors with each new piece he learns, regardless of the style or notational texture? What happens when David begins to memorize a piece? Is his ear involved? Often problems occur when a student first begins to memorize a piece. Remember two guidelines: 1) beginning perceptions affect the total process; and 2) memory problems indicate that learning has occurred with very little aural involvement. Memory should be the result of proper learning habits as opposed to being a completely separate type of practice. Diagnosing the root of the problem, if only in these two areas, will help improve a student's progress tenfold.

The Physical Aspects of Making Music

Aural direction has a mammoth effect upon physical coordination in piano playing. As is often said, "One plays the piano with the mind and ears, not with the fingers." This statement is true because fingers do not contain any brain cells that can direct any mental or physical endeavors. Developing only the physical aspects fails to develop any type of musical artistry at the piano. The word *technique*, in the past, has referred just to the physical aspects of piano playing. Gradually, the meaning of the word *technique* has changed from the purely physical connotation in the 19th century to one referring to the overall music-making process. Heinrich Neuhaus, the teacher of a number of renowned pianists, including Sviatoslav Richter and Emil Gilels, believed piano technique to be *all-encompassing*.[1] Artur Schnabel considered it to mean the avenue by which sounds heard inwardly were realized, thus the channel between soul and body.[2] To Adele Marcus, technique and purely technical practice are two entirely different things. She thinks pianists are always wrong to think that having physical facility at the keyboard automatically implies that one has technique.[3]

Numerous artist-teachers and pedagogues during the 20th century have denounced the old idea of technique being only a physical aspect of piano playing. Leon Fleisher maintains that problems worked out from purely a technical standpoint never support the weight of a musical conception.[4] Celia Mae Bryant agrees, stating that the development of technique depends upon the physical, intellectual and musical factors which are all very closely integrated in the basic foundation of musical artistry.[5]

When the system of learning begins on the right track, the technical/physical aspects develop more naturally. The whole body coordinates as one entity. It doesn't divide into fingers, wrists, arms, elbows, torso, legs and pedaling feet. Dividing the body up is what causes the wrong tonal relationships to occur. Separate motions make separate sounds. Different kinds of motions produce different kinds of sounds. A young student should learn during his early years of study that *like motions* produce *like sounds*. In other words, physical motions must be organized in a rhythm or otherwise the sounds produced by these motions will not relate tonally. For example, if the down-up motion (simulated or real) of the wrists is not synchronized with the pulse pattern, the motion of the wrists will "pump" at random causing numerous unwanted accents. Technical exercises will not necessarily correct this problem.

The problem has to do with what the mind decided upon originally because physical motions are responses to mental perceptions. If the task of reading the symbols is unorganized, thus the physical motions will also be unorganized, resulting in unrelated tonal relationships.

Pedaling

Pedaling, like mind-body synchronization, aural awareness and rhythmic pulse, is another aspect of piano playing that should not be neglected during the early years of study. Many students only move the foot up and down, according to the pedal markings or teacher suggestions. This approach leaves the student with very little knowledge of the "why, when and how" of pedaling. The process develops purely as a mechanical procedure, one that doesn't involve the ear. As a student progresses into more advanced music, it is difficult to incorporate the aural aspect into the pre- and post-hearing. The pedal remains outside the student's realm of aural consciousness. To avoid the problem, proper aural and physical habits must begin when the pedal is first used.

Since pedaling adds one more dimension to the physical coordination in piano playing, some aural awareness should be developed before even the simplest of pedaling procedures are introduced. Correct pedaling can usually be understood and heard more easily by a child than an experienced player if that experienced player learned to pedal without the ear. Moreover, pedaling can be added to a young child's aural gestalt more easily than an adult's aural gestalt because the child's mental and physical habits are just in the early stages of being formed. For mature students working on advanced literature, the pedal will receive a subordinate role unless aural pedaling has already been mastered. Too many details, such as articulation and phrasing, occur in advanced music for one to begin understanding the elementary concepts of pedaling. The use of the pedals should become second nature long before the student is playing advanced level music. Early on, the ear must guide the how, when, where and speed of pedal changes. Sequencing the rise in pedaling complexity should go hand-in-hand with the rise in the complexity of the music. Pedaling must enhance the sound, not cover up the faults!

First, students should experience pedaling in simple settings where special attention can be given to learning how to pedal. Give attention to how the pedal works, explaining the mechanics of notes, dampers and the pedal mechanism, and noting what happens with the sound when the pedal is used correctly and when it is not used correctly. The talented students will hear the difference immediately, while the difference may have to be pointed out for others. Some students will feel awkward getting their fingers and foot coordinated, thus causing the fingers or the foot to be released early.

Teaching a student to pedal single keys, one after the other, is the best approach to use when first introducing pedaling as a new concept or when reteaching transfer students. The process should begin with letting the student pedal one key at a time, continuously using the third finger with one hand and then the other. Then have the student pedal parallel triads in one hand at a time, using only the white keys. This can be followed by having the student pedal parallel triads hands together.

Teaching the student the timing aspect of depressing and releasing the pedal is of utmost importance. The process can be outlined for the student in the following way:

1. Make the sound
2. Depress the pedal
3. Make the new sound before releasing the pedal

    4. Then change the pedal. (As the student's pedaling skill improves, steps 3 and 4 should evolve into a play/pedal action that happens almost simultaneously.)

Some students understand the play/pedal process more clearly when it is described as a depress-release motion rather than a down-up motion. The down-up motion indicates to some students that the foot should go down to depress the pedal and come up—completely off the metal—to release and change the pedal. Obviously, coming completely off the pedal produces a "hit" sound when the foot returns to the metal again. Whereas, the depress-release or a down-relax motion promotes a quieter and smoother approach to pedaling. Students with keen aural awareness usually learn the timing aspect of depressing and releasing without any problems as the ear tends to guide the foot automatically.

For advanced level students, sophisticated pedalings may be suggested in literature that is already much too complex. The result will be similar to an overloaded electrical circuit. The ear and emotions will turn off immediately. The facial expression turns to a distraught or anxious look. The body language will say, "Look, there are more things happening at one time than I can handle." The teacher may need to rethink the assignment. Does the pedaling raise the musical complexity level far beyond the student's present learning and performing level? Does the student first need to experience this type of pedaling in an easier setting? How about the student's ear—is it involved? Will the student's progress be slowed, at times, because of the difficulty of the pedaling? There are limitless possibilities. A careful diagnosis by the teacher should produce some logical answers. One rule to remember is that all students need to experience a variety of pedalings before they reach the more advanced levels of literature. Even before going into the intermediate level of literature, a student should have had some experience pedaling various mixtures of articulations, voicings, nuances and numerous characteristics inherent in music composed in different styles.

Musical Understanding and Interpretation

Developing a sense of musical understanding implies that one has the ability to understand the what, when, where and how of music. As musical motion unfolds, the interaction of the elements—melody, harmony, rhythm and form—plus the overall musical texture create the fluctuating tensions and resolutions in music. Learning how this process works is the essence of musical understanding. Some advanced pianists can study a score and understand it intellectually, yet not be able intuitively to take the understanding and turn it into an aural image. Other advanced students can look at a score and intuitively pre-hear how the music should sound but not be able to explain why. Both processes, the understanding and the pre-hearing—intuitively or consciously learned—should go hand-in-hand in the early stages of study. A student's intuition can be clarified by understanding, and understanding can help promote the intuitive aural aspect. With a large majority of students, the pre-hearing has to be fostered unless the student is super-talented. Even the super-talented will have "lazy ears" or poor concentration at times.

To create an atmosphere of musical understanding with a student, the ear should be promoted first, then the facts or the how and why. An excellent method of creating this atmosphere is the demonstration of sound: play a phrase correctly and then incorrectly. Ask the student to decide which is the better one. It will be a game of discovery. "Victoria, do you think my first version or my second version sounded better?" Victoria may reply, "The second version was definitely better." Various students may give a variety of answers, including, "The two versions sounded exactly the same to me!" This answer indicates that the student is still unable to react emotionally to what's happening in the music. Whereas another student may say, "Oh yes, the second version sounded so much better and I can tell you exactly why." The why doesn't need to be said in a technical language; it only needs to describe the student's reaction to what was heard. If the reaction is correct, then the student is learning to react emotionally to the musical phenomena just heard.

For most students the concept of tension and resolution must be explored. It can be done by demonstration, explanation and/or by analogy. For instance, "Sam, does this chord (demonstrating a fully diminished chord) have a sound of tension or a sound of relaxation?" Two chords also can be played—a fully diminished chord and its resolution. Have the student discover aurally, in both cases, which chords have a sound of tension and which ones a sound of resolution or relaxation. This directed listening will promote the aural aspect of the student's musical understanding. The student, though, must have an intellectual understanding of the two different kinds of sounds before the proper identifications can be made. Until one experiences ownership of the concepts of tension and resolution, logical emotional reactions cannot occur.

To foster musical understanding, teach the basic characteristics of what creates tension and resolution. For young students, points of tension and resolution that affect phrase shapes, both dependent and independent, may be taught first instead of the points that may affect the rise and fall of intensity at the note-to-note level. Concern at the local level can occur later after the student becomes oriented to phrase thinking.

What is more important is for students to grasp concepts that will help shape phrases from the concept of the whole. This probably will be the shaping of dependent phrases. Usually the phrases that beginners encounter are simple four-measure dependent phrases that begin relaxed, reach a point of tension or climax on the downbeat of measure 3—many times involving the V7 chord—and from that point of tension (with a slight feeling of relaxation in measure 4) continue into the second dependent phrase (mm. 5-8) toward a point of relaxation on the downbeat of measure 7. When students are learning to understand and hear phrase shapes, it is advisable to have them concentrate on phrase goals: moving from a point of repose toward a point or area of tension or from a point of tension to a point or area of relaxation or repose. After a student understands and hears phrase shapes and plays them with some artistry—regardless of the stage of advancement—style interpretation may be introduced.

Style characteristics sometimes appear in the early stages of elementary music. Whether to incorporate the explanation of these characteristics at this time depends entirely upon each student's individual level of understanding and performance control. Getting a student to be cognizant of how musical motion and phrase shapes unfold should be the higher priority. Style interpretation will be of no value until a student is playing with some artistry and understanding of phrase shapes.

Artistry

The development of artistry in piano playing involves the total involvement of music-making. Artistry refers to the level of musicality and refinement in one's playing. It includes the treatment of:

1. Tone color
2. Dynamics
3. Touches—attacks and releases
4. Voicing
5. Pedaling

6. Nuance—both tonal and rhythmic
7. Gauging of dynamics both from the concept of the whole and the pattern inside
8. Style awareness
9. Understanding and treatment of the rise and fall of intensity levels in music

Artistry includes learning to perform convincingly in a very musical manner. When should artistry be considered? It should begin as soon as a student learns the basics of reading, rhythm, range of keyboard and has the mind and body thinking and playing in a rhythm. Beginners cannot be concerned with how musical a piece sounds if they are still not rhythmically deciphering the notes. Likewise, aural awareness should also begin early in a child's musical experience or pitch errors will not be detected. Neither can any artistry be considered without the ear being involved. The mind and the ear must guide the physical processes or the physical motions become disjointed and awkward. The slow learners will have more trouble playing artistically, yet they can be guided in that direction. They will enjoy playing the piano more, and friends will be more interested in listening to them if they play with some artistic flavor. Some pedagogues suggest that teachers should not be concerned with the development of artistry in those who are not musically gifted. The author believes that everyone who studies piano should be exposed to learning to play artistically, otherwise many students will leave music lessons thinking that music is nothing but skills and drills.

Making music evokes feelings or emotions within the participants: the performer and her audience. Even slow learners can succeed in communicating musically and draw a response from the listener. The teacher has to make value judgments in regard to each student. A performance may be considered very musical for a particular student at a specific level of advancement. Yet for another student, the same level of artistry may not be acceptable because of that student's superior innate musicality. Thus not artistry itself, but the level of artistic development will vary from student to student.

The foundation of artistic development is much easier to teach during the elementary years of study because the music is less complex and the pieces are short. Phrase shapes are easy to understand and hear. Gauging the rise and fall of intensity levels in short pieces is excellent training for understanding phrase shapes later on that are longer and more complex. Learning to pre-hear attacks and releases in a tonal context should be accomplished during the early stages of training or the student will become a visual/physical player rather than an aural one. Many times the potential of playing artistically is there, but it fails to get outside the person because of other difficulties. Reading problems, including the omission of reading holistically in metered-pulse patterns and lack of ear involvement, lead to frustration rather than artistic playing. Adding artistry to a student's playing after she has studied numerous years makes the playing sound artificial or prefabricated. That is to say, the student again thinks, "I'll learn the notes first and later become concerned with sound." Now that piano teachers understand more about the learning process, that approach to learning is obsolete and should be avoided. The total mental and physical involvement of playing the piano is so interwoven that the whole process of mind and body in a rhythm, guided by the ear, should be set into motion very early on. Without this conditioning, development of a student's artistic potential is inhibited. Playing the piano artistically is far too complex to be changed totally at the more advanced levels. Artistry, although it may be in an unrefined state, must begin early.

Musical Style

A student is ready to learn about the interpretation of musical styles as soon as there is a thorough grounding in the basic fundamentals of reading, rhythm and range of keyboard as well as a holistic perception of the symbols in a metered pulse. There also needs to be a basic understanding of how the interaction of the elements creates the rise and fall of intensity levels in music. In other words, the complete music-making process should be in progress. Without it, going into styles with a student is a little forbidding. Perhaps this explains why some students decide they want to stop lessons when they are faced with learning how to play in different styles. The question arises, "How can they cope with all the complexities of a sonatina or a baroque piece when their basic foundation is so poor?" For some, the answer will be to progress through the stages to a point where the teacher may decide to consider giving students music that is attractive, fun to play, but with only a few of the complexities that are present in the classics. The easy baroque dances from the *Notebook for Anna Magdalena* or the *Two-Part Inventions* of J. S. Bach will not be the right selections for everyone. Some students may need to follow a *literature curriculum* of mood music or music that relates more to "pop" sounds, including jazz and blues. As a student progresses through the elementary level of study, the teacher will have to decide which curriculum direction is most logical for that student. "Should I guide Gail through the more classical route or through music that displays more of the sounds of today's pop music?" Directing a student into music that she is not prepared to play or music that she finds completely nebulous will encourage her to turn away from music lessons entirely. This seems to happen particularly to students in the 12 to 14 age bracket.

A large portion of the dropout problem can be traced directly to misguided literature selections: music that is too complex for the student or music that the student has no interest in learning. The teacher may have to "sell" a student on the idea of learning the Bach *Inventions*, and with many of today's students, this may be the case. Yet no type of persuasion will make up for a student's poor foundation for learning music. That must be solved first. There will be a limit to how much a student will be willing to struggle with "getting the notes off the page" before stylistic characteristics can be considered. Consequently, it is more advantageous to foster the *interest* of the student, within the realm of his musical curiosity and learning level, than it is to see him become a dropout.

Regardless of which curriculum track is chosen for a student, many musicians feel that a student should become knowledgeable in both worlds—the classical as well as the "pop" field, including jazz and blues. Perhaps a piano student's literature curriculum should not be totally void of either. In today's world, a well-rounded musician is expected to be in touch with all styles of music.

The Elementary Level

The elementary level of piano teaching and learning can be described overall in terms of six stages of complexity as opposed to grade or book levels. This is advantageous for the teacher because different piano method series use varying leveling and grading systems. Moreover, students advance on such an individual basis that it makes the entire system of leveling very problematic, especially at the elementary level of study. Some students advance very quickly while others seem to need more time at each level of complexity. Progress is not always orderly, and a teacher cannot know in advance how long it will take a student to progress to the next stage of complexity. Teachers find it hard to describe a student's advancement level other than labeling it as elementary, intermediate or advanced. This is because phases within a level are not easily described. Placing musical progress into separate units or time frames is very complicated since learning occurs in a continuous but unorderly fashion. There may be problems labeling Sally as a third year student or one who is in Book III. More appropriately, Sally may best be described in terms of the complexity of her music, both notational and musical.

Different piano method series have different standards and criteria for deciding levels for books. This makes the Book III description valid only when describing progress within that specific set of books. Stating that someone is a third year student reveals only that fact. In three years of study one student may show enormous progress in reading and performing music, whereas another student may have progressed very little. Book III or Level III labels usually describe only the level of notational complexity contained in one book of a particular series, disregarding the musical complexities or the intangible complexities, such as tonal and rhythmic nuance, degrees of staccato and legato, the level of pedaling sophistication and the tension and resolution within phrases and the complete piece.

Although the process of learning to play the piano doesn't easily divide into self-contained units or time frames, the process can be described in stages of complexity. The key concepts within a stage can be outlined systematically and described in a series of learning structures which depend upon what has previously been learned. A description of the phases within a stage can be extremely helpful for teachers in guiding the learning experiences for individual students. Even though each student understands learning and performing concepts at a different rate of progression, certain phases of development need to be experienced by all learners. With some students, the phases may need to be divided. Yet with talented students, the phases may be combined according to an individual's ability and needs.

The following chapters will present six stages of complexity within the elementary level of piano study. These stages illustrate a learning system in sequence of selected key concepts, emulating that of the prodigy or model learner. The instructional sequence presented in these chapters will provide a guideline for promoting a system for learning and is an exemplar or model from which each student's basic musical aptitude, experience and learning capacity can be judged. The teacher, though, must always keep in mind that the model must be adjusted to correlate with each student's basic musical aptitude, experience and learning capacity. The teacher must always consider differences in learners. Repetition or elimination of specific phases of the sequence may be necessary, thus some of the concepts may need to be divided and simplified whereas other ones may need to be combined. For example, there is little value in having students practice individual steps of a learning strategy if their basic intuitiveness would allow them to combine those steps. Progress will be hindered though, if more complex music and complicated learning strategies are presented while the student's present complexity level is already problematic. Students, nonetheless, may have severe problems with one specific aspect of their playing, but that aspect should not dominate over all other aspects of their lessons nor their practice. *Teaching should never ignore the total process of learning and making music, the projected goal for every student.*

Notes

[1] Heinrich Neuhaus, *The Art of Piano Playing,* trans. K. A. Leibovitch (London: Barrie & Jenkins, 1973), 10-11.

[2] Konrad Wolff, *The Teaching of Artur Schnabel* (New York: Praeger Publishers, 1972), 22-23.

[3] Adele Marcus, comp., *Great Pianists Speak with Adele Marcus* (Neptune, N.J.: Paganiniana Publications, 1979), 7.

[4] Leon Fleisher, "About Practicing and Making Music," *Clavier* 2 (September, 1963), 12.

[5] Celia Mae Bryant, "Solving Technical Problems Thru an Intellectual and Musical Approach," *Clavier* 3 (October, 1964), 44.

PART TWO

The Six Stages of Complexity

Chapter IV

STAGE I

Young children's musical experiences in Stage I should include not only the fundamentals of learning to read music, but also some basic music-making ideas. Although the beginning results may not always be satisfactory, a student's early impression of what lessons are all about should include concepts of how to make music at the piano as well as the basic concepts of learning to read music. The talented student may automatically approach lessons with making music the number one goal, while many others will approach it from a more technical standpoint, thinking constantly about where the next note is. Their first attempts in making music, e.g., playing rote tunes and simple one line melodies, may be musically unsatisfactory. Most talented students, however, can immediately copy the teacher's version of a rote tune and play it in a convincing rhythmic swing. Many of the slow or normal learners' versions may include both wrong notes and poor rhythm. What causes the difference? Many teachers believe it is due to the innate musical ability that some children possess, which many writers refer to as "natural musical talent."

"Prodigy," "super-talented" and "musically gifted" are all labels given to children who demonstrate an unusual ability toward learning and performing music at a high rate of proficiency. These children appear to have the ability to 1) perceive music symbols from the beginning in a rhythmic swing; 2) respond emotionally to what they perceive; 3) imagine aurally how that perception should sound; and 4) coordinate physically to produce those sounds. They begin to make music right from the start with very few complications.

Although keeping in mind that there are different types of learners, the music-making process should be presented to all learners during the beginning weeks of lessons. The results will vary widely with different children; however, the exposure is most important. All new students should begin lessons believing that the process will not be all skills and drills but one that will involve having fun with learning to make music. Naturally some students will have trouble imitating all the pitches and rhythms in the simplest of rote tunes. Yet it is the experience that is important as opposed to the exact imitation of the tunes.

Rote tunes will make music come alive in the eyes of a beginner. Ron may say, "I'm making music already, and it is only the first lesson." This is the response that all teachers would like to hear after the first lesson. The child is beginning lessons on a "high note." Ron continues, "I think I'm going to like taking piano lessons really well." Ron's playing of the rote tunes may not have been as good as Sam's version, but the main consideration is that Ron felt the excitement of making music from the first lesson.

Playing rote tunes, learning to work with pre-staff notation and reading the staff will all be a part of the goals for Stage I. The results of the very talented student can be used as a model for most all of the students, but with an understanding that individual goals must be considered for each student who studies. The slow or normal learners will have to approach Stage I from a more practical view, though this does not imply in any way that the slower or normal learners should be exposed to a different type of process than that of the model learner. The difference should be in the proficiency only. Thus, the presentation can be done in simple terms and the expectations and results judged accordingly.

Interviewing the Student

An interview is the most efficient way a teacher can evaluate a child's potential as a piano student. It also offers an opportunity for meeting the child's parents. This is a time that the teacher can become acquainted with the student's general musical ability and background. The interview should include learning about the student's:

1. Personality
2. Family, including parents and siblings
3. Previous musical experience in general music classes, school or church choirs, band, orchestra or private lessons in other instruments
4. Reasons for piano study
5. Other activities and hobbies
6. Rhythmic awareness (response to clapping out rhythmic patterns and imitation of rote song rhythms)
7. Aural awareness to contrasts (high, low and middle pitches on the keyboard), extreme dynamics, intervallic songs, happy and sad or bright and dark triads (major and minor), scale duets (harmonized scale patterns; see Example 14, Chapter IV) and rote tunes. (The teacher must remember that children respond more easily to sound contrasts if the examples are played in the middle range of the keyboard as opposed to the extreme ends.)
8. Mind and body awareness—that is whether the response to instructions proceeds from the mental/visual to the aural before the physical or whether the aural is completely by-passed

Even during the interview, a teacher can sense if the student has any of the natural attributes of the prodigy—the model learner. Decisions concerning the type of learner the student may be can be based upon observation plus other factors, such as 1) general comprehension of instructions; 2) attention span; 3) level of ease with the new teacher; 4) desire to take lessons; and 5) general interest in the music-making process during the interview. All of these considerations will help guide the selection of method series materials for the student. Also, it will give the teacher much insight into how the student will function in a teacher-student situation.

Musical Experiences for Stage I

After the interview the teacher is ready to begin planning out the student's musical experiences for Stage I. A compendium of Stage I experiences should include the following:

1. Introduction to music and playing the piano, including a demonstration of how piano sounds are made
2. Acquaintance with the relationship among the keyboard topography, direction of sound and direction of notes on the score
3. General keyboard orientation
4. Explanation of how the fingers are numbered
5. Presentation of pre-reading
6. Presentation of a system for saying rhythm
7. Demonstration of rote tunes
8. Presentation of directional reading, line and space notes, neighbors and skips, the concept of intervallic map-reading, the Grand Staff and the music alphabet

9. Demonstration of positions on the keyboard, such as G position, C position and/or landmarks on the staff

10. Presentation of a "thinking and doing" system for making music: "Where do I place my hands?" "How do I say my rhythm?" "How do the music symbols relate to the keyboard in both pre-reading and in reading the Grand Staff?"

Making Music with Pre-Reading

Pre-reading experiences should not only be considered as preparation for reading the staff, but they also, along with rote tunes and scale duets (see Example 14), should serve as an avenue for getting the musical process started: preparing the mind, body and ear to "think and do" in a rhythm. Through the pre-reading process, teachers should attempt to get the normal and slow learners to duplicate what the super-talented student does from the beginning lessons: play tunes in a rhythm without having been taught the basic fundamentals of reading. In other words, many times the talented student will begin to read groups of symbols holistically as a matter of course as opposed to having been instructed to go through a set of rational processes. They are able to bypass the preliminary stages of learning to read (perceiving symbols one-at-a-time) and go directly to reading by groups of symbols. These groups are usually perceived in a metered-pulse pattern, such as by the measure in 2/4 or 3/4 meter. Accordingly, all the other students should learn to read by groups as soon as the preliminary stage of reading is conquered. Mastering the preliminary stage of reading, though, may take several weeks or months, and in some cases, even longer. The proficiency level of reading in a rhythmic grouping may be different, but the process should be the same. This can best be achieved by having students begin making music through pre-reading experiences with familiar tunes like the following:

Example 1. "Merrily We Roll Along," from *Alfred's Basic Piano Library*, Lesson Book 1A, Palmer, Manus and Lethco.

LEFT HAND POSITION

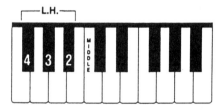

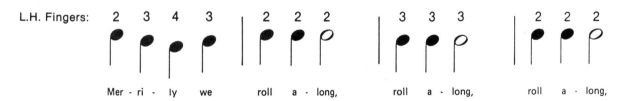

DUET PART: (Student uses black key groups ABOVE the middle of the keyboard.)

THIS PAGE:

44

Example 2. "Jolly Old Saint Nicholas," from *Alfred's Basic Piano Library*, Lesson Book 1A, Palmer, Manus and Lethco.

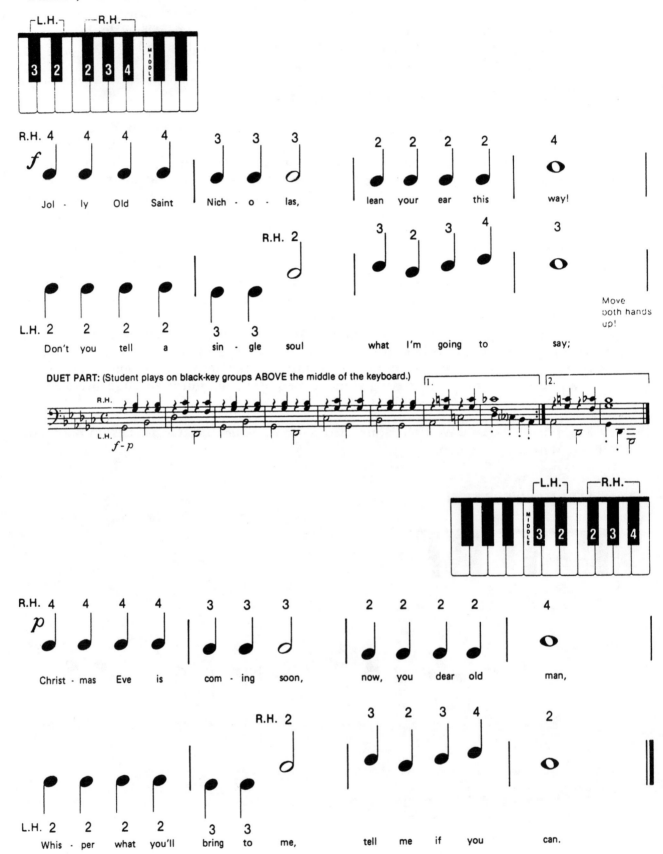

Pre-reading experiences allow a student to tackle a new task—playing the piano—with a known quantity, which is a familiar tune. It is also a task that can be undertaken without having to read the Grand Staff, while providing the teacher with an opportunity to observe the student's reaction to learning to read, his sense of aural awareness and his feeling for rhythm and overall musical intuitiveness. The experience can help the student to recognize the direction of notes, rhythmic note values and left and right hand stem direction. In other words, this is a time for promoting the mind, ear and body processes in a rhythm without the cumbersome task of deciphering notation on the staff. Since the tunes are familiar, the child will often approach the task partially by perceiving how the pre-reading works and partially from knowing the tune previously.

The pre-reading, in most beginning method books, includes duet parts which offer the student the opportunity of playing a familiar tune in a harmonic-rhythmic setting with the teacher or a parent. This type of experience provides rhythmic security and encourages students to react emotionally to the rise and fall of intensity levels, especially at cadential points. It serves as an opportunity for the student to make "big music" even from the beginning lesson at the piano.

Rhythm and Reading

Although the rhythm in both pre-reading and staff reading experiences sometimes can be accomplished by singing the words of familiar tunes, a system for saying rhythm should be introduced from the beginning. The more gifted can sing the words or say the rhythm. Usually both will be successful. However, for many students, singing the words may not work successfully because the student will stop and start either to decipher the notation or to find the next word. The saying of note values normally is the best system, because "the quarter note is a quarter note is a quarter note," regardless of where it appears in 2/4, 3/4 or 4/4 metered pieces. (How a quarter note functions within a 6/8 rhythm or in a triplet figure will have to be explained when it first appears in the student's music.) The way the words relate to the note values must be explained and demonstrated in order for the student to understand the relationship between a quarter note and two-eighth notes; two quarter notes and a half note; three quarter notes and a dotted half note; and four quarter notes and a whole note. The length of note values and their relationship can be clapped out with each new piece for the student to grasp the concept. Whereas numerical counting—1 and 2 and 3 and—fails to relate to the length of note values as they occur in different contexts, the system of saying the note value names does relate.

From the first lessons, students should say the note values aloud (unless they already understand and feel rhythm in a pulse) before and during the time that pieces are played, both during lessons and practice time at home as follows:

Quar-	ter,	Quar-	ter,	Quar-	ter,	Quar-	ter
Half	-	Note,		Half	-	Note	

Quar-	ter,	Quar-	ter,	Quar-	ter
Half	-	Note	-	Dot	

| Quar- | ter, | Quar- | ter, | Quar- | ter, | Quar- | ter |
| Whole | - | Note | - | Four | - | Counts | |

| Quar- | ter, | Quar- | ter |
| Two- | eighths, | Two- | eighths |

| Quar- | ter, | Quar- | ter |
| Quar- | ter- | Dot- | eighth |

The rhythmic duration of saying the words, "quar-ter, quar-ter," must correspond to the rhythmic duration of saying, "half-note." The same would be true with the other relationships: "quar-ter" must equal "two-eighths" and "quar-ter, quar-ter, quar-ter" must equal "half-note - dot" and so forth. The teacher should be concerned with having the student sense the rhythmic durations rather than understand them mathematically. This will be too early for the student to grasp the mathematical bookkeeping of rhythmic notation. (It is neither practical to explain the bookkeeping aspects of rhythm at this time nor necessary.)

The main objective for a student's saying rhythm out loud is to foster a feeling for note value relationships. Yet when playing from memory, beginners gradually should be able to retain the rhythm while only thinking the rhythm silently. Some students, nevertheless, may need to continue saying it out loud when playing from memory, especially in situations where the rhythm "goes out the window" every time the *out-loud-procedure* changes to the *thinking-silently-procedure.*

Feeling note value relationships is necessary before rhythmic-pulse groupings can be felt and understood. Although saying note values is the most common system for teaching rhythm, the best system is whatever works most successfully with a teacher and his or her students. The process always works more effectively without the use of an iron clad rule. Be flexible and allow some of the students to use other methods of counting if they work more efficiently for them. As each student progresses, the beginning system of counting can merge gradually into words, letting the syllables of a word enhance the chances of pulse perception, such as Cho-co-late for three quarter notes in a 3/4 meter measure, Huck-le-ber-ry for a 4/4 meter measure and Ap-ple for a 2/4 meter measure. As the teacher, be sure that the words are said in a rhythmic swing with the first syllable being said slightly louder than the others. This fosters the mental and aural suggestion for remembering where the beginning of each new rhythmic pulse starts and also helps with the transition from note-value thinking to pulse-group thinking.

Some students may want to begin with traditional counting, especially those whose parents instigate the idea because "that is how they learned to count." A majority of the young students, though, will play more consistently in rhythm by saying the syllables of words to match-up with the pulse grouping. Counting by the numbers tends to forestall a student's grasp of pulse rather than enhance it because it draws students more toward note-to-note reading and playing.

Although a number of students will be capable of reading and playing in a rhythmic swing by Stage I or II, there will be many others who will be struggling for some time with feeling the length of simple note values. Those who are struggling will need to delay learning to read in a pulse. When pulse grouping is begun, the new concept should be installed gradually, perhaps with only one or two pieces a week. Then the concept can be extended gradually to more pieces until the student is perceiving all of his literature assignments in that fashion. This approach should be considered also when suggesting memory work; pieces that are easiest to sight-read and play should be the same pieces students are asked to memorize.

As a means of fostering a student's rhythmic sense, clapping out rhythms, saying rhythms aloud and walking rhythms may assist a student in learning to feel and sense rhythmic grouping. This may fail though, as mentioned previously, to transfer automatically when students begin reading from a score. The relationship between feeling the swing of rhythm as a listener versus feeling the rhythm as the player becomes two entirely different processes for many individuals. Consequently, the teacher must draw attention to what the student experienced and felt when being a listener and how that experience can apply rhythmically to making music from written notation.

Introducing the Grand Staff and Map-Reading

Reading the staff can be approached by introducing the student to positions on the keyboard or by emphasizing landmarks. With any system—positions, landmarks or Middle C—the purpose is to familiarize the student with where to begin playing a piece. From that starting point, neighbor-and-skip-note (seconds and thirds) and line-and-space-note concepts can be presented, all of which are an integral part in getting a student to read the staff like a road map, thinking direction and distance. Using the map-reading concept places attention upon the relationship of notes, thus stressing the direction and intervallic relationship as opposed to the isolation of note names. Emphasizing the individual letter names of notes at the very beginning tends to direct a student's reading approach more toward perceiving and playing notes one-at-a-time.

Intervallic Reading

Once the student understands a system for saying rhythm, finding landmarks, positions or guideposts, and comprehending directional map-reading, including the neighbor-and-skip-note concept and the line-and-space-note concept, intervallic reading can be introduced, sequentially. That is to say, as soon as the student recognizes neighbors (seconds) and skips (thirds), that student is ready to make the transition from thinking neighbors and skips to thinking intervals and recognizing not only seconds and thirds, but also fourths, fifths, sixths, sevenths and octaves. The most effective way for teaching a student the intervallic approach to reading is to introduce the intervals one at a time. Allow the student to become at least slightly comfortable with the melodic interval of a second before the melodic interval of a third is introduced.

Throughout the presentation of intervals, the pieces should be in simple, familiar rhythmic settings. With the presentation of each new interval, the texture should alternate hands no more than once per two or four measures. This will give the student a chance to concentrate mainly on one new interval at a time before the texture becomes more complex. The next group of examples illustrates an appropriate way of introducing intervallic reading in a sequenced manner:

Example 3. "Just a Second!" from *Alfred's Basic Piano Library*, Lesson Book 1A, Palmer, Manus and Lethco.

Moderately fast

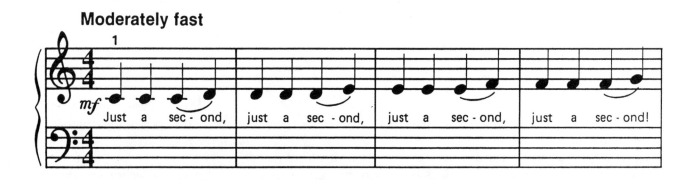

Example 4. "Who's on Third?" from *Alfred's Basic Piano Library*, Lesson Book 1A, Palmer, Manus and Lethco.

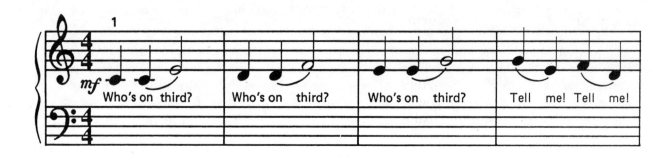

Example 5. "Play a Fourth," from *Alfred's Basic Piano Library*, Lesson Book 1A, Palmer, Manus and Lethco.

Example 6. "My Fifth," from *Alfred's Basic Piano Library*, Lesson Book 1A, Palmer, Manus and Lethco.

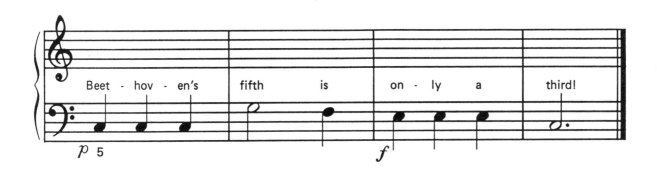

Introducing Imagination and Creativity

Creativity and imagination should be encouraged during Stage I. This will offer the student a chance to "paint pictures" with sound and experiment with "big" sounds and "little" sounds. Students enjoy making sounds that depict thunder, rain or the trickling sound of a flowing brook. This will encourage sound experimentation and emotional reaction to musical phenomena. Concepts dealing with imagination and creativity can easily be left out of lessons, especially those lessons where there are numerous reading or rhythmic problems. In actuality, the opposite should occur. When reading problems begin to cloak the atmosphere of a troubled lesson, this can be one of the most favorable times to introduce imagination and creativity into the learning situation. For example, as a teacher begins to press a student to make correction after correction, the student's mind sometimes becomes blocked. Confusion begins to control the student. The distinction gets blurred between what the errors are and what the corrections should be. The reaction becomes one of "will this lesson ever end so I can get out of here and go home?" This could be the perfect time for the teacher to switch the student from reading notation to making up songs by ear. Allowing a student "to make up her own songs" not only gives the student creative and imaginative experience, but it also takes the pressure off an otherwise tense moment in the lesson. The student can go home feeling proud of her creative accomplishments rather than embarrassed about her reading problems.

Guiding the Physical in a Rhythm

Even during the early stages of reading music, the more gifted students tend to perceive music in a rhythmic grouping. In turn their physical actions, including wrists and fingers, respond in a coordinated fashion, especially with regard to wrists' synchronization. The opposite may be true with many of the slow and normal learners. Their physical actions will reflect a less organized type of perception, usually relating more to individual note-reading. These students will need special help in fostering perceptions that will promote organized physical motions. This is when the application of words, used to foster rhythmic grouping— such as *Cho-co-late*—may gradually be changed to the words, *Down-and-up*, in order to promote physical organization and coordination. For example, the words, *Down-and-up*, will remind the student that any body or wrist motions should be corroborated with the rhythmic pulse grouping or rhythmic swing of the music. This enhances the continuous motion of musical sound and prevents the wrists from pumping at random or with each note that is played. Curtailing the "pumping of the wrists" and fostering pulse grouping should be two of the Stage I goals for a majority of the students. Nonetheless, those who are struggling with "reading the notes and guessing at the rhythm" will be overwhelmed with just the reading process. Consequently, they will not be ready to be concerned with whether their music is being played in a swing or whether the wrists are synchronized with the pulse. In approaching a piece like the next example, a talented beginner will "see and play it by the measure" without even considering the notes one at a time. Most slow learners and many normal beginners, though, will have to perceive it one note at a time, because any other way would be much too complicated.

Example 7. "Position C," from *Alfred's Basic Piano Library*, Lesson Book 1A, Palmer, Manus and Lethco.

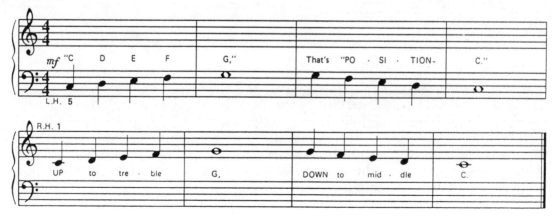

In most cases, the common goal for the slower learners will be to understand and play the pitches and note values correctly. Perception and playing by the measure will be far too difficult; therefore, how should the teacher proceed—by note values or by measure pulse? By note values will be the answer for many of these students, but the teacher may experiment some with the measure pulse. The result may be surprising. If the result is a positive one, the teacher knows that the student is ready to proceed at a little faster rate than normal. All the same, if the result is partial or total confusion, the teacher will recognize that the student probably needs to proceed, as most slow learners do, needing many, many months of note value instruction before any concepts of grouping can be presented.

Evaluating Textural Settings

The texture of beginning pieces should be easy-to-read notational patterns with simple note values and with no articulation. The patterns should make use of two or four measures in one hand before the musical idea switches to the other hand, as is demonstrated in the following example:

Example 8. "Balloons," from *Alfred's Basic Piano Library*, Lesson Book 1A, Palmer, Manus and Lethco.

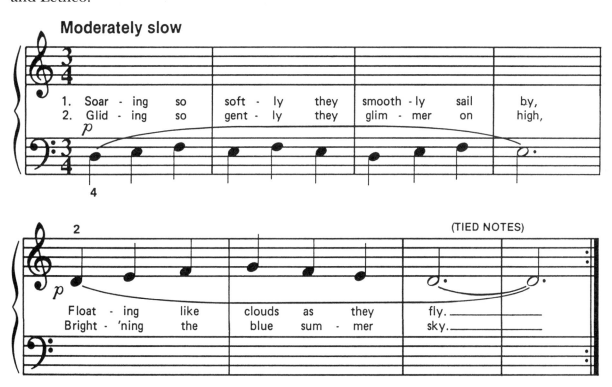

Additional note values can be introduced as soon as the child feels comfortable with simpler patterns, such as mostly quarter notes except a minimal number of whole or half

52

notes. With pieces in 3/4 meter, patterns of quarter notes with a few dotted half notes are preferred. This can be followed with pieces using eighth notes or quar-ter-dot-eighth patterns. (Both eighth notes and quar-ter-dot-eighth patterns appear at different times in different series. Some include it in the first level books; others wait until the second level.) When eighth notes are added, they should appear in easy notational settings. The next two examples have simple textures but the settings are slightly more complex than the previous example. The first one adds eighth notes and the latter one contains more frequent hand alternation:

Example 9. "Goldfish," from *Bastien Piano Basics*, Piano for the Young Beginner, Primer B, Bastien.

Example 10. "Now I've Done It!" from *Alfred's Basic Prep Course*, Solo Book A, Palmer, Manus and Lethco.

Pieces that alternate hands more frequently than at two- or four-measure intervals appear in primer books at different times. In some of the primer books, there are some examples where frequent, alternating hand patterns occur as early as by the third or fourth piece. This obviously will be very confusing to a beginner. The same would be true when eighth notes are introduced during the first few pieces of a child's primer book.

Harmonic intervals usually are presented after melodic intervals. They too will need to be experienced in a number of pieces before they are recognized, heard and executed without difficulty. The easier the setting is, the less trouble the child will have going from one harmonic interval to the next. Harmonic intervals which first appear without an accompanying melody are grasped much more easily by a student, such as is illustrated in the following example:

Example 11. "More About Intervals, No. 2," from *Alfred's Basic Piano Library*, Lesson Book 1A, Palmer, Manus and Lethco.

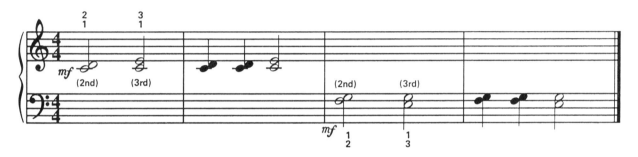

Playing several pieces similar to "More About Intervals" will make it easier for students to approach pieces combining both types of intervals, melodic and harmonic. These next two examples are excellent pieces for introducing the combination:

Example 12. "Rockets," from *Alfred's Basic Piano Library*, Lesson Book 1A, Palmer, Manus and Lethco.

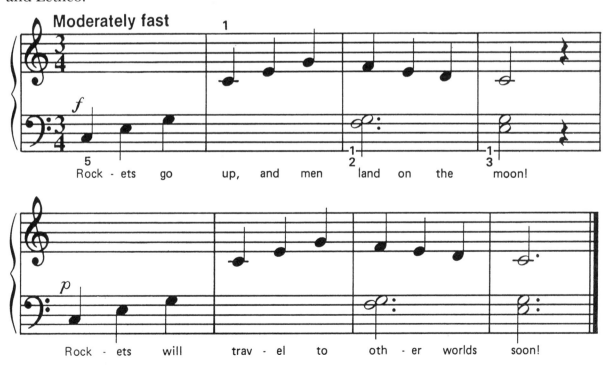

Example 13. "Quiet River," from *Alfred's Basic Piano Library*, Recital Book 1A, Palmer, Manus and Lethco.

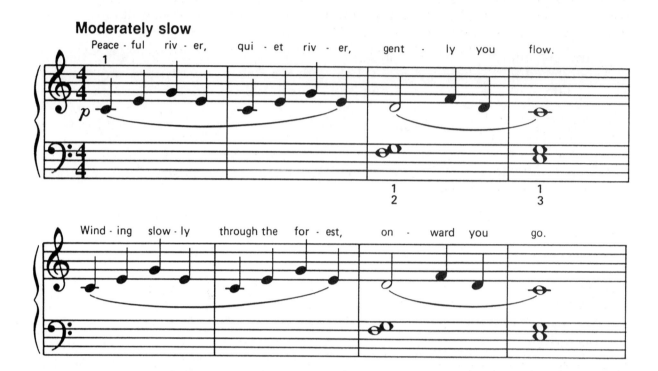

In pieces such as "Quiet River" and "Rockets" the student should begin to feel comfortable with recognizing how the intervals look and sound. In both pieces, there exists only seconds and thirds in the right hand melody and harmonic seconds and thirds in the left hand. The combination of these intervals should become easy for the student to recognize and play before fourths, fifths and other simple intervals are introduced. Students can learn an interval such as the fifth by rote, but there is no transfer value unless the student relates to the way the fifth looks and sounds in relationship to other simple intervals. As a student recognizes the melodic third, e.g., C and E, that recognition will gradually meld into the recognition that the C and E are the first two notes of the root position of the C Major triad. Subsequently, all of these early reading concepts become part of the basic foundation of learning to read and understand the components of music.

Shaping Phrases

For some students Stage I will be too soon to be concerned with phrase shapes involving the rise and fall of intensity levels. For others, the concept of phrasing may be introduced with the previous two examples using a very simple explanation, such as, "Let's consider the beginning of this piece as being at home, a place of relaxation or repose." This can be followed with, "Let's think about leaving home and going to the shopping center, a place of excitement and fun. After the place of excitement, we will go toward home again, a place of rest and relaxation." In other words, home would represent the tonic harmony. The exciting trip to the mall would represent going from the tonic to the dominant, causing a rise in the intensity or dynamic level. From the dominant, the arrival back home would signify a return to a point of repose. This approach allows the teacher to use analogies with the child to promote the understanding of phrases—both dependent and independent. Phrase concepts do not necessarily have to be explained at this time, only the analogy. The purpose of using the trip promotes the concept that phrasing is similar to a continuous journey as opposed to traveling only from note-to-note. The students who are struggling with the basics of reading will find the phrasing concept to be an overload for an already overtaxed mind. Those who are more imaginative will be ready and willing to explore the idea of "making stories out of their music." Playing duets or accompanying the student at a second piano is another way to foster the student's hearing of phrase shapes. The teacher can dynamically emphasize the changes in harmony, denoting the rise and fall of intensity levels. Playing tetrachord scale patterns in duet form with the teacher also promotes the same phenomenon. Playing scale duets helps to awaken the student's intuitive sense of hearing what notes belong together in a specific tonality, such as F Major or D Major. (The teacher must learn to transpose the following harmonic progression into the different keys where the teacher's part can be played with the student as he or she deciphers by ear what notes belong together in the different scale patterns.)

Example 14. "Scale Duet," from *Developing Piano Performance: A Teaching Philosophy*, arranged by Camp.

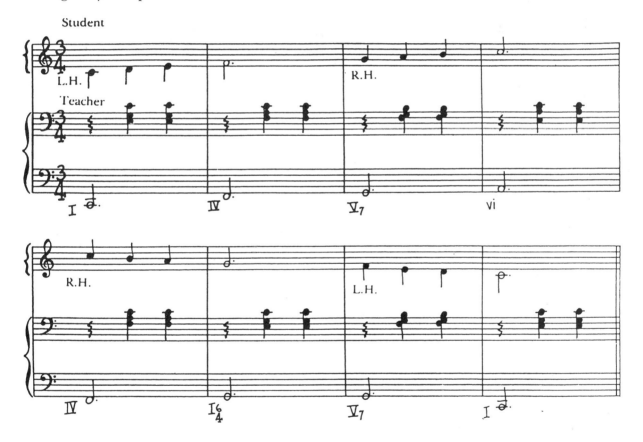

Here again, the student is experiencing the rise and fall of harmonic tension and resolution in a setting without having to read the staff. The scale duet concept can be presented first at a child's interview and continued on during the first couple of years of study. (Playing scales with thumb crossings can be delayed until this type of scale pattern appears in their music.) The scale duet concept is a wonderful way to present an aural version of pitch relationships within a given tonality. For example, after the scale duet is played in the key of C, place the student's fingers (L.H. 5-4-3-2 and R.H. 2-3-4-5 fingerings) on the F position, and let the student decide which one of the pitches sounds incorrect, suggesting that a black key is needed. This can be followed gradually throughout the different tonalities until one day that student will have an aural concept of "what notes belong together" in all of the major and minor tonalities. How to write and recognize the key signature patterns can be presented later in theory books and in musicianship classes.

Teaching a student the pitch pattern of a specific scale by having that student memorize the key signature is a visual–tactile approach to teaching scales and keys. This is why piano teachers are constantly having to correct the pitches that should be flatted or sharped within a given tonality. The aural aspect of the tonal relationships among the pitches is missing. Learning what key a piece is in by memorizing how many flats or sharps are in that piece results in the concept of tonality being only visual, whereas the aural concept of the tonality is what becomes valuable to the student.

In grasping the tension and resolution idea or the rise and fall of phrase shapes, some students may respond very quickly to the previously mentioned "shopping center" concept of phrase shapes, moving from a sense of home toward excitement, and then returning home again. Others may understand more easily from hearing the teacher demonstrate the concept or by experiencing it in scale duets and harmonized rote tunes. Hypothetically, it is to a child's advantage to be lead intuitively first, because that can be done even before the child is capable of understanding an analogy. As a rule, the teacher should always appeal first to a child's innate sense of reacting emotionally to musical phenomena. This process can lead students to begin thinking intuitively about tonal quality and quantity as well as the character and mood of pieces.

The Initial Approach to Legato and Staccato

Playing legato or staccato comes very naturally to some beginners, while other beginners with finger coordination problems experience a number of difficulties, particularly with playing legato. When this occurs, the teacher can lessen the problem by having the student play non-legato for the first few weeks of lessons. This will allow for greater concentration on the sound of the succession of pitches rather than on the touch. Playing all pitches non-legato will not be confusing because staccato notes usually do not make their appearance until near the end of the child's first book. Some of the less coordinated students may play in a non-legato fashion naturally, depressing the key on the first part of the note value (Quar-) and releasing on the second part (-ter). When children are forced into playing legato before they hear what the teacher is describing, the result normally causes tension in the fingers and hands, a condition that should be prevented. After a student begins to hear the need for connecting notes, legato playing can be attained more readily. Legato playing achieved only as a physical concept produces a superficially connected sound, because legato versus a detached sound is an aural concept that is only carried out by the physical, not created by it.

Some students will connect a series of pitches yet the result sounds like individual attacks. This is due to a student's continuing to approach the reading task thinking in note values long after the teacher has stressed the grouping concept. When this occurs there are problems to be diagnosed concerning the dichotomy between what the instructions were and what the student is actually doing. The problem may be the result of an error in perception as well as a lack of aural involvement.

Staccato playing can be understood and executed more easily if it is introduced in a piece that has all staccato notes. Otherwise the student becomes confused trying to remember which touch to execute. "The Popcorn Man" is an excellent piece for approaching staccato playing for the first time because all the pitches are marked staccato:

Example 15. "The Popcorn Man," from *Alfred's Basic Piano Library*, Recital Book 1A, Palmer, Manus and Lethco.

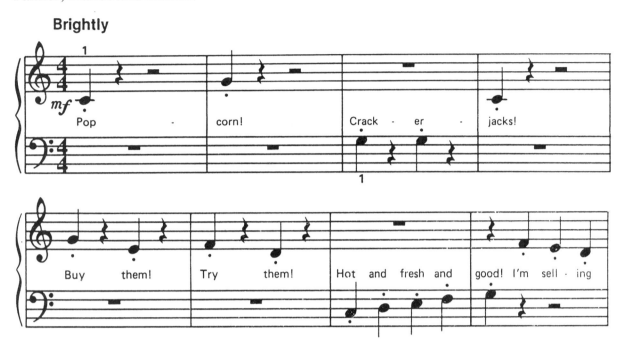

The next nine examples illustrate how staccato notes and other concepts should be sequenced throughout the six stages of complexity. Each example contains staccatos in increasingly more difficult contexts. A majority of the students will need to learn several pieces at each complexity level before they progress to playing staccato pitches in a more complex setting. For example, most students should experience several pieces similar to "Raindrops" before they attempt pieces like the "Minuet and Trio" or the "Toymaker's Dance" which are both from more complex stages of music. All nine of these examples are from *Alfred's Basic Piano Library*, Level 1A through Level 5:

Example 16. "Raindrops," from *Lesson Book 1A*.

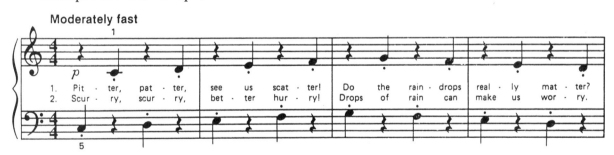

Example 17. "Ping-Pong," from *Lesson Book 1B*.

Example 18. "Minuet and Trio," from *Recital Book 1B.*

Moderately fast

Example 19. "Toymaker's Dance," from *Recital Book 2.*

Allegro

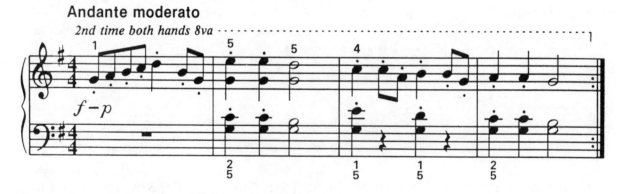

Example 20. "18th Century Dance," from *Lesson Book 2.*

Andante moderato

Example 21. "Tango Staccato," from *Recital Book 2.*

Andante moderato

Example 22. "Alpine Polka," from *Recital Book 3.*

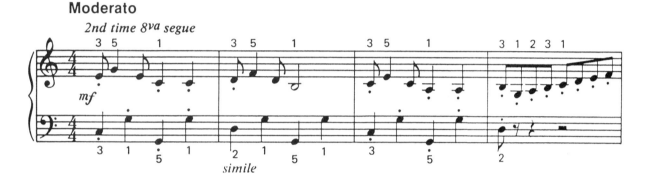

Example 23. "Calypso Holiday!" from *Lesson Book 4.*

Example 24. "Chromatic Polka," from *Recital Book 5.*

Staccato notes should be demonstrated as sounds that are detached as opposed to sounds that are connected. The detachments, at first, may be explained as notes that are released during the second half of a note value, e.g., playing on the "quar-" and releasing on the "-ter." (This is similar to the non-legato style which was suggested for the beginning student who has finger coordination problems.) This approach will prevent the student from getting the impression that staccato notes are played like "touching a hot iron," an idea that was popular at one time. The hot iron concept is not recommended because it suggests to a student to play staccatos with no aural concept of what the detachment sounds like. Also, the hot iron suggestion will make it difficult for the teacher, in more advanced music, to instruct the student to play different degrees of staccato and legato in such pieces as early classical dances and sonatinas. The teacher should instruct the student to play staccato or *portato* notes in a way that each one will sing or have a "lilt" sound before being released. Suggesting to students that they play staccatos as very quick releases implies to those students that all

60

detached notes are alike. This first impression will be difficult to change later on when the student progresses to intermediate and advanced level literature.

Understanding Accidentals and Key Signatures

Key signatures usually appear in beginning books after accidentals are introduced as a means of establishing a tonality, such as F Major. For example, the key of F Major is introduced as F position with Bb appearing as an accidental. In this way, the student is reminded each time B appears that the B needs to be flatted, similar to the following:

Example 25. "The Dragon's Lair," from *Bastien Piano Basics*, Piano Primer, Bastien.

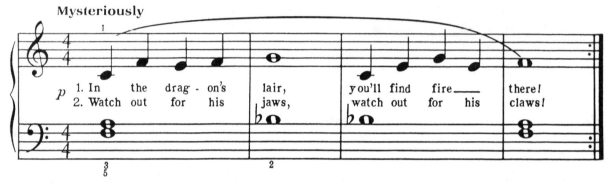

Playing in different positions that require familiarity with different tonalities will be understood and executed easily if the student has already experienced the concept aurally through the scale duets. Learning to play in a specific key, such as F Major or A Major, is much more difficult for a student if that student is approaching the task strictly from the visual standpoint. Using the scale duet concept encourages the student to approach all tonalities from the aural concept.

Reading Concepts and Physical Coordination

Up to this point in Stage I, most recommended concepts have been of an aural or rhythmic nature. As the student progresses into music similar to the next example, "My Robot," some special guidance may be needed not only in reading and understanding accidentals, but also in coordinating the fingers:

Example 26. "My Robot," from *Alfred's Basic Piano Library*, Lesson Book 1A, Palmer, Manus and Lethco.

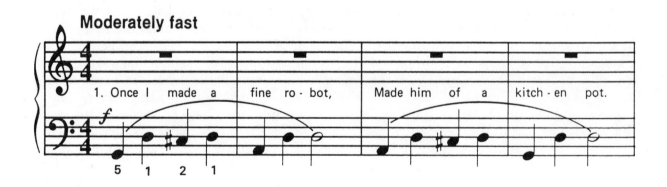

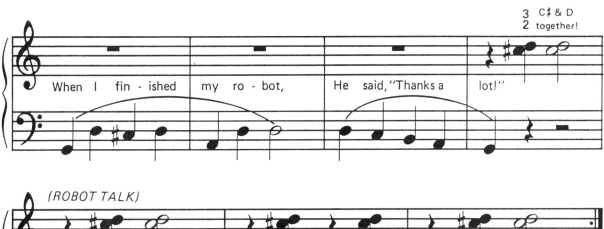

3rd time gradually dying away -

"My Robot" illustrates a left hand pattern that probably will require some physical guidance by the teacher. The rhythmic grouping and musical motion should travel by the measure, thus requiring the physical motions to do the same. The use of saying words will help foster the needed corroboration among the rhythm, the musical motion and the physical motions. Words reflecting the rhythmic pattern, such as *Huck-le-ber-ry*, may be changed gradually to words reflecting the physical motion, one overall wrist motion per measure. Saying the words, D*own-and-up-and* or *reLax-and-up-and* will foster this motion. As the child progresses into more complex musical concepts, the series of *Down-and-up-and* motions will need to be taught as one continuous motion similar to walking. For instance, as a child walks, his individual steps glide into one continuous type of motion rather than into a type of marching or polka step. Playing a group of single notes is similar. When playing the keys by a measure grouping, the wrists usually dip slightly on each downbeat, but there isn't a separate or "frozen" attack for those keys. Instead, the downbeat attack is only part of a continuous motion like the motion that occurs when a child walks. Talented children will play this way automatically because they will hear the musical motion traveling by the measure: a primary pulse feeling on beat one and a secondary pulse feeling on beat three as opposed to hearing it one note at a time. If the musical idea is expressed in individual pitches, the student will play measure one as four separate motions, measure two with a downbeat on beat one and another downbeat on beat three. With most students, the rest of the piece will also be played similarly. Although the *Down-and-up-and* practice procedure may mean different things to different students, the *down* concept only signifies the beginning of a new circle of musical motion as opposed to a big drop with the wrists or a down "hit" sound.

All students frequently lower their wrists slightly at times and it is usually at random when using the thumbs and fifth fingers. Suggesting words like *Down-and-up-and* organizes that lowering of the wrists to coincide with the rhythmic pulse grouping, which becomes more and more important as a child advances. After a student receives instruction for promoting physical coordination, the tendency to "hit" the *down* or make a large, jerking down motion

62

should lessen. If there is a tendency to jerk the wrist down on the downbeat, the word *down* may be changed to re-L*ax.* The saying of words will serve as a mental reminder that the wrists should be synchronized with the rhythmic grouping—the rhythmic swing of the piece.

Suggesting the use of words, like *Down-and-up-and,* is a tangible way to help organize a student's perceptions and physical motions. Although the *Down-and-up-and* is referred to as a physical practice procedure, the words serve only as a practice reminder for helping organize the mind in directing the physical. The actual wrists' motions will be minimal. The teacher will be attempting to prevent the student from pumping the wrists for each note, or in the case of "My Robot," from pumping the wrists when the notes are played with the thumb. Pumping the wrists is very common among young piano students. Not only does this make a student's music sound "notey," it also is an indication that the student is perceiving the score one note at a time or outside a pattern reflecting the pulse grouping.

The Older Beginner

With the adult or older beginner, learning to read differs with each individual just as with the young beginner. Older beginners, therefore, can be treated in a similar, individualistic fashion as were the younger students. One quickly realizes, though, that adults already have established patterns of approaching a task or situation, thus complicating the process of teaching them how to practice. Often they immediately desire to play difficult pieces which require corrections on most every aspect: pitch, rhythm, fingering, articulation, plus the mental, aural, emotional and physical.

Adults have a tendency to "pick out what they can," at a tempo that is much too fast, being completely undisturbed by numerous starts and stops. This makes it frustrating for student and teacher alike. Unless an adult is willing to approach learning to play the piano in some kind of organized framework, the process is rather unsuccessful. Nonetheless, if an adult really wants to learn to play, and not just play some tunes "kind of correctly," the same sequential order of concepts for the young beginner can be followed. Music may be selected, however, from books that are more appropriately designed for the older beginner or adult, such as the following four examples:

Example 27. "A Friend Like You," from *Alfred's Basic Adult Piano Course,* Lesson Book 1, Palmer, Manus and Lethco.

Example 28. "Beautiful Brown Eyes," from *Alfred's Basic Adult Piano Course,* Lesson Book 1, Palmer, Manus and Lethco.

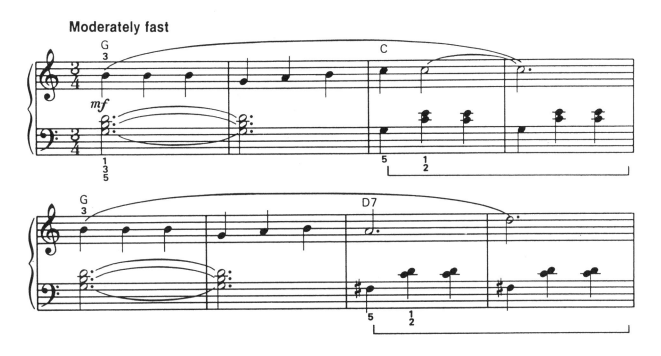

Example 29. "Sonatina in Two Positions," from *Alfred's Basic Piano Library,* Chord Approach for the Later Beginner, Solo Book 1, Palmer.

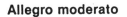

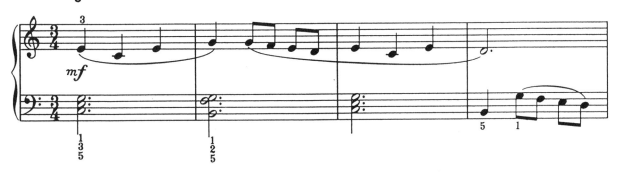

64

G POSITION

Example 30. "Nocturne," from *Alfred's Basic Piano Library*, Chord Approach for the Later Beginner, Solo Book 1, Palmer.

C POSITION

Andante moderato

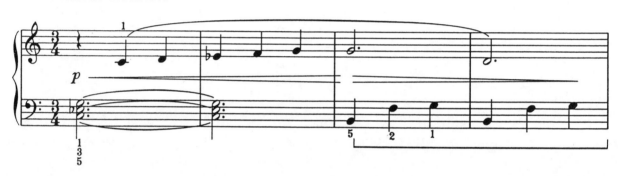

G POSITION

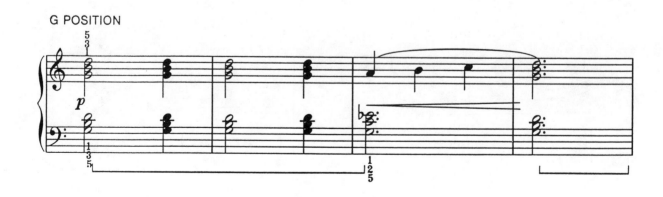

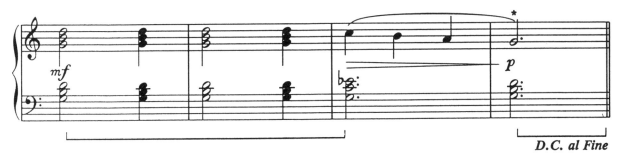

D.C. al Fine

*Here the last notes may be released by the hands while you are moving to the new position, since the notes will continue to be sustained by the pedal.

Some adults are capable of working on music that increases in complexity at a faster rate than literature designed for young children, thus allowing for conceptual presentation to progress with only a minimal amount of reiteration. Just like young beginners, the older ones will have to be assigned literature that is designed to relate to their individual ability so that new concepts can be absorbed and integrated with the old ones.

Evaluation of Stage I Progress

The concepts from Stage I will need to be experienced in numerous types of contrasting settings before the student is advanced to the Stage II level of complexity. If the notational settings become too complex too quickly, the student's sight-reading of new pieces becomes very labored and full of starts and stops. When this happens, it is time to rethink what is being done. Are the pieces getting too complex too soon? Is the student losing concentration when pieces are first read? Is the student reading a rhythm by note values or pulse? The student's progress should be evaluated before continuing or the student's ear and emotions will "shut off" and progress will be disrupted. Some of the pieces may be corrected a number of times and finally learned, but this will indicate to the teacher that the learning and performing progression is functioning improperly. Remember, the student needs to perceive new pieces with some ease or the fun and excitement of learning diminishes. When lessons begin to be more corrective than instructive, the student's literature curriculum needs to be reevaluated.

The reading and learning of music is an ongoing process where formerly learned concepts appear in new, slightly more complex settings—thus the importance of sequencing. This enables the student to feel some accomplishment instead of being reminded constantly that a large portion of what is being read has been incorrectly perceived. Students must be challenged, yet the complexity level of pieces should coincide with the student's present learning level.

When a teacher becomes aware that progress has come to a standstill, additional books, usually of a slightly less complex nature, are needed. The interruption in progress indicates that new concepts are appearing in the pieces faster than the student can absorb, a situation that occurs frequently in Stage I since the student is just beginning to learn to read. Finding additional books at the same level with a similar reading approach is the best answer. The problem does not necessarily indicate that the teacher has made mistakes in instruction or literature selections; children simply react differently to learning to read. Most students need many experiences with familiar settings before being challenged further. This is a common problem and it may occur also a number of times within the other stages of learning.

At Stage I, there are only a few appropriate supplementary books from which to choose. The choice of books, consequently, will be either from the same piano method series, such

66

as recital, solo, Christmas or technic books, selections from other series, or books that display a chord approach to reading. At this stage, technic books should be considered as additional books for grasping reading concepts. In any case, do not complicate the already problematic situation by adding books that will produce additional reading and rhythmic problems. For instance, be very careful about assigning primer books that contain pieces using single notes in hands-together settings, mixing parallel and contrary motions and using a variety of intervals. These are most confusing for young beginners. Also, some primer books introduce intervals and note values with no consideration for a sequential order.

Sequencing all facets of the texture of the music is of utmost importance for most young beginners because a solid reading foundation is needed before they experience concepts out of sequence. Although it was stated earlier that "method series do not necessarily fail," beginner books from some of the series are designed more effectively than others, particularly for the normal or slow learner. With the super-talented, there can be less concern because this type of student computes the symbols quickly and turns them into music intuitively, regardless of arrangement. But for most of the other learners, the presentation of concepts in some type of sequential order is extremely important.

Chapter V

STAGE II

Students are ready for Stage II concepts and literature as soon as they understand the Stage I complexities, such as 1) the relationships among the Grand Staff (the direction of sound and the keyboard topography); 2) directional map-reading; 3) a system for saying rhythm; and 4) the process of getting the mind and ear to direct the emotions and the body in a rhythm. To a large extent, the Stage I concepts will have to be fostered over and over again with most students, this being especially true with many of the normal and slow learners. Some of the concepts may need reiteration continually throughout a student's musical training because the level of competency will vary with each individual who studies piano. One student will read pitches very easily but will fail to play in a rhythm. Another student will read the pitches in a rhythm but will have no aural awareness of pitch errors. Students have to be paced according to the positive and negative aspects of their individual ability to learn music and to play the instrument.

With this stage as with the other stages, the teacher must always remember that the six stages of complexities should never be considered as self-contained units, nor as having any given length of study time associated with the individual stages. One student may be comfortable with beginning concepts and literature from Stage II before Stage I is completed. Other students may need to continue working in Stage I for quite an extended period of time. If very little is being grasped in Stage I, moving on to the Stage II literature will only complicate the situation. On the other hand, students will have to be evaluated very carefully for they may lose all motivation if left in the Stage I literature for too long a time. Moving on to a slightly more complex level may provide just the motivation that is needed. Other students may "drown" in the more complex music of Stage II. What is best for each student will have to be decided very carefully by the teacher.

Increasing the Complexity Level

Advancing students to the next stage of complexity should always be approached with the following in mind:

1. Teaching material should be selected on the basis of what is within the realm of possibility for each student.
2. Selections should offer a student the opportunity for eliminating weaknesses from the previous stage in addition to presenting new challenges when applicable.
3. Teaching material should not advance the student into areas which will amplify weaknesses, e.g., pieces that would include a mixture of motions—parallel, oblique and contrary—in a hands-together setting if that student is still having problems with reading patterned textures utilizing one hand at a time with very few directional changes.

If the student is ready for Stage II literature and concepts, the teacher will need to begin (or to continue in cases where it was started in Stage I) the awakening of musical intuition and/or musical understanding, e.g., to teach the shaping of phrases by intuition or through understanding how musical motion is created. The student should become aware aurally of the tension and resolution in phrases, such as a real or implied harmonic progression from tonic to dominant and back to the tonic. The beginning concepts of artistry should be approached by the more talented students, such as treatment of phrase shapes, points of tension and repose, different levels of sound and intensity and an understanding of the difference in touches, such as slow and fast attacks and releases.

In regard to rhythm, performance tempos can be increased slightly within pieces that are easy to read and play in a pulse grouping. An understanding of pulse grouping can be fostered by having the student listen, clap and write pulse groupings within a meter. The pie-system of saying rhythm in 6/8 meter should be introduced when the student first encounters any compositions in 6/8 meter. This includes saying *cho-co-late* for ♩♩♩ ; *pump-kin* for ♩ ♪ ; and *pie* for ♩. .

For many of the students, melodic and harmonic intervals may need to be reviewed, especially as they are presented in different settings and combinations. The notational texture in the Stage II music normally includes:

1. The mobility of five-finger patterns through the use of 8va signs,
   resulting in the expansion of the keyboard range
2. The inclusion of more accidentals
3. The continuation of short melodic patterns, but with more directional
   changes
4. The mixture of unpatterned notation along with the previously learned
   five-finger patterned notation

By the second level of books, method series begin to differ in the timing of the extension beyond the familiar five-finger positions. Whenever the extension does occur, this will demand either some thumb crossings or the use of consecutive fingers on nonconsecutive notes, for example the use in the right hand of finger 1 on C, finger 2 on E, and finger 5 on A. For some students this expansion will be premature because they still may be struggling with remembering that G is a second up from F or that C is a second down from D. Having to remember that an interval larger than a neighbor note may have to be played by a neighboring finger can be confusing to some, especially those who have failed to gain ownership of the five-finger patterns.

The teacher must correlate a student's present reading potential with the new demands of the literature. The challenge that the notational patterns produce should be in the general range of the student's grasp. If the challenge overextends this range, it may interrupt a student's reading progress for awhile. For instance, some method books introduce contrasting articulation between the hands at the same time the notational patterns are extended. For some students, this produces a challenge that is far greater than can be absorbed at one time. The result may cause the student to stop and start rhythmically as each new piece is approached.

These demands plus other musical ones, in turn, will place more pressure upon the coordination of the physical. Moreover, some of the pieces will require singing or resonant sounds (ones that have prolonged vibrations) to be convincing musically. These are sounds that have a singing quality, sometimes referred to as "fat" sounds, versus "lean" sounds that tend to die immediately. Tones that have a singing quality will be needed especially for the first, louder tone in two-note slurs and for long melodic notes on strong beats. The areas of creativity and imagination should also be encouraged, unless the student is continuing to struggle with basic reading and rhythmic concepts. To what extent the teacher should proceed with these new demands will depend entirely upon the learning and performing ability of each student. These ideas offer the teacher a compendium of possibilities for the hypothetical student as opposed to a model example of what should be considered as a normal attainment for the majority of students. The compendium includes:

1. Development of rhythmic pulse and faster tempos
2. Extension of the familiar five-finger patterns
3. Introduction of musical understanding
4. Increase of musical demands brought about through the inclusion of musical understanding

Melodic and Harmonic Intervals

For a student to become secure with any concepts, especially those concerning map-reading and intervallic relationships, there will be a need to experience each concept in many different kinds of settings. In reference to intervals, most students will master melodic intervals long before mastering harmonic intervals. Harmonic intervals may at first require an extra thought process for some students because of the added physical problem, sometimes called "finger locking." Playing consecutive fifths is usually easy for a student. Alternating seconds, thirds, fourths, and fifths, though, will be difficult for many young students. Their fingers may tend to lock on each different size interval when the next interval is larger or smaller. Some students appear to add an extra thought process in order for their hand to make the change. Once a student perceives and hears a series of changing harmonic intervals as a second-nature process, the fingers, in turn, stop locking. Thus the finger locking or freezing on a harmonic interval translates into a mental–aural perception problem instead of a physical problem. Physically the fingers fail to move in a continuing fashion when the mental–aural fails to perceive the different sized intervals in a continuous rhythm. This problem can be attributed to the student's inability to hear the harmonic-intervallic progression. To help alleviate the problem, pieces in easy rhythmic settings should be experienced, such as in the next three examples:

Example 31. "Good Sounds," from *Alfred's Basic Piano Library*, Lesson Book 1B, Palmer, Manus and Lethco.

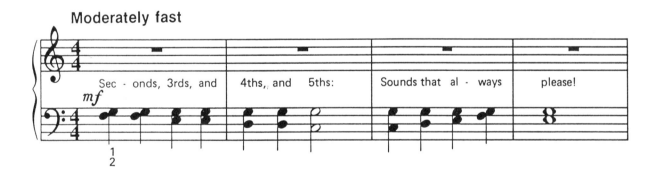

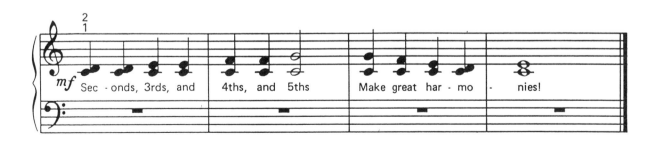

70

Example 32. "Mumbo-Jumbo," from *Alfred's Basic Piano Library*, Piano Solo 1A, Palmer.

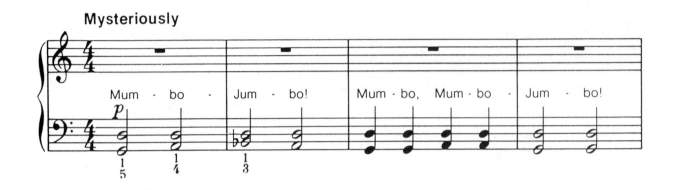

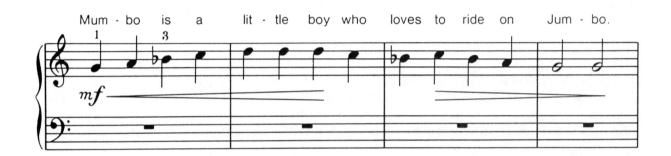

Example 33. "Hayride!" from *Alfred's Basic Piano Library*, Recital Book 1B, Palmer, Manus and Lethco.

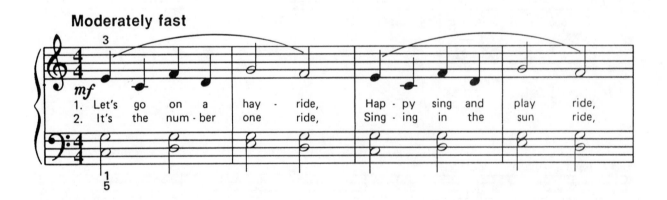

Working on several pieces similar to the next example will also help alleviate the problem because the left hand has a complete measure of rest before a different harmonic interval has to be played:

Example 34. "Money Can't Buy Ev'rything!" from *Alfred's Basic Piano Library*, Lesson Book 1B, Palmer, Manus and Lethco.

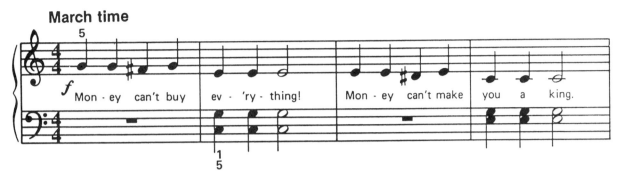

Settings similar to these are much easier for the young student than pieces that require three different harmonic-intervallic changes within one measure. Having the same harmonic interval for a measure and a measure rest between the harmonic-intervallic changes gives the student time to disengage the left hand before the mind has to command, physically, the fingers to change intervals. The measure rest also gives the ear more time to perceive aurally the next interval.

Harmonic intervals and accidentals are two aspects of the notational texture that commonly cause reading problems during this stage, particularly if students continue to recognize symbols separately instead of in units. This separate thought process will cause a delay in execution of each interval, which in turn throws the musical idea out of rhythm. The same thing happens with accidentals. Some students will tend to recognize accidentals separately from pitch symbols. Here again, the double thought process delays the mental–aural command of the physical, resulting in rhythmic stopping and starting. To overcome these problems, students need to experience both the harmonic intervals and accidentals over and over again in simple settings before these are approached in more complex textures. There has to be an integration of the thought processes in both cases, which can come only through much experience with the concepts. The following examples from Katherine Beard's book, *Creepy Crawly Things and Some That Fly*, offer an excellent opportunity for integrating the thought processes involved in playing consecutive harmonic intervals:

Example 35. "Pinching Bug," from *Creepy Crawly Things and Some That Fly!* Beard.

Example 36. "When Mr. Skunk Stamps His Foot --- Look Out!" from *Creepy Crawly Things and Some That Fly!* Beard.

Excerpts are from *Creepy Crawly Things and Some That Fly!* by Katherine K. Beard from a collection of 27 elementary pieces—used by permission of the publisher: The Boston Music Co., 172 Tremont St., Boston, MA 02111.

Example 37. "Ants on Parade," from *Creepy Crawly Things and Some That Fly!* Beard.

"Conversation With a Woodpecker!" is an example using the harmonic interval of an augmented fourth. This can be explained to a very young student as being "The Big Fourth":

Example 38. "Conversation With a Woodpecker!" from *Creepy Crawly Things and Some That Fly!* Beard.

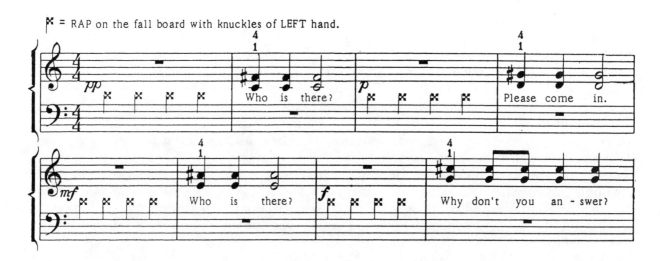

Example 39. "Dancing Dragonflies" from *Creepy Crawly Things and Some That Fly!* Beard.

"Dancing Dragonflies," displaying harmonic intervals of a fifth, may be preceded by a piece composed of melodic intervals of a fifth, such as is found in the next example:

Example 40. "Don't Touch Me! Said One Porcupine To Another!" from *Creepy Crawly Things and Some That Fly!* Beard.

(m.m. 1–4)

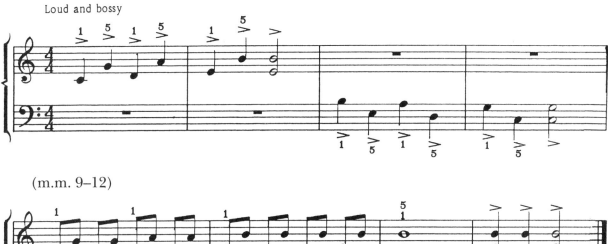

(m.m. 9–12)

With these pieces, the student has a chance to experience perceiving a complete page of seconds, thirds, fourths and fifths. The student's concentration will not be divided among numerous single notes and a variety of harmonic intervals. Most of the 27 pieces from this book are built around one interval, harmonic or melodic. As an added touch, the pieces display some wonderful 20th-century characteristics. Since method books have to be written for the hypothetical student, supplementary books, similar to *Creepy Crawly Things*, can be used to offer added experiences for those who need additional work on specific concepts. Also, books like this one can be exciting to a student because the pieces are composed as fun pieces, yet they are serious in intent. In addition to the interval pieces that emphasize a particular interval, there are several other compositions which emphasize a specific concept, such as the chromatic scale, with the presentation being achieved in an amusing manner:

Example 41. "A Long Wiggly-Worm!" from *Creepy Crawly Things and Some That Fly!* Beard.

Here again, the accidentals are used in a repetitive way, similar to the interval pieces. With all of these examples, it will be important for students to integrate new notational symbols, such as accidentals or harmonic intervals, into their reading and learning gestalt. When this fails, problems will occur in all areas: mental, rhythmic, physical and aural since sound is produced physically from aural images conceived by mental perceptions.

74

One of the basic premises of Stage II is to have the student experience an increase in the complexity of musical ideas, but in easy settings. The same should be true for the notational texture. When there is an increase in the notational complexity, the musical complexity should be less demanding, such as in the following examples:

Example 42. "First Etude," from *Bastien Piano Basics*, Performance 1, Bastien.

The notation in the next example reveals an increase in intervallic combinations (seconds and thirds), a few accidentals, rests and triads. Though the page is filled with staccato markings, the pitch and rhythmic patterns are very similar:

Example 43. "Tap Dance," from *Bastien Piano Basics*, Performance 1, Bastien.

Although there is an increase in the use of triads and the staccato touch, most of the triads and the melodic notes are all staccato. This avoids the problem of having to cope with an increase in both triadic activity and contrast of articulation simultaneously. The inclusion of more triads is made less threatening, to a large extent, because the notation remains very patterned, both in pitch and rhythm.

The notation in the next example will be more challenging for the student because of the single-note patterns occurring in both hands using a mixture of quarter and eighth notes with a few accidentals:

Example 44. "The Caravan," from *Alfred's Basic Piano Library*, Recital Book 1B, Palmer, Manus and Lethco.

The easy part of learning this piece will be reading the left hand pitch-and-rhythmic pattern. The accidentals in the right hand, although a little troublesome for some, also should be easy. From the hands-together point of view, the real culprit will be the physical coordination or synchronization between the hands. The rise in physical demands is an aspect of the music score that is not readily recognized, but the teacher will quickly find it apparent when the student begins to play the score. The piece can be conquered, though, without too much struggle because there is only one new concept: the synchronization of hands (getting the hands to stay coordinated in a rhythm in spite of the notational arrangement).

This brings up the question, "What would be the best pulse pattern to use for this piece?" A whole measure, two primary pulses per measure or a primary and a secondary pulse per measure? Perhaps two primary or strong pulses will be the best choice. Examine the left hand pattern. The five- to one-finger pattern, at a more or less andante moderato tempo, dictates two primary pulses. The teacher might think of the two in a hierarchic fashion, but that thinking will be too complicated for most students in Stage II. Since the pulse pattern must help organize the physical coordination between the hands, a longer pattern—a primary and secondary measure feeling—would be too long for the student to perceive aurally and execute physically as one rhythmic grouping. This would augment the physical problems rather than help to alleviate them.

Incorporating many notes, motion changes (parallel, contrary and oblique), accidentals, and articulation changes may suddenly cause a child's mind to overload similar to an overloaded electrical circuit. Correction of minutiae follows. Transfer of learning will be negligible. The student starts on the road to "just learning pieces" rather than "learning how to learn." Nevertheless, when the changes or additions are sequentially ordered in simple settings, the mind overload will not develop. The complexity of the notational texture, if it occurs gradually, can rise without causing the "stopping and starting" syndrome to appear. The key to preventing an overload of the system is to avoid adding complexities in several areas at one time, such as notational, musical and physical. As long as the complexity rise is mainly in one area, as is evident in the "Caravan," Example 44, the student's progress will continue normally.

An Approach to Developing an Inner Sense of Rhythmic Pulse

As soon as a student grasps the intervallic map-reading concept and plays correct note values, concepts for developing an inner sense of pulse should be introduced. Remember, the talented ones will sense and feel pulse intuitively during Stage I. Yet for a large majority of students, the development of an inner sense or feel for rhythmic grouping or pulse will have to be taught. This brings up the question of when to introduce it. Stage II will be the right time for many students; however, many others will not be ready until Stage III or later. Although pulse is very basic to becoming a musician, it is that elusive ingredient that is missing in many students' playing. Holistic perception, correct physical coordination and aural images all require a sense of pulse because pulse is the organizer and conductor of the total operation of music-making. For those who do not have an inner sense of pulse—and that will be many students—step-by-step practice procedures should be outlined to foster the understanding and execution of it; for most, pulse will have to be fostered throughout their musical training. When pulse is missing, mind and body unity and control of tonal relationships always will be problematic.

In the initial stages of teaching rhythmic pulse, compositions should be used that are in simple notational settings and in 3/4 or 2/4 meter. This affords the student the opportunity to concentrate fully upon one concept: grouping note values into strong and weak beats. The process can be started with only one or two pieces, allowing the other pieces still to be played in note values. As the student begins to feel secure with the concept, all pieces can be practiced in a pulse. (Each new piece will have to be sight-read initially in note values, then changed to a pulse grouping either during the first week of practice or at the next lesson.) As suggested in Stage I, teaching the grouping of notes into pulse patterns can be initially approached by using words that contain syllables corresponding directly to a meter signature, such as *Cho-co-late* for a piece in a 3/4 meter. This process is easy to teach if the student has a natural sense of rhythm, but very complex if the natural sense is missing. Some of the more talented students may begin to sense and feel pulse groupings even as pieces are being sight-read. With others, the process will take much longer to grasp.

Specific procedures may be used for students who demonstrate an enormous problem with understanding and sensing pulse. This will be true especially when, for instance, a nine- or ten-year-old student has taken lessons for two or three years and pulse remains a problem. Although these procedures are being suggested for presentation during Stage II, a number of students may not be capable of working on them until Stage III or IV. In other words, teaching rhythmic grouping must be very flexible. One cannot say definitely in which stage it should be taught. As a rule, the author suggests the following: present rhythmic grouping in Stage I or II, using words, but not necessarily going into step-by-step practice procedures. Simply present the grouping of notes into small pulse-units. How well the student instinctively hears and feels simple groupings should be used as a guide in deciding whether or not to go further with the concept.

In many cases, the step-by-step procedures will be handled more easily by a majority of students in later stages. The reason the procedures are mentioned in this stage is that the more talented students will be ready by Stage II to read and play in a pulse grouping. Some will sense the grouping intuitively and others will be capable of learning to sense it through the use of the pie-system of saying rhythm. The grouping concept leads students to hear and play in phrases, and many students in this stage certainly are capable of phrase playing. The teacher must be sure, though, that the concepts are not understood artificially. This will make the student physically uncomfortable and draw attention away from hearing the music.

The first step in organizing individual note values into metered-pulse patterns is teaching a student to perceive symbols holistically. For this to happen, a student's individual system of "rhythmic bookkeeping" has to be framed inside measure pulse-units. The use of accentual treatment (dynamically accenting the beginning of a pulse grouping) provides students with a mental–aural reminder, between lessons, of the pulse organization. The small dynamic accent prompts the student to remember the need for grouping, thus that note values should be perceived in metered pulse-units, not as separate note values. This in turn provides a basis for physical coordination, especially for wrist motion.

The purpose of the accentual treatment is to offer a mental–aural suggestion of how the physical should be organized, similar to a conductor being the organizer for musicians in an orchestra or choir. The accentual treatment should be done only as a mind organizer as opposed to being used as a mechanical device. The teacher must constantly monitor the student's response to the procedure. Ugly "hit" sounds indicate that the student is applying the procedure mechanically without any aural involvement. More appropriately, the correct execution of the accentual treatment demonstrates that the student is pre-hearing the tonal relationships within the grouping, giving some dynamic emphasis to the pitches occurring at the beginning of each strong-weak rhythmic grouping.

As a student becomes comfortable with sensing and feeling the rhythmic swing of the groupings, the need for exaggeration, i.e., dynamic accenting, decreases. Thus this exaggeration should evolve into de-emphasis and internalization; as the student begins to sense and feel the grouping internally, there will be less need for performing a dynamic reminder at the beginning of each recurring pulse pattern. The exaggeration may have to be used for some time with the less talented students, particularly with the reading of newly assigned pieces. When pulse grouping does take an extended period of time for a student to understand and internalize, the dynamic accents should be continued, but executed rather lightly. The need for continuing to exaggerate pulse groupings dynamically over a long period of time usually indicates that there is a total lack of aural involvement. Producing heavy accents or "hit" sounds indicates that the student is only going through the motions of understanding the pulse feeling. Attempting to do the accentual practice procedures without any regard for sound is similar to saying or counting rhythm aloud unconsciously. The student has to hear and feel it or the "sayings" have no affect on the rhythmic organization. Saying rhythm aloud and using the accentual treatment are both mental and aural reminders of what must be done rhythmically.

With lively pieces in 2/4 or 3/4 meter, there is only one pulse-unit per measure. In 4/4 and 6/8 rhythm, there are usually two basic pulse-units: one primary and one secondary unit. (Pieces played at slower tempos may sound more convincing with two primary pulse-units, such as, (♩♩♩♩). A beginning attempt with a new piece in 4/4 meter may have to be practiced in two primary pulse-units (♩ ♩), which can be referred to as Learning Metric Units. As the student progresses with understanding rhythmic grouping, less difficult 4/4 meter pieces can be practiced in one primary and one secondary pulse-unit (♩♩), referred to as Performing Metric Units. Another way of describing pulse grouping to a student would be to say that there is one primary half note and one secondary half note. (If the student plays in the school band, she would understand it more easily by saying, "Let's take it in a one.") The same procedure can be used with pieces in 6/8 meter. Each student should move on to the Performance Metric Unit both in 4/4 and 6/8 as soon as possible because the music motion "bogs down" very quickly at fast tempos when the measure is divided into two primary pulse groupings.

The following procedures may be applied to students at any level of advancement and age other than very young students. The procedures are too complex to be used with very young children, and would automatically defeat the purpose of assisting students in learning to play in a phrase rhythm or musical rhythm.

Step-by-Step Practice Procedures for Promoting
Rhythmic Grouping and Mind–Body Synchronization

STEP I. Organizing note values into strong-weak pulse groupings

Pulse grouping: ♩ ♩ ♩

Example 45. "Sing, Bird, Sing," from *Bastien Piano Basics*, Piano 1, Bastien.

Exaggeration (accentual treatment): Playing *Loud-soft-soft* as a mental-aural reminder of the Strong-weak-weak rhythmic grouping

De-emphasis of the *Loud-soft-soft* accentual treatment: Making only a slight accent as a mental–aural reminder of the Strong-weak-weak rhythmic grouping

Internalization of the Strong-weak-weak rhythmic grouping: Changing the slight dynamic accent to an inner feeling for pulse grouping

[Internalization of a rhythmic grouping refers to one's ability to sense and feel the recurring rallying point of rhythm—the recurring beat or rhythmic swing in music similar to a human heartbeat. Remember, the use of the accentual treatment—the dynamic accent— should evolve gradually into a feeling for the recurring pulse as opposed to using an audible reminder for the beginning of each new circle of rhythmic motion.]

STEP II. Organizing pulse groupings into primary/secondary units within a measure

Pulse grouping: ♩ ♩ ♩ ♩ (When sight-reading a piece initially, the student may need to use the simple pulse grouping, the Learning Metric Unit.)

Measure grouping: ♩ ♩ (The Performance Metric unit)

Example 46. "The Clown," from *Alfred's Basic Piano Library*, Lesson Book 1B, Palmer, Manus and Lethco.

Exaggeration (Primary Strong-weak, secondary strong-weak): Playing *Loud-and-soft-and* as a mental–aural reminder of the Primary Strong-weak and secondary strong-weak.

Fine

(In order to avoid confusion, the dynamic accents in measures 4 and 7 should be eliminated when this piece is used for teaching pulse grouping.)

De-emphasis of the *Loud-and-soft-and* accentual treatment: Making only a slight accent as a mental–aural reminder of the Strong-weak, strong-weak rhythmic groupings

Internalization of the Strong-weak rhythmic grouping: Changing the slight dynamic accent to an inner feeling for pulse grouping

During the early stages of teaching a student to perceive and play in pulse patterns, some beginner books may include pieces containing musical motion that appropriately unfolds, more convincingly, in two-measure Performance Metric Units (primary/secondary two-measure units). Yet because of the difficulty of "thinking and doing" in two-measure patterns, most students will need to use a one-measure Learning Metric Unit, especially during the initial stages of learning to group notes rhythmically. A two-measure grouping will be too long of a time span for most students to perceive aurally and execute physically in a successful manner. Take, for instance, this next example:

Example 47. "Japanese Story," from *Guidelines for Developing Piano Performance* Book 1, Olson.

Rather than considering a two-measure grouping, a learner who is just beginning to understand grouping should approach the piece first with Step I procedures (organizing individual note values into two primary pulse groupings: (♩ ♩); then apply the practice procedures from Step II (organizing pulse groupings into one-measure primary/secondary units: ♩ ♩). Just as individual notes organize to form pulse groupings and pulse groupings organize to form measures, measures sometimes organize into larger groupings to form primary/secondary measures. The tendency of the musical motion of measures pulling to organize into larger units is due commonly to the interaction of harmonic motion—real or implied—and of texture.

In situations where measures do organize logically into primary/secondary measures, most students should start first with Step II practice procedures, then apply the Step III procedures. That is to say, the Step II practice procedures of organizing notes within one measure would be done with Learning Metric Units (♩ ♩ | ♩ ♩) followed by Step III practice procedures, for those who are capable, using the Performance Metric Units (o | o). The Step III procedures would be applied only if the student is capable of hearing through the two measures as one aural entity. As one may observe, the size of the Performance Metric Unit— the rhythmic unit for deciding on tempo—and the sub-phrase grouping are sometimes identical, especially in fast-paced pieces using slow harmonic rhythm. (This is usually not the case in slower-paced pieces that make use of frequent harmonic changes). This is true in the case of the "Japanese Story." For students who are ready to play in two-measure rhythmic groupings, "Japanese Story" or pieces similar to the following example can be used for organizing primary/secondary measures into sub-phrase groupings.

82

STEP III. Organizing measures into sub-phrase groupings

Pulse grouping: ♩ ♩ ♩ (The Learning Metric Unit from Step II)

Sub-phrase grouping: ♩. ♩. (The Performance Metric Unit and the sub-phrase grouping, in this particular piece, are identical.)

Example 48. "Waltzing Elephants," from *Bastien Piano Basics*, Piano 1, Bastien.

Exaggeration (Primary Measure, Secondary Measure): Playing a Primary *Loud-soft-soft* and a secondary *loud-soft-soft* as a mental–aural reminder of the Primary Strong-weak-weak and the secondary strong-weak-weak rhythmic grouping

De-emphasis of the accentual treatment: Making only a slight dynamic accent on the first beat of each two measures as a mental–aural reminder of the two-measure rhythmic grouping

Internalization of the two-measure rhythmic grouping: Changing the slight dynamic accent on the beginning of each two-measure grouping to an inner sense or feeling for the rhythmic grouping

As soon as a student is comfortable with learning and playing pieces in pulse groupings outlined in the first three steps, phrase concepts can be introduced. (Earlier, phrase concepts

were discussed from the intuitive standpoint for the more talented students who are capable of grasping the concept practically from beginning lessons.)

In many elementary pieces, most phrases are made up of four measures. All phrases, dependent or independent, normally have directed musical motion from a point of repose towards a goal of more tension (a focal point or axis needing some type of musical treatment) or from a point or area of tension towards repose. Each musical goal or focal point is a place where the musical motion is directed. A goal can be a point or area of greatest tension (climax) or a point or area of greatest repose (resolution). One of the simplest of phrase shapes begins with repose and is directed towards a point of climax, usually a four-measure dependent phrase. From the point of climax, a second four-measure dependent phrase is directed back towards a point of repose. The two dependent phrases form what is referred to in formal terms as a "period." This could be explained to a young student as "a complete musical sentence." Another simple phrase concept, specifically used many times in children's music, is one that moves from repose-to-climax-to-repose, all within four measures. This would be an independent phrase or a complete musical sentence within itself.

Needless to say, there are other types of phrase shapes, such as a phrase that begins with the point of greatest tension, e.g., the opening phrase of the first movement of Beethoven's *Pastoral Sonata*, Opus 28, and moves towards a point of repose. Obviously, there are also local points of tension and repose along the way from the main point of tension to the main point of repose. These local points of interest should be considered only after the concept of the whole phrase has become secure. This would be the case in both dependent or independent phrases. Although the more gifted students may be able to hear and sense both levels of interest at the same time, the concept of holistically perceiving four-measure phrases should be learned first.

The teaching of phrasing is presented many times from the concept of eight full measures with the idea that all phrases begin with a feeling of repose, progress towards a climax and from the climax return to a feeling of repose. There are several built-in problems with this approach. First and foremost, an eight-measure phrase is longer than most beginning students can focus upon aurally; therefore, the phrase can be achieved only by imitating the teacher over and over again. Any transfer of learning is negligible because this approach provides no basic understanding for future decisions on shaping other phrases. The student will have to depend always upon how the teacher has wanted each and every phrase shaped. The student would be only an observer. The phrase-teaching scenario would continue lesson after lesson, year after year with, "Susan, please stop doing it wrong for the fifteenth time and listen once again to how I play the phrase as this is absolutely the only way it can be played." Continuing on, "I learned how to shape it from Professor Friedman who learned it from Madame Molinski." Susan may begin to think out loud, "I sure wish I knew the magic of the phrasing that my teacher learned from Professor Friedman who learned it from Madame Molinski!" The next thing that comes to mind is, "I don't know what it is my teacher wants, but if I can just get out of here I certainly will try to find it before I return." This apostolic succession approach to teaching phrasing is very limited because the student is being asked to execute a musical idea that has been conceived aurally by a teacher several generations past. This is where the problem is. How can the student imitate a full eight-measure phrase when the student is still having problems hearing tonal relationships among the pitches within one measure?

There will always be some difficulty in teaching a student a musical idea that is longer than the student can conceive aurally. Teaching phrasing, consequently, from a step-by-step approach is much more successful. Although presented as a step-by-step approach, the phrase concept is actually being taught from the concept of the whole. The only difference is that the size of the whole becomes larger as the smaller steps are understood and heard. Step IV procedures promote this process.

STEP IV. Organizing sub-phrases into phrase groupings

Learning Metric Unit: ♩. (One measure)

Performance Metric Unit: ♩. ♩. (Two measures, one **Primary Measure** and one **Secondary Measure**)

Four-measure musical phrase: ♩. ♩. ♩. ♩.

Example 49. "German Dance," from *Guidelines for Developing Piano Performance,* Book 1, Olson.

First: Most students will need to apply Steps I and II procedures before Step III procedures are applied. (These steps will be identical in 3/4 meter pieces.) The exaggeration, de-emphasis and internalization versions will need to be continued until the student begins to acquire an inner feeling for rhythmic grouping.

Second: Apply Step III procedures.

After the student has somewhat mastered the Step III procedures with the "German Dance" and other similar pieces, the student is ready to experience the Step IV phrase groupings.

Third: Apply Step IV Procedures.

[These practice procedures on accentual treatment are taken from outlines developed in books previously published. See Max W. Camp, *Developing Piano Performance: A Teaching Philosophy* (Van Nuys: Alfred Publishing Co., 1981), 67–71; and Camp, *Guidelines For Developing Piano Performance*, Book I (Van Nuys: Alfred Publishing Co., 1985), 4–16.]

With Step IV, the student is being guided in this particular piece from individual notes to a one-measure Learning Metric Unit pulse (♩. or ♩ ♩ ♩); a two-measure Performance Metric Unit (♩. | ♩.); and on to a four-measure dependent phrase (♩.| ♩.| ♩.| ♩.). These two-measure groupings—primary/secondary pulse units—will serve as the basis for establishing a performance tempo for this piece as well as the basic sub-phrase unit of the four-measure phrase. That is to say that the musical motion, when performed up-to-tempo, travels in a two-measure, primary/secondary pulse grouping. Any real or simulated body response to the rhythm, including head, torso and wrists, should be synchronized with the pulse pattern. The student's *emotional response* will gradually expand from the pulse to the sub-phrase on to phrases, sections and the complete piece. The student's basic *body response*, however, will continue to corroborate with the rhythmic grouping.

The size of the basic pulse grouping of this or any piece depends upon tempo. The faster the tempo travels, the larger the pulse grouping will be; the slower the tempo, the smaller the pulse grouping will be. Pulse groupings are somewhat subjective, but the more experience one has in making pulse grouping judgments, the easier it is to sense or feel what size grouping will be the most logical. The key is hearing how the melody, rhythm, harmony, form and texture all interact among each other. The pulse grouping is the result of the interaction of the basic musical elements, form and texture. Pulse is the aspect of music that has to be sensed and felt by the student or taught by the teacher as opposed to an aspect of music that is actually seen on the score.

A musician must remember that the length of the grouping must always relate to the tempo. For example, if you are playing a movement from a classical sonata, a grouping that is too long will make the performer's body feel uncomfortable. There will be a need to feel the recurrence of a new circle of musical motion before it is due to occur again. If the grouping pattern is too short, the beginning of the circle comes around too quickly. The player will feel that he is being "bombarded by notes." Actually, when notes are being grouped into patterns that are too long, the student is shifting the strong-weak rhythmic relationship into a higher architectonic level than is logical. The strong-weak pulse grouping must be one with which the body feels comfortable. Pulse grouping always can be related to "nodding your head" or "patting your foot" to music. It is the rhythmic swing or avenue by which audiences listen.

With Step IV, the student will be learning how four measures relate to form musical phrases, dependent and independent. In children's music, many of the easy pieces move rhythmically in two-measure pulse-units because of the very slow harmonic rhythm and thin texture. (This does not mean, however, that all easy pieces nor more advanced compositions move rhythmically in two-measure pulse-units.) This, consequently, becomes the basic sub-phrase unit of the four-measure phrase. As these two-measure sub-phrase units become understood, heard and felt, the student will be capable of understanding and hearing how four measures group to form phrases. For example, in the "German Dance," presented earlier, the opening phrase begins with a repose on the tonic. In measure 3, the musical motion travels to the dominant harmony and to the highest melodic tone in the phrase, producing a feeling of climax or tension. In measure 5, the musical motion travels from this point of tension back to a point of repose in measure 7. The rhythmic grouping will have helped the student to think and hear in longer groupings, allowing him to leave the individual notes—the "nickels and dimes" of the phrase—and to concentrate on the phrase from the concept of the whole. As previously mentioned, this can be compared to learning to read words and sentences by chunks. These rhythmic grouping practice procedures can lead a student to read and perform music in chunks as opposed to reading and performing symbols one-at-a-time. This helps teach students that music is always going somewhere: moving from repose towards more tension or away from tension towards repose.

Musical Understanding and Artistry

Musical understanding, phrase shaping and artistry normally will be continued throughout Stage II. More realistically, though, some students may continue to be baffled by the process of learning to read, attempting to understand and execute rhythms, and trying to coordinate the fingers physically. For these students, shaping phrases and artistic concepts will have to be delayed. There will be many students, however, who will be ready. The teaching of artistry is approachable from a number of different angles. Usually the question arises, "When should I be concerned with a beginner's sound?" There is no simple answer since all learners are individuals. Normally one should be concerned with a student's sound as soon as possible. Some Stage I students immediately become conscious of tonal quality and quantity, and it should be nurtured at that point. For example, the author has worked with five-year-old students who were wonderful with tonal quality and dynamic levels. Yet those are rare cases, for even after three years of study, the fundamentals of reading may still dominate the lessons of many students. Tonal quality and quantity, to some extent, will have to be delayed until the student has mastered the very fundamentals of reading and playing in a rhythm. As a result, guiding a young child's musical intuitions may or may not be a common practice by Stage II. For a majority of normally gifted students, it most definitely should be, but for others the musical understanding and artistry may have to be delayed.

Fostering the imitation of tonal qualities, character, mood and dynamic levels should be a part of every lesson plan. Suggesting that the student imitate the teacher's interpretation of each piece, however, is not a wise decision. This promotes the idea that the student always must hear through the teacher's ears. The imitative concept of interpretation is limited somewhat because it fails to develop emotional reaction to musical phenomena as well as aural images of that phenomena. Interpretation by imitation obviously does have to be employed from time to time, especially with the less talented students, when intuition and musical understanding both fail. A majority of the normal learners and the musically gifted, though, can be taught to react emotionally to musical phenomena. Ensemble playing, particularly with duets, is an excellent way to foster a student's understanding of the rise and fall of the intensity levels in music. The duet, "Dumka," is a good example because the harmonic progression in the second piano part so vividly illustrates the need for changes in the intensity levels:

Example 50. "Dumka," from *Kaleidoscope Solos*, Book 1, George.

88

* DUMKA (do͞om′ kä): Ukrainian folk ballad, usually sad or contemplative.

As the harmonic tension rises in "Dumka," the teacher may increase the dynamic level, as in measures 3 and 4. The student, hopefully, will also react emotionally to the harmonic tension or to the dynamic rise in the teacher's playing of the duet. In that way, even without instruction, the student is beginning to react to changes in the rise and fall of the intensity levels in the music or to the dynamic changes made by the student's duet partner. Students, in some cases, will have the intuitive ability to follow the teacher's dynamic rise and fall throughout a piece. There are some students who may even intuitively sense a need for some rhythmic nuance at cadential points, such as at the half-cadence on the dominant in measure 8. Many times when this occurs, students gradually will begin reacting emotionally in all their pieces to the harmonic progressions as well as to the melodic direction.

This approach is usually the most effective technique for developing musical understanding and fostering the student's musical intuition. The teacher is attempting to spark the student's gradual, sometimes unconscious, intuitive reaction to musical phenomena in an osmosis or fluid fashion before presenting one that is more structured. Learning through intuitive means is the ideal way for students to begin their journey into musical understanding. As students progress, the intuitive approach can be supplemented by teaching the understanding of what is happening musically in the score—how the melody, harmony, rhythm, form and texture are all interacting to cause the rise and fall of intensity levels and the changes in mood and character.

Less Patterned Notational Settings

Since most method books present a specific reading approach, students in Stage II should be exposed also to some pieces that will require them to read outside their familiar positions or reading patterns, such as the following:

Example 51. "Maple Sugar Praline," from *Assorted Chocolates*, Poe.

Experience with this type of setting ensures that the student is gradually understanding the full Grand Staff, not just pieces beginning on the G position or on what is Landmark F. The pitches, in the previous example, are not located in a patterned position. The left hand begins on Db with the third finger, the right hand begins on Gb with the second, and leger lines are also present. In addition to the notational pattern being unusual, the texture is thin, requiring some creative thinking in deciding phrase shapes. Although the student may find the pentatonic setting slightly unfamiliar, the piece will be easy to read for most Stage II students.

Students should study a number of unpatterned pieces during this stage or they will progress into more advanced literature feeling uncomfortable anytime they have to begin a piece on notes other than in G, F or C position. These thin-textured supplementary pieces, consequently, can serve not only as experience with less patterned music, but also as an avenue for broadening a student's experience with both musical understanding and artistry. Rather than placing emphasis on more complex notation at this point, musical understanding and artistry can become the main thrust with pieces similar to the next example, as well as examples 53 and 54:

Example 52. "Prune Danish," from *A Baker's Dozen*, Poe.

Within some of the thin-textured compositions, different mixtures of articulation, such as two-note slurs and staccato notes, gradually make their appearance. The mixtures may be introduced to the student in very simple settings, especially if the articulation is patterned with the measure pulse, as is true in this next example:

Example 53. "Banjo Tune," from *Kaleidoscope Solos,* Book 2, George.

The student's first attempt with "Banjo Tune" probably will involve saying the rhythm aloud in note values: Quar-ter, Quar-ter, Quar-ter, Quar-ter. This approach can be changed, by the next lesson, to saying pie-system syllables aloud as a means of promoting the perception of the piece by the measure, rhythmically, aurally and physically. Using syllables of words from the pie-system of saying rhythm can be adapted to fit the note-value relationships of the piece:

(If the need arises, the pie-system can be used in a slightly different way from how Hazel Cobb advocates its use in her books on teaching rhythm, *Rhythm with Rhyme and Reason* and *Rhythm to Count, Sing and Play*; the only criterion being that the note-value relationships must remain the same.)

By using a combination of syllables for each measure, the teacher is instructing the student to use one overall physical motion for the measure rather than one motion for the opening two-note slur, one motion for the first staccato note and one motion for the last staccato note. A similar situation occurs in this next piece:

Example 54. "Candy Mints," from *Musical Moments*, Book 1, George.

As soon as the note values are understood, "Candy Mints" can be practiced in a similar way using the words, *Down-and-up-and*, emphasizing once again the organization of the physical to coincide with the rhythm, the measure pulse:

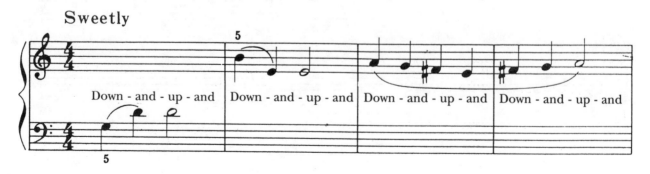

These words will help coordinate the wrists' motions and help prevent dropping or pumping on each note that is played, causing unwanted accents especially on the half notes. The down part of the wrist motion gradually should change to become *through-and-up-and*, similar to the description of the wrist motion for Example 26, "My Robot," in Stage I. In other words, the student would need to be **hearing and playing through** the down part of the wrist motion as opposed to **freezing or hitting** as the wrist go down.

As a student experiences articulation, phrasing and artistry in the forthcoming stages, a number of other notational concepts will be added to the texture. These may include musical accents, chord progressions in root position and inversion and pitch and rest combinations, all of which may appear in increasingly more complex settings.

Ensemble Playing

Ensemble playing, especially duets, offers some of the best experiences for making music in all stages not only for beginners but for all students. First, ensemble playing will excite the student. Second, it helps foster an inner sense for feeling rhythmic pulse and phrase shapes. And third, if the music is easy enough to read, the student will become more involved with music-making rather than finding each note or "getting caught up" in note values. The teacher, nevertheless, should avoid assigning duet books that are difficult to read. If there is a struggle with the reading, all the fun is gone before the music begins. The notation of pieces in duet books should be at such a level that the student can read the symbols acceptably at sight. And in some cases, the students may even be able to sight-read the pieces and play them with the teacher's part before they take them home. This will serve as a great incentive for practicing. For example, the Duet Book 1B of *Alfred's Basic Piano Library* by Dennis Alexander can be read easily at sight during Stage II. The solo parts are arranged so that they sound musically convincing even without the accompanying parts. Consequently, attention can be given to performing and making music fun and exciting. The following duets are recommended examples:

Example 55. "Sonatina For Two," from *Alfred's Basic Piano Library*, Duet Book 1B, Alexander.

Secondo

Primo

Brightly

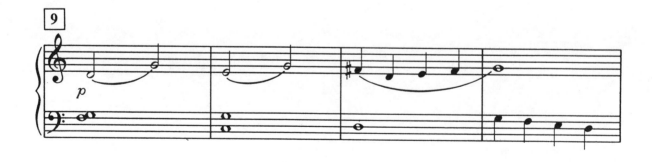

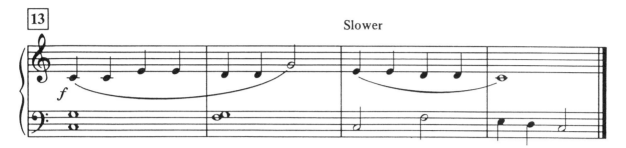

The next example illustrates a duet, as did the previous one, in which the student will have to become accustomed to playing longer note values while the duet part is moving in shorter note values. This setting will demand that the student hear and feel the rhythm of the solo part as it sounds against the accompanying part. The teacher-student parts may be switched for the talented students who are reading well. The teacher will delight in the student saying, "Hey, let me try your part!"

Example 56. "Ballad," from *Alfred's Basic Piano Library*, Duet Book 1B, Alexander.

Secondo

94

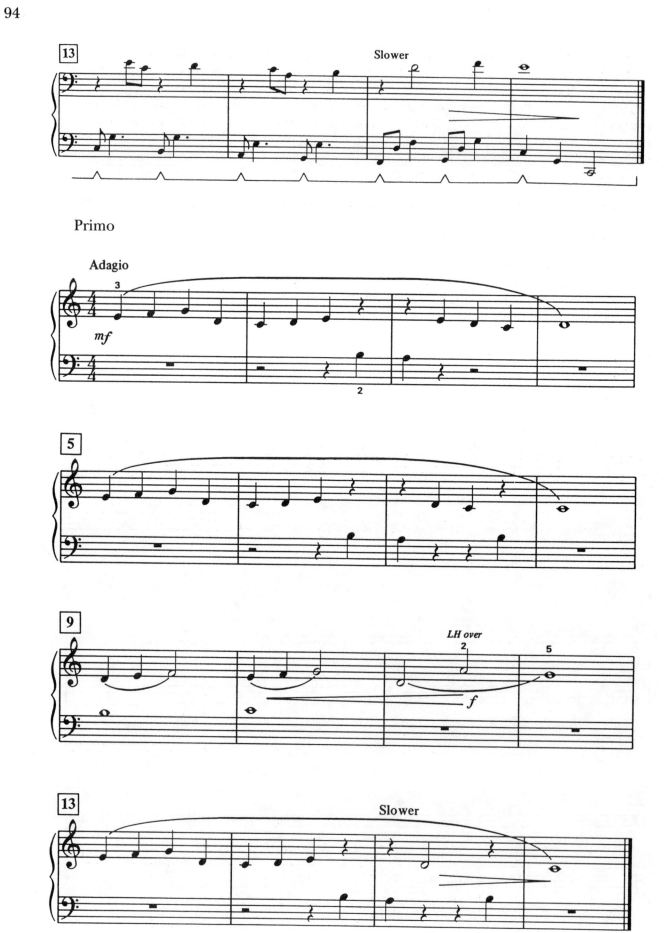

Primo

How intriguing it will be to hear a student say, when perusing a new duet book, "Please, let's try this piece as I believe I can read it without even having to practice it." This may be true even with a piece similar to the duet, "Rockin' Roberta." Why is this such a surprise? Well, if a teacher examines the rhythms between the two parts, the duet looks rather complex because of the syncopation. Will the student find this easy? No, not entirely, but the student may immediately become enthralled with working on it, especially if she has a good sense of rhythm. This piece will be easy to read and the desire to play it will help the student overcome any problems with the rhythm:

Example 57. "Rockin' Roberta," from *Alfred's Basic Piano Library*, Duet Book 1B, Alexander.

Secondo

Primo

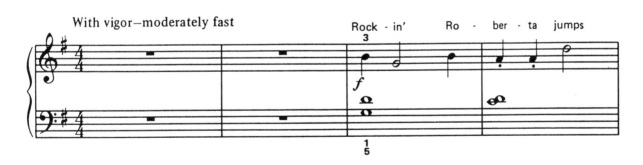

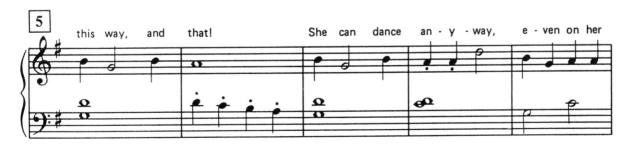

Culmination of Stage II

The Stage II literature selections increase the musical complexity considerably, adding:

1. Internalization of pulse
2. Musical understanding
3. Emotional reaction to the rise and fall of intensity levels
4. Artistry
5. An increase in contrast of touches
6. Changes in articulation within longer pulse patterns
7. Tonal quality considerations

The notational complexity has also increased. Yet in examining this chapter, one quickly realizes that Stage II music has been more concerned with adding more *music* as opposed to adding more *notes*. Stage I sets up the foundation and Stage II continues that foundation and adds some musical complexities. Within Stage II, music-making will become a reality for some while others may continue to struggle with the basic foundation of reading notes and note values.

How complex should the pieces get in Stage II? This is difficult to answer. As a rule of thumb, the pieces should display a combination of previously learned concepts from Stage I and a number of newly introduced concepts from Stage II. The combination should offer a challenge to students, but one that will have quick rewards. If the challenge produces confusion, the new concepts are appearing perhaps faster than students can absorb them into their learning gestalt. Let us examine the next example and discover what demands the combination of old and new concepts produce:

Example 58. "Minuet and Trio," from *Alfred's Basic Piano Library*, Recital Book 1B, Palmer, Manus and Lethco.

Minuet

Moderately fast

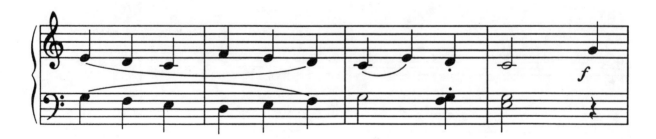

Fine

Trio

Play R.H. ONE OCTAVE HIGHER 2nd time.

D.C. Minuet al Fine

The notes and note values will be easy to read, but there are some examples of melodic and harmonic intervallic changes occurring at the same time. What about the articulation? For the most part, the articulation will be easy because most of the staccato notes occur simultaneously in both hands. If one looks closer, though, there are a few measures in which staccato and legato touches will have to be executed simultaneously, which will make the piece difficult for some students. The demands of the piece, therefore, will be challenging but *most definitely* in the range of what should be expected from Stage II students. For the slower learner, more supplementary literature in a less complex setting may be needed, whereas the more talented student probably will be able to play the piece at sight without any problems.

Chapter VI

STAGE III

The texture of the Stage III compositions should include concepts that have been studied in the first two stages, but in settings that are slightly more complex, from both the notational and musical standpoints. Five-finger patterns should be extended to include the intervals of sixths, sevenths and octaves. Much of the literature should include scalar thumb crossings, a number of pieces in 6/8 meter and many examples of the quar-ter-dot-eighth rhythmic pattern. The various method series introduce these two rhythmic concepts at different times. Regardless of when they are introduced, the important thing is learning not only to be able to comprehend the ideas, but also to be able to pre-hear them. Both rhythmic concepts will transfer very easily to other pieces if the concepts have been learned aurally. Counting out 1 - 2 - 3 - 4 - 5 - 6 in 6/8 meter or 1 & 2 & in a quar-ter-dot-eighth pattern will not guarantee the correct playing of either rhythm. The student will need to have an aural conception of how the note values relate rhythmically as opposed to just having a mathematical understanding of the relationships.

The complexity of the notational patterns between the hands will rise, and series of consecutive eighth note patterns will occur with more frequency. This in turn will demand additional physical dexterity. Articulation will change from legato to staccato more frequently in settings that are much less patterned. Some pieces may call for faster tempos than experienced previously and melodies may appear more in combination with primary chord progressions. Syncopation, mobility (position changes) and style characteristics will also begin to become evident.

The sequencing of concepts and materials will require closer examination than before in order that the literature offer a challenge to the student, but one that is not overwhelming. If the challenge becomes too complex, the student's progress quickly will come to a standstill, resulting in more errors than is usual with each piece. One might summarize Stage III with this thought in mind: although the texture of the literature selections basically still may be patterned, the overall demands—rhythmical, aural and physical—will increase. To avoid major problems, each student's learning level will have to be assessed with regard to which concepts may cause difficulties and which ones have already been mastered. Examine the pieces and decide if the new complexities will produce problems in the reading, rhythmic understanding and/or aural control. Remember to consider the physical demands. Keep in mind that the student must be challenged, or both lessons and practice will become boring. The student's reaction to reading Stage III music is the best guide. If it is utter confusion, the change has been too drastic; more likely though, the new challenges of Stage III literature will be welcomed.

The cyclical sequence—the sequential ordering of concepts into more complex settings—of the many aspects of notation involving melody, harmony, rhythm, form, articulation, texture and phrasing begins to loom larger and larger. If the sequential order is right for a student, she will notice very little difference when she begins to read a more complex score. The student will continue to perceive the symbols as easily as she did in the previous level of literature. If the system obviously begins to break down during any phase of a stage, the teacher must diagnose what the problems are. Have the pieces suddenly become too difficult? Has the student continued to maintain a keen interest in learning to play the piano? Are the problems due to poor preparation on the student's part? Am I, the teacher, doing a good job with preparing and directing the lessons? Am I giving off "vibes" that I have lost interest in teaching the student? These and many other aspects of teaching the student should be examined. The teacher must discover the answers, or the student will decide that he no longer has the time for piano and will ask to discontinue lessons. Perhaps it is the frustration with reading music that has squelched the student's enthusiasm for taking lessons, rather than the fact that he actually does not have the time for lessons.

Rise in Notational Complexity

Rhythm. For some students, following the author's suggested correlations among the pieces in the different method books may fit perfectly. Yet other students may succeed more easily if the teacher selects a combination of pieces that best adheres to that student's present learning and performing needs. In any case, it is best not to select a combination of pieces at random, involving the presentation of several new concepts at one time. For example, when dotted-quarter-eighth patterns are presented, the new rhythm should be experienced in a number of different settings, displaying a gradual increase in notational complexity. If the student is assigned only one piece using the new rhythmic pattern before another new concept is assigned, the sound of the new rhythmic pattern will have less of a chance of being retained. The newly learned rhythm may have to be taught again and again when it appears in other pieces. However, if the student experiences the rhythm in a number of pieces, in increasingly difficult settings, the student has a chance to master the concept, both mentally and aurally. The following examples illustrate how a rhythmic concept can be reiterated several times in increasingly complex settings:

Example 59. "Silent Night," from *Alfred's Basic Piano Library*, Lesson Book 2, arranged Palmer, Manus and Lethco.

Example 60. "Alouette," from *Alfred's Basic Piano Library*, Lesson Book 2, arranged Palmer, Manus and Lethco.

Example 61. "Cockles and Mussels," from *Alfred's Basic Piano Library*, Lesson Book 2, arranged Palmer, Manus and Lethco.

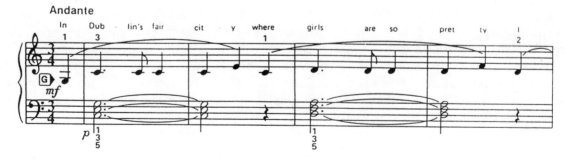

Example 62. "Kum-ba-yah!" from *Alfred's Basic Piano Library*, Lesson Book 2, arranged Palmer, Manus and Lethco.

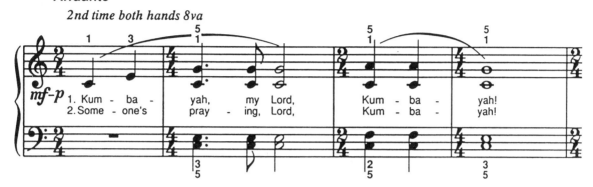

Example 63. "Bell Song," from *Alfred's Basic Piano Library*, Recital Book 2, Palmer, Manus and Lethco.

mm. 1–4

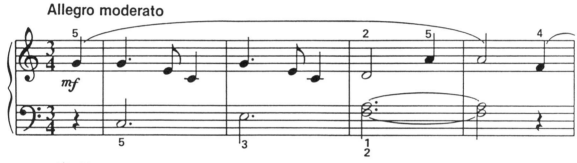

mm. 17–20

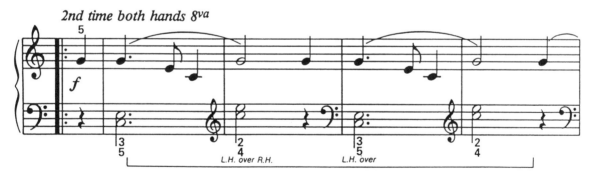

Example 64. "Michael's Fanfare," from *Alfred's Basic Piano Library*, Technic Book 2, Palmer, Manus and Lethco.

These examples are fairly similar, but they are all slightly different. For instance, "Kum-ba-yah" has a thicker texture than the first two examples. The "Bell Song" does require some left hand crossings while "Cockles and Mussels" does not. Yet both the "Bell Song" and "Michael's Fanfare" include more complex textures than Examples 59–62. "Michael's Fanfare" may be the most difficult of all the examples because of the contrary motion between the hands.

Intervallic Expansion. A similar sequential order needs to be considered with regard to pitches, including the intervallic extension from a fifth to the octave. First, the interval of the sixth should be experienced in a number of pieces, displaying a gradual increase in complexity, and in more than one position. The other two simple intervals, sevenths and eighths, should follow the same pattern. The next dance illustrates the harmonic interval of a sixth in a somewhat complex setting:

Example 65. "18th Century Dance," from *Alfred's Basic Piano Library*, Lesson Book 2, Palmer, Manus and Lethco.

This piece is in the G position with most all notes marked staccato except for the half notes. The harmonic interval of a sixth appears among thirds, fourths and fifths. This way the student will gain experience in recognizing the difference in the appearance of all four intervals. (Some students will recognize and hear harmonic intervals before melodic ones.) Through the use of 8vas, the hands change position on the keyboard several times. The phrases may be taught intuitively by demonstrating how the rise and fall of the intensity levels is created by the rise and fall of the melodic line and the harmonic progression. The student also can recognize how the tension to resolution—each IV to I progression—becomes less and less spread out on the page, going from an open to a closed position. This indicates that each tension to resolution in this piece may be played at a decreasing dynamic level. As for tempo rhythm, the basic character of the piece suggests a measure Performance Metric Unit (o), i. e., one primary and one secondary pulse (♩ ♩).

The "18th Century Dance" offers the student active participation in learning a simplified imitation of a standard classic dance from a specific style period—the early classical. Consequently, learning this composition will offer experience not only with the interval of a sixth, but it also will introduce some stylistic characteristics in a more complex texture. The new interval, however, should be introduced first in a setting that contains no other new concepts before approaching it in a piece such as the "18th Century Dance." When a new interval is first introduced, it should be the focus, the main concept that the student is to perceive and hear. For the first appearance of the sixth, a piece like "Lavender's Blue" would be most appropriate:

Example 66. "Lavender's Blue," from *Alfred's Basic Piano Library*, Lesson Book 2, arranged Palmer, Manus and Lethco.

This could be followed by the next example:

Example 67. "Lone Star Waltz," from *Alfred's Basic Piano Library*, Lesson Book 2, Palmer, Manus and Lethco.

mm 1–4

mm 9–12

mm 21–24

D.C. al Fine

In "Lavender's Blue," the interval of a sixth is the only new concept on the page, therefore making it simple for the student to comprehend. In the "Lone Star Waltz," the fact that some of the melodic intervals of the sixth resolve to a fifth makes it easier for the student because the fifth is already a familiar interval. The harmonic interval of a sixth appears several times in the right and left hand parts. Whereas the new interval appeared in the "18th Century Dance" in a rather complex setting, "Lavender's Blue" and the "Lone Star Waltz" textural settings are quite simple. As the teacher begins to recognize small or large differences in textures such as in these examples, much better choices can be made with regard to which pieces a student should be assigned next. The teacher will recognize that piece X shows a much more complex setting of a concept than piece Y.

In the next example, intervals of the fifth, sixth and seventh appear with the tonic to dominant-seventh progression. When the student is first sight-reading the piece, the left hand part can be blocked while the right hand is becoming comfortable with its new expanded position. (Having to expand the hand out beyond a five-finger pattern can be explained to the student in this manner. "Human beings only have 10 fingers to play 88 keys, therefore, this will require each hand to get accustomed to leaving its comfortable five-finger pattern.")

Example 68. "Our Special Waltz," from *Alfred's Basic Piano Library*, Lesson Book 2, Palmer, Manus and Lethco.

The notational setting will make it easier for the student to perceive and hear the new interval, because of 1) slow harmonic changes (the L. H. pattern is the same for three measures); 2) the use of only two harmonies (until the last section); and 3) the simple melodic pattern (E-C to G; E-C to A; and E-C to B). The difficulties will be conquered easily because students will grasp the stepwise motion as the intervals get larger going up the page and smaller as the melodic line falls.

Introducing Compositions with Scalar Patterns

Most composers include a scale pattern using finger crossings when presenting the octave or interval of the eighth. Students handle the combination of the new interval and the scale and finger crossings quite easily if the crossings have been presented earlier in short scalar patterns, such as in the next example:

Example 69. "The Galway Piper," from *Alfred's Basic Piano Library*, Lesson Book 2, Palmer, Manus and Lethco.

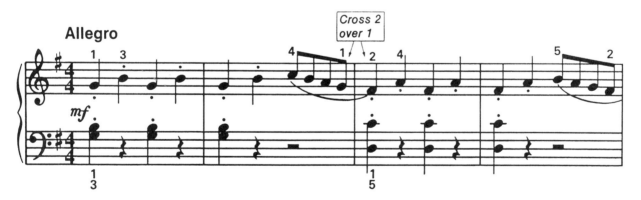

The partial scale patterns appear on an upbeat to a downbeat setting. With the crossing occurring on G down to F# (using the second finger to cross-over the 1), the procedure is very simple to execute. This presents the crossing-over concept in its simplest form. Needless to say, the awkwardness of most beginners' thumbs makes it difficult to teach crossings when one of the first examples involves crossing the fourth finger over the thumb—playing C down to Bb in the descending F Major scale. Although the crossing in the F Major scale is not easy to manage, it will be much easier if the student has experienced simpler crossings beforehand. In the next example in C Major, the crossings are easier than the ones needed in the R. H. of the F Major scale:

Example 70. "Scaling the Rockies," from *Bastien Piano Basics*, Piano 2, Bastien.

The next example, "Scale Improver," is a wonderful piece for preparing students for thumb crossings in playing scales:

Example 71. "Scale Improver," from *Alfred's Basic Piano Library*, Technic Book 2, Palmer, Manus and Lethco.

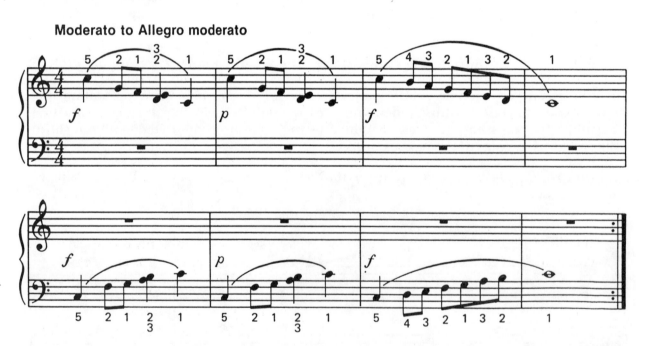

During the process of learning to play scale passages hands alone and together, students gain additional insight into how the patterns are designed by playing scales in contrary motion. Some students are able to grasp the fingering patterns more readily in contrary motion than in parallel motion because they are able to observe the similarity of the fingerings in both hands as in the following:

Example 72. "See You on 'C'," from *Alfred's Basic Piano Library*, Technic Book 2, Palmer, Manus and Lethco.

Andante to Allegro moderato

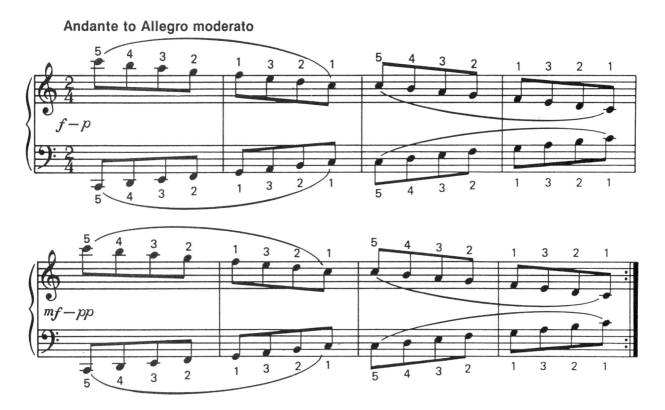

Learning to read, hear and play scale patterns in contrary motion is very appealing to most students. They usually play them with pride, relating, "Look at me do this!" Remember the first experience with scales was during Stage I, using the tetrachords in an aural context as opposed to a written one. The student found, by ear, what black keys were needed when the pattern began on a given note. This introduced the orientation of tonalities through the aural aspect of learning as opposed to just memorizing key signatures. Recognizing the tonality concept from the score should come after the student recognizes the tonal relationships aurally.

Introducing Melodies with Chord Accompaniments

Melodies with I-V7-I or I-IV-V7-I chord accompaniments are commonly found in much of the music at this advancement level. If the student is reading well, it is appropriate to have the student transpose some of the simpler settings into other keys. Transposition can be done also in Stages I and II with the very simple, patterned pieces. Most "ear" students transpose pieces naturally, but the experience is also valuable for those who are not as aurally-oriented. Transposing usually helps draw students more into the aural aspect of reading music and away from viewing music strictly as a visual task only.

Pieces that combine simple melodic patterns with primary chords are helpful also in teaching elementary level students how to shape phrases. Students have an easier time deciphering the rise and fall of tension and resolution when the full triad is present. Explaining phrase shapes with music that only contains implied harmony is much more difficult, unless the student has a strong intuitive sense toward feeling tension and resolution.

"Oh! Susanna" is a good example of a piece that can be used for transposition as well as for teaching phrase shapes:

Example 73. "Oh! Susanna," from *Bastien Piano Basics*, Piano 2, Foster, arranged Bastien.

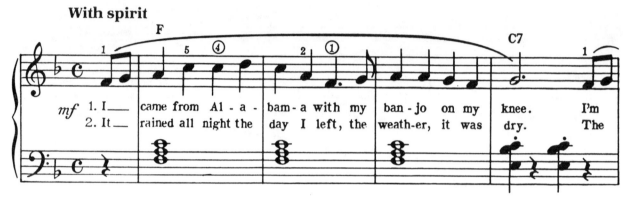

By this stage, students need to be introduced not only to triads in root position but also to their inversions, illustrated in the next two examples:

Example 74. "Flying Fish," from *Bastien Piano Basics*, Technic 2, Bastien.

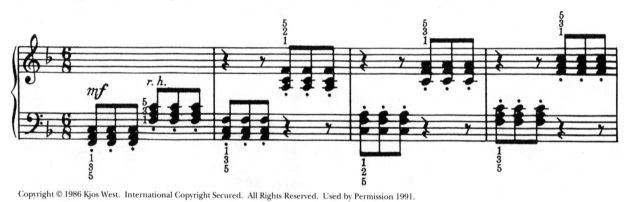

Example 75. "Old Plantation," from *Piano All The Way*, Level 4, Gillock.

"Flying Fish," obviously, is an easier setting than "Old Plantation." For those students who had problems changing positions in "Flying Fish," "Old Plantation" would need to be assigned later in the stage or during Stage IV or V. "Old Plantation" does include some examples of voicing of lines, but the voicing will not be complicated to execute. The slow tempo, Adagio, will be helpful to the student in executing the position changes. Students generally react differently to playing inversions: some students, at first, struggle with having to change positions of chords, whereas others handle the chord changes quite splendidly. The key to playing inversions easily appears to be related directly to the student's ability to approach the task aurally rather than physically. When the task is approached aurally, the ear tends to direct the hand to the next position without hesitation, and it does so with the hand remaining relaxed. While on the contrary, when the hand is directed only by the mind and the eye, the task is much more difficult to execute and the hand tends to tighten as it moves. In many cases, the teacher may need to delay assigning pieces with inversions, particularly to those students who have small hands.

As one can readily see, by Stage III there is a synthesis of the basic materials of musical composition and the notational settings of music: intervals (melodic and harmonic), basic note values and different size pulse patterns, triads and their inversions, keys, scales and harmonic progressions. These materials should always appear first in simple settings and gradually be integrated, *sequentially*, into the general notational fabric of the score. By adding the materials sequentially, students are able to absorb them into their learning gestalt— the "pool" of previously learned concepts. For instance, the presentation of melodic intervals is normally followed by harmonic intervals and partial triads—C and E going to F and G and back to C and E. The partial triads gradually appear as full 3-note triads: C-E-G to B-F-G, returning to C-E-G. The sequence of introducing triads, partial and full, into a student's learning gestalt is of utmost importance because of the physical awkwardness. For many young students, playing a full triad is very uncomfortable. They have difficulty both in playing all three notes at one time and changing from one triad to another. Consequently, it is as important to sequence the presentation of the triadic concept (partial and full triads) as it is to sequence the presentation of intervals.

Emergence of Physical Problems as a
Result of the Increase in Notational Complexities

As notational complexities rise, more demands are made upon the physical aspects of learning to play the piano, thus resulting in problems with physical coordination and dexterity. In evaluating literature from the different method books, some series' authors appear to consider the physical demands while other authors appear to be less cognizant of its importance. This dictates a strong need to examine all books with regard to the correlation between the notational arrangement and the demands of the physical realization of that arrangement. Forcing the use of some finger combinations can cause students to tighten both the fingers and the hands. This is a condition created partly by literature with too many physical demands, such as pieces containing full three-note chords, which appear early on in some beginner books before the student has had a chance to master simple harmonic intervals.

Also, combinations of notational patterns, such as alternating staccato and legato passages in alternating chordal and scalar settings, should be experienced first in easy arrangements to avoid physical confusion. "Galway Piper" illustrates these combinations, but in a simple setting:

Example 76. "The Galway Piper," from *Alfred's Basic Piano Library*, Lesson Book 2, Palmer, Manus and Lethco.

The "Galway Piper" will not be an easy piece to learn, but the alternating staccato and legato sections are mostly patterned and simple to read. The scalar passages include only a partial scale pattern and the position changes are prepared by two half notes. The combination of complexities, consequently, is diminished somewhat by how the composer has arranged the patterns. In addition, the musical ideas fit the meter extremely well, which will assist the student in playing the piece in a measure grouping (𝅝) with one primary (𝅗𝅥) and one secondary pulse (𝅗𝅥).

Any mixture of harmonic and melodic intervals for one hand, within a continuous eighth note pattern, will often cause physical problems when it is first introduced. The fingers sometimes balk or tighten when having to alternate back and forth between a double and single note pattern. This subsides, though, as soon as the student begins to perceive the pattern aurally. When it is first introduced to a student, the presentation should be in a very simple setting similar to the following:

Example 77. "8 Bar 'Pop' Pattern," from *Alfred's Basic Piano Library*, Lesson Book 2, Palmer, Manus and Lethco.

The "8 Bar 'Pop' Pattern" should be followed by some compositions which use similar but slightly more complex textures like the next piece:

Example 78. "Got Those Blues!" from *Alfred's Basic Piano Library*, Fun Book 2, Palmer, Manus and Lethco.

Although these two settings may be a little difficult physically, it is definitely time for the student to gain some finger dexterity with patterns alternating single and double notes. In actuality, the problem stems more from being influenced by *seeing* the pattern as opposed to *hearing* the pattern.

112

During Stage III, experiencing pieces that call for more finger dexterity is important because all of the next three stages will place more demands on the physical. Pieces similar to the next three examples will be appropriate for developing the needed dexterity to meet these demands. The design of these examples from the *Piano Etudes*, Book I may be more appropriate, in some cases, for Stage IV, V or VI students. Again, the teacher will have to make that decision for each individual, because all students approach reading music so differently. The teacher must always keep in mind that the sequence of literature examples in these six stages is a model from which individual curriculums can be developed. It is nearly impossible to design a compendium of literature and concepts—combining supplementary material with a core curriculum of literature—that would correspond to the needs of all types of students. Choices, instead, will have to be made in regard to each student's needs. For example, when a recommended piece or book in any of the stages is too difficult for a student, that recommendation will need to be placed in a later stage *for that particular student.*

The reading ability of students can be described in a number of different ways. One student may read chord structures quite easily, whereas a more linear pattern will completely baffle that student. Another student will be capable of reading a rather complex texture as long as the notational patterns make logical sense, aurally, to that student. Yet that same student may be totally frustrated when reading very simple notation that has a number of unusual dissonances. For instance, with the next three examples, a good linear reader will be perfectly comfortable with pieces "Three" and "Four," though "Ten" may be difficult to read because of the changes in harmony:

Example 79. "Three," from *Piano Etudes*, Book I, Bartók, compiled by Olson.

Example 80. "Four," from *Piano Etudes*, Book I, Bartók, compiled by Olson.

Example 81. "Ten," from *Piano Etudes,* Book I, Schytte, compiled by Olson.

(mm. 1–4)

     Pulse Grouping: Two Measures
     Smallest Musical Idea: Two Measures

Allegro moderato

(mm. 13–16)

     Pulse Grouping: Two Measures
     Smallest Musical Idea: One Measure

In comparing these examples, one can easily spot the problems. In "Three," the hands will be playing in parallel motion, but at a *Moderato* tempo. As a result, the pulse will need to be the measure pulse: one primary and one secondary accent (♩ ♩). Having to pre-hear and play the motivic pattern in both hands, in a measure pulse, will cause some students to make unwanted accents on the *portato* notes at the end of each slur and produce some locking of the fingers. The difficulty will be with the physical as well as the aural. The tendency will be to drop the wrists and accent on each set of *portato* notes without aurally recognizing the error. (There is a tendency for students to execute both *portato* and staccato notes with a quicker attack and release than what is used for the surrounding notes, resulting in unwanted accents. The unwanted accents will be difficult to avoid since the pattern must be perceived and imagined aurally by the measure instead of by the individual slurs.) Although not an easy texture to play, it is one that will be invaluable to the student, because this type of texture occurs very frequently in most all music in the classical style.

In "Four," the difficulties will be similar, but more complex because of the mixture of parallel and contrary motions. The student will automatically want to drop the wrists each time the right hand thumb and the left hand fifth finger strike the keys. In spite of the mixture of motions, the musical ideas should be perceived by the measure as opposed to being perceived by the thumbs and fifth fingers.

"Ten" appears to be simpler, and it really is, but most students will break down aurally and physically on the last score because the pulse grouping in the piece will need to be two measures—one primary measure and one secondary measure. Whereas the smallest musical idea in the first score is identical to the pulse grouping (two measures), the smallest musical idea in the last score is one measure. Thus, there will be a tendency to shorten the pulse grouping in the last score (mm. 13–16) to agree with the shorter musical idea. This would be incorrect. The size of the pulse grouping (two measures) must remain the same throughout because the piece continues in the same meter and tempo without examples of hemiola or other rhythmic irregularities. Changing a pulse grouping from two measures to one measure would give the aural impression of a faster tempo because the pulse grouping sets up tempo rhythm! The change in the pulse grouping would disrupt the feeling for the four-measure phrase in the last score. In many respects, working on "Ten" will be as valuable to the student as learning "Four," because there are many pieces at the intermediate and advanced levels where this type of situation occurs. (As has been suggested previously, the less talented student may have to play "Ten" with a one-measure pulse if two measures proves too difficult rhythmically, musically and physically.)

If these examples from *Piano Etudes* prove to be too challenging for the student, new demands in finger dexterity can still be approached during this stage, but with pieces which display much simpler settings like the following six examples:

Example 82. "Fanfare," Op. 117, No. 8 from *Everybody's Perfect Masterpieces*, Vol. 1, Gurlitt.

Example 83. "Sounds from Switzerland," from *Alfred's Basic Piano Library*, Fun Book 2, Palmer, Manus and Lethco.

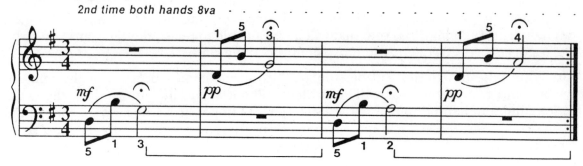

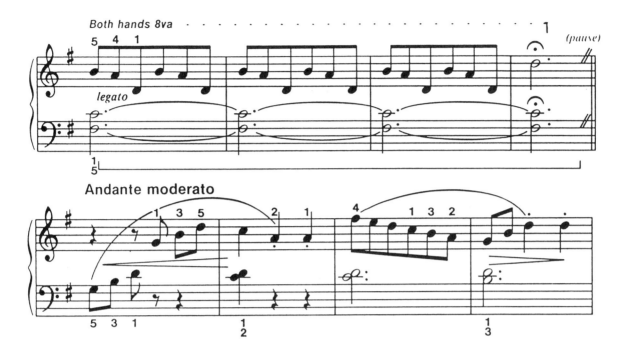

Example 84. "Stroll in the Park," from *Alfred's Basic Piano Library*, Fun Book 2, Palmer, Manus and Lethco.

116

Example 85. "Hoe-Down!" from *Alfred's Basic Piano Library*, Recital Book 2, Palmer, Manus and Lethco.

mm. 1–4

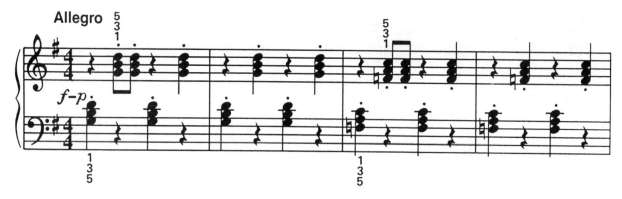

mm. 9–12

Example 86. "Hot Peppers," from *Alfred's Basic Piano Library*, Technic Book 2, Palmer, Manus and Lethco.

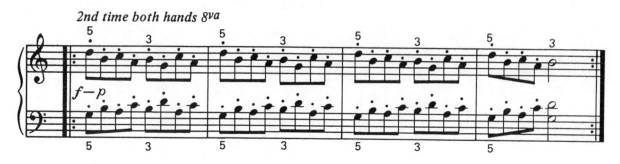

Example 87. "Etude in Imitation," Op. 218, from *First Steps in Keyboard Literature*, Köhler, edited by Olson.

In addition to some physical demands, the "Etude in Imitation" will offer the student some experience, in a very simple setting, with imitation, a contrapuntal device found in many advanced compositions in the baroque style.

The following example is another composition which will produce special demands on physical coordination and finger dexterity, even if only a moderately fast tempo is used. This is because the repeated use of the thumb and fifth finger in the left hand will be detrimental to physical coordination in the measure pulse grouping (one primary and one secondary pulse grouping). The piece is easy to read and offers no rhythmic complexities, yet the continuous use of the thumb and fifth finger, in rotation, will lend itself easily to grouping physically and to shaping musically within that two-beat grouping. This will negate the feel for the measure pulse and longer phrase idea:

Example 88. "Dining at a Foreign Restaurant," from *Trip to a Faraway Place*, McGraw.

The five-to-one repeated finger pattern may throw the 4/4 meter measure into a 2/4 meter, disrupting the musical motion of the long line. The mind and ear, therefore, must perceive it by the measure even from the first attempt. Once the "dropping wrist" forms the

118

habit of playing in groups of twos, the teacher will be faced with the difficult task of correcting the student's initial perception.

Learning to Play New Rhythms

Inclusion of 6/8 meter into a student's learning and performing gestalt can best be achieved if the settings used for the presentation are of a simple nature. Take, for instance, this next example:

Example 89. "Tarantella," from *Bastien Piano Basics*, Piano 2, Bastien.

The musical ideas and the rhythm are very patterned. In addition, there are only three positions used: the i, iv and V7 triads in G Minor. No key signature is present, only accidentals. The syllables of words should be taught (or reviewed) for the 6/8 rhythmic patterns: *Cho-co-late* for the three-eighth-note pattern (♪♪♪); *Pump-kin* for the quarter-eighth-note pattern (♩ ♪); and *Pie* for the dotted quarter note (♩.). A similar composition in 6/8 meter would be the following example:

Example 90. "Penguin Parade," from *Bastien Piano Basics*, Technic 2, Bastien.

The next piece will be somewhat more difficult because the right hand melody is not in an easy five-finger pattern:

Example 91. "Scottish Bagpipes," from *Bastien Piano Basics*, Piano 2, Bastien.

In discussing 6/8 rhythm, the student needs to understand that there usually are only two beats or pulses in each measure: one primary and one secondary. When using the words, *cho-co-late, cho-co-late*, follow this up with the concept that the two *cho-co-lates* will be hierarchical in nature. In other words, the two *cho-co-lates* will be considered as being primary and secondary units (♩. ♩.), within the concept of the whole measure. The student may comprehend what you are talking about very easily if it is described as follows: "The *chocolate* on the downbeat (count one) is down and the other one is up." Continuing with an analogy, "Pat your legs on the down—the first *chocolate*—and say earth; and follow it by pointing your fingers toward the sky—the second *chocolate*—and say sky." The student will understand the measure as an "earth-sky" concept. This gives the student a sense of one rhythmic circle per measure, whereas perceiving both *chocolates* as down—having two starting points—divides the student's perception and aural image into two parts, cutting the musical line in each measure into two segments. For the piece to be played and phrased successfully, the measure, as opposed to half the measure, must be the smallest phrase-unit, the smallest musical circle.

In the next example, the musical circle involves eight quarter notes with a primary pulse feeling on the first quarter note and a secondary pulse feeling on the fifth quarter note (♩♩♩♩♩♩♩♩):

Example 92. "Trying Not to Get Scared While Going Through the Tunnel," from *Wishing That Vacation Would Last Forever*, Poe.

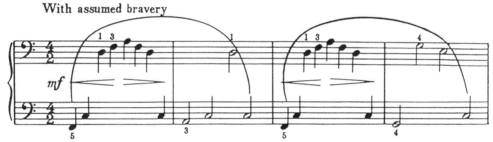

Here the rhythmic circle of musical motion has many separate pitches inside, but the pitch and rhythmic notation both are quite simple. A majority of the pitches involves the intervals of thirds and fifths, and the note values are mostly quarters and half notes.

Introducing the Jazz Element

As the student approaches tunes that illustrate jazz rhythms, an inner sense of pulse should already have been established. Aspects of jazz rhythms, such as syncopation, cannot be played very convincingly without a sense of pulse, because jazz music and most pop music require a feeling for pulse or the rhythmic swing in music, as seen in the next two examples:

Example 93. "Neophyte Rag," from *Jazz Fragments*, Richie.

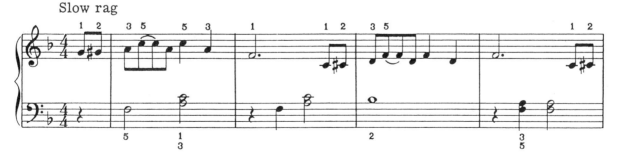

120

In the "Neophyte Rag," the upbeat notes (the two eighth notes leading into the downbeats) will fail to sound correct unless the student hears and feels where they belong in relationship to the downbeat. Moreover, the syncopation produced by the ties will sound "manufactured" unless there is a feeling for how the syncopation works within the feeling of the measure pulse.

Example 94. "Ragtime Man," from *Alfred's Basic Piano Library*, Fun Book 2, Palmer, Manus and Lethco.

A similar situation occurs in "Ragtime Man." Here again, for the syncopation to sound convincing, there must be a feeling for how the syncopation works within the measure pulse. All the tied notes must have an upbeat sound as they all occur on weak beats within the measure pulse.

Artistry and Pedaling

In working on tonal control, balance, clarity, touches and pedaling, it will be best, in Stage III, to continue using short pieces in easy settings and simple rhythm similar to the following two examples:

Example 95. "Lonesome Journey," from *Ready For Reading*, Book 2, Grove.

Example 96. "Evening Tide," from *Ready For Reading*, Book 2, Grove.

"Lonesome Journey" demands a clear balance between the hands as well as some tonal control. Students often want to strike or "hit" the right hand chords with no sound concept in mind. "Evening Tide" illustrates the use of the pedal in a very easy setting, demanding very little of the student other than playing simple phrases with only one pedal change per phrase.

If the student has not been introduced to the speed of attack concept, now is the time to demonstrate and explain how it affects the dynamic level of sound. Some of the super-talented students may hear intuitively that clarity, balance and expressive tonal quality are all affected by a key's speed of attack, but for others, they will show no awareness of any connection. The concept, therefore, will not only have to be demonstrated and explained, but it will also have to be fostered constantly with most all students. Through analogies, demonstrations and discussions, the concept of playing a faster attack with one hand than the other hand must be understood, imagined aurally and executed many times before it becomes second nature with a student. Demanding these controls too early will cause some students to react with tightness, especially if the ear is not involved. The ear—the pre-hearing— must come into the picture before many demands can be made of tonal control.

One exercise that commonly helps promote tonal balance is having a student play the third finger, in each hand, on middle black keys, e.g., the A-flats, with varying degrees of speed. First, while disregarding balance, get the student accustomed to playing with a fast attack while maintaining contact with the key—not attacking from above the key. With this, demonstrate the difference between a very fast attack and a slow attack, relating the two to the degree of loudness and softness of the sounds. It is imperative that the student hear the difference between notes that "ring" or "sing" and notes that have a "hit" sound. Then suggest that the student balance the two notes, playing the right hand louder by using a faster attack in that hand.

The concept of a ringing tone versus one sounding "hit" will have to be reiterated numerous times before the student can conceive tones aurally before striking the keys. As long as the tones sound hit, a teacher will know that the striking is being guided by the mind and the physical, not the ear. The refining of tonal control and balance must be approached on a very individual basis. What may have to be considered as acceptable for one may be far below the capability of another student and vice versa.

The same is true for pedaling. Some will find pedaling very logical. Yet others, who have developed at a slower aural pace will find pedaling an added inconvenience. Pieces similar to "Evening Tide" will be the best choices for most students, because the process involves long pedals, eliminating the need for a number of changes. The eye-ear-foot coordination will be particularly difficult for the visual learners who want to think of it in separate steps without anticipating the next change. This occurs because their ear is not alerting them of the need to change. They are trying to pedal by seeing the page and then physically moving the foot. Normally before any pedaling is needed, the student should learn to hear pedal changes one note at a time, hands separately as described in Chapter III. In teaching the pedaling process, the teacher should stress that the student should not hold the leg tightly or attempt to balance the body with the pedaling foot, both of which make pedaling changes more cumbersome. The student's body should be balanced on the bench (some children will have to lean against the bench because of their short stature) and be able to play the pedal without grabbing the leg or attacking the pedal from above. The student should be instructed to keep the foot on the pedal while making pedaling changes to avoid striking the metal from above after each change. The student should also be reminded to keep the heel on the floor while making pedaling changes.

Refinement of pedaling will occur gradually and on an individual basis. For those who find it very intimidating, simply delay refinement. If refining the pedal is added at the expense of damaging tempo and aural control, then it serves no purpose. The use of the pedal can be delayed or the student can pedal compositions which require only one pedal throughout or very few pedal changes, such as the following whole-tone scale piece:

Example 97. "The Planets," from *Alfred's Basic Piano Library*, Lesson Book 1B, Palmer, Manus and Lethco.

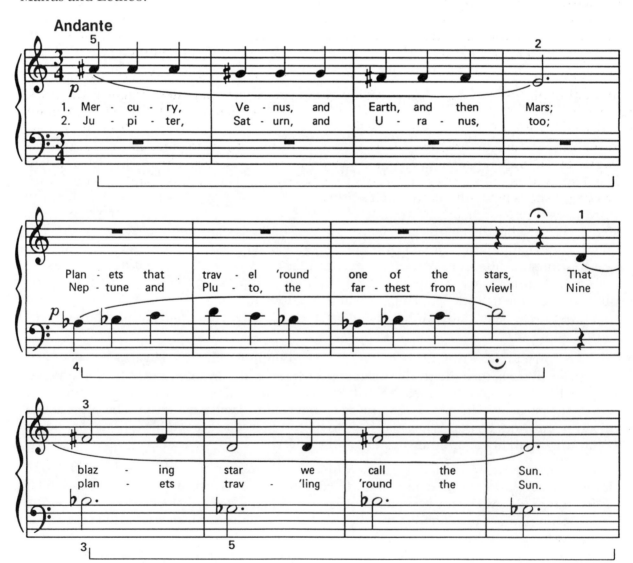

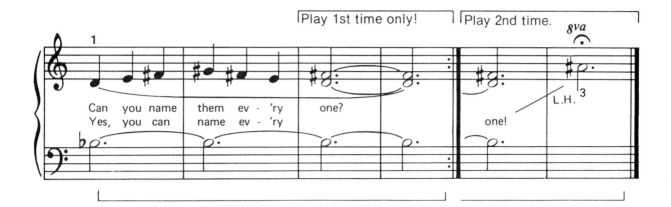

Conclusion

Stage I stressed establishing a reading, rhythm and range foundation in addition to getting the mind, ear and body to perceive, hear and play in a rhythm. Stage II added numerous musical complexities and slightly increased the notational demands. Stage III involved adding some musical complexities, but the notational texture became much more substantial than was found in the previous stages. In turn, the physical coordination became more demanding as did the total concept of learning and performing music.

As one progresses through the guidelines for the other stages, it will become apparent that although the musical and notational complexities are integrated, Stages I, III and V are more concerned with the basic foundation of reading notation and II, IV and VI are more concerned with adding musical complexities and style characteristics. All of the stages, though, are somewhat integrated, but a teacher will find the general outline of the individual stages very helpful in placing students at specific complexity levels. The teacher must realize that a student, at times, could hypothetically be working on literature and concepts from two stages, especially consecutive ones.

Chapter VII

STAGE IV

The music in Stage IV shows a definite rise in complexity in comparison to the music of Stage III. Whereas Stage III broadened the basic foundation of notational complexities, musical complexities were held to a minimum. Stage IV places emphasis upon adding more musical complexities as opposed to adding more notes. The Stage III literature was basically patterned in pitch, rhythm and articulation. These pieces used a narrow range of the keyboard and contained phrase shapes that were easy to decipher. Now is the time for the student to experience music that will be less patterned, will cover a wider range of the keyboard and will have a number of added musical demands. Although there is always the possibility of leaving patterned music too quickly, students will become bored if they are left for too long a time playing music that is all very similar in design. This is the reason several unpatterned supplementary pieces were introduced in Stage III. They were suggested as a means of acquainting the student with music that did not necessarily start on a familiar landmark or in a specific position, such as G, F or C. Most of these pieces were very thin-textured with implied harmonic progressions. Full three-note triads were missing, thus calling upon the student to hear implied harmonic progressions as opposed to seeing and hearing the harmony spelled out, e.g., C-E-G and C-F-A.

The majority of the Stage IV literature suggestions will continue this trend, offering the student a chance to experiment with new notational settings and new types of sounds. As a result, this will bring about the needed evaluation of several aspects of the student's reading process. Is the student ready to learn music that will challenge him musically and at the same time be of a less patterned nature? Were most of the combinations of symbols in Stage III perceived and executed without many problems? Is the student comfortable with playing in a pulse? Does the student approach new literature assignments with excitement or reluctance? If the answers are mixed, more experience may be needed with music similar to the Stage III examples. The teacher, though, should not be guided always by the weaknesses of the student, or the assignments for that student will become tedious and uninteresting. In other words, "do not play it too safe or students will become completely apathetic to their music." Moreover, the teacher should not take for granted that a specific student is going to have problems with a piece or a book because of that student's past experiences. Students are unpredictable: with some challenges they may "fall on their faces" while with other challenges they may "succeed with flying colors."

Stage IV Supplementary Materials

With some of the Stage IV supplementary music, there may be some difficulties with hand synchronization because of the unfamiliar textural settings. One hand may be coordinated perfectly with the pulse pattern while the other hand may approach a piece playing tightly in a note-to-note fashion. Normally students more or less keep their wrists synchronized with the pulse as opposed to the wrists moving in opposite directions. When wrists do become disorganized, it often is due to the diverse pitch or rhythmic patterns between the two hands. This dissimilarity may cause the wrists to pump up-and-down at random or pump up-and-down independently of each other. When this occurs, the teacher must attempt to diagnose why. The diversity of patterns often causes the student to lose a sense of holistic perception and a feeling for pulse. In addition to diverse patterns, an increase in the keyboard range and an absence of a specific tonality all may make it difficult for some students to maintain physical coordination and musical direction.

Many of the Stage IV supplementary literature suggestions are basically linear, thin-textured and unpatterned, making it difficult for some students to sight-read. If the student becomes too engrossed in trying to read the unusual settings, the aural part of learning will become completely subservient to deciphering the score. A student's repertoire at the beginning of Stage IV, consequently, should only contain a minimal number of these pieces. The student may struggle with the reading at first because compositions from the method books mostly make use of familiar notational patterns, which is necessary for a majority of students. If they were composed differently, too many students would have problems with sight-reading new assignments.

Supplementary materials, if chosen carefully, can serve as an added dimension to the student's method series core literature. One key point, though, to remember in coordinating the two kinds of materials is that the pieces in supplementary books are often not sequenced as carefully as the pieces in the method series. The challenges of the supplementary material, to a large extent, will have to be monitored very carefully or the new types of settings will confuse the student. The better designed method books present the student with a sequenced progression of notational complexities, such as intervals, scales, triads, inversions, finger crossings, key orientation, primary chords and textural settings. The progression offers security for the student because newly assigned pieces will look familiar, which is less true with some of the supplementary books.

Although pieces from the method books offer both notational and musical challenges, the notational challenges often dominate. The method books generally are written for the "middle-of-the-road learner" as a majority of students fit into this category. If the method books contained a wider variety of notational and musical complexities simultaneously, the pieces would be too difficult for most students. The idea of using a method series as the core curriculum is normally the best choice for most learners, allowing the supplementary books to serve as a needed addition.

Adding Supplementary Materials to a Student's Core Curriculum

When adding supplementary literature to a student's core curriculum during Stage IV, both a student's strong and weak points should be examined. Regardless of the additional musical complexities, even a small rise in notational complexities will affect some students' ability to cope. Some of the different aspects of the notation to consider include the presentation or juxtaposition of the following concepts:

1. The use of primary chords in both hands
2. The inclusion of a number of different hand positions and tonalities
3. The addition of textures which require more frequent pedal changes, causing a need for very careful voicing, clarity and balance
4. The inclusion of ostinato patterns against simple melodic patterns, causing a rise in complexity of controlling synchronization between the hands, voicing and, in some cases, longer pulse patterns
5. The use of thicker textures in both hands
6. The increase in keyboard range, demanding more physical mobility of the student
7. The suggestion of faster tempos
8. The increase in linear writing, causing problems with perceiving and hearing thin-textured passages as musical lines
9. The increase in contrasting articulation within each hand and between the hands

10. The increase in the number of pieces composed outside five-finger
positions and using less familiar fingerings, such as the finger 2 on
Middle-C in the right hand or finger 3 on G in the left hand

The Extension of Five-Finger Patterns

As one or both of the hands extend beyond the familiar five-finger patterns, coordination among the eye-ear-hand may become more difficult to retain as will be the case in the next example:

Example 98. "On Top of Old Smoky," from *Alfred's Basic Piano Library*, Lesson Book 3, arranged Palmer, Manus and Lethco.

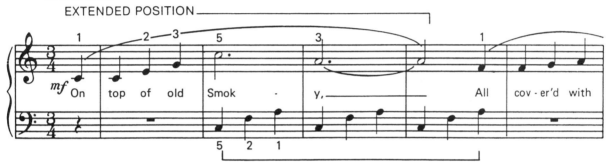

The right hand extends to the octave while the left hand extends to a sixth. The octave, rather than appearing in a scalar texture, is now presented as a full four-note arpeggiated chord. Although the extensions in both hands basically change a student's view of the score from easy five-finger patterns to a more open score, there are some aspects of this example that will make the transition easier: 1) the rhythmic pattern is very simple; 2) the tonality is C Major; and 3) there are no accidentals. Blocking can be used to promote a holistic perception of the symbols when they are first read, enabling the mind and ear to direct the physical in extending to the octave. Although the extensions add a new dimension to reading and to the tactile aspect of playing, the other aspects of the notation allow the student to concentrate mainly on one dimension—the extension of the triadic pattern to the octave.

A General Rise in Complexity

In the next example, the melodic pattern, including pitch and rhythm, may be slightly more difficult, but the left hand pattern is all chordal. The *more* in one hand will balance out with the *less* (the blocked L.H. being simpler) in the other hand. Also, the chordal left hand pattern will allow for more concentration on the balance and clarity of the melody and accompaniment pattern. A good rule of thumb, concerning musical refinement, is that the less difficult the setting is to read and play, the more refinement may be expected. This will not hold true for all students, but it should be considered for the majority of learners.

This next excerpt, from "Light and Blue," appears to be an easy setting. The crossings, the alternation between melodic and harmonic intervals and the mobility of the pattern (the 8vas), however, make both the musical and technical/physical controls slightly cumbersome to manage. Although one can recognize that some of the new concepts are balanced with some concepts that the student already has mastered, the notational pattern still looks slightly more difficult:

Example 99. "Light and Blue," from *Alfred's Basic Piano Library*, Lesson Book 3, Palmer, Manus and Lethco.

The following composition also appears to be more challenging, and it is because the composers include a number of scale passages moving in both directions and intermingling with harmonic intervals. Let's consider, though, some other factors: 1) the octave scale patterns and crossings have already been experienced; 2) the key signature is C Major; and 3) the rhythmic pattern will be easy to understand. Subsequently, this example will be challenging, but within the range of the Stage IV student:

Example 100. "Prelude in 18th Century Style," *Alfred's Basic Piano Library*, Lesson Book 3, Palmer, Manus and Lethco.

The teacher must recognize whether the challenges of newly assigned literature are balanced by items on the score which have been previously mastered. The challenges may look entirely forbidding when in actuality the trade-offs, or items that balance the challenges, may make the literature very approachable. Realizing the multiplicity of complexities, with or without any trade-offs, permits the teacher to make more logical literature selections for the individual learner. All presentations of new concepts or new textural arrangements should be balanced with aspects of the score that have been mastered previously and some aspects that will present a challenge. In this way, the student will be able to absorb the new concepts and reorganize her learning and performing gestalt at a slightly more complex level. For instance, the introduction of pieces in the key of Bb Major is sometimes delayed until the third or fourth level. This delayed introduction, nevertheless, still needs to be presented in a setting that displays some concepts familiar to the student like the following piece:

Example 101. "Little Prelude in B-Flat," from *Music Pathways*, Piano Discoveries Book D, Olson, Bianchi and Blickenstaff.

The notes will be easy to read and the touch remains legato throughout. Rhythmically there is nothing new to comprehend; therefore, the only new concept will be the key of Bb. There are some hand crossings, but the notation is very patterned. Some young students do have problems playing in the key of Bb because of the awkward hand position, but being introduced to the new tonality in this type of setting will make the playing easier. The same considerations would be true with the next two pieces:

Example 102. "Drifting in Outer Space," from *Music Pathways*, Piano Discoveries Book B, Olson, Bianchi and Blickenstaff.

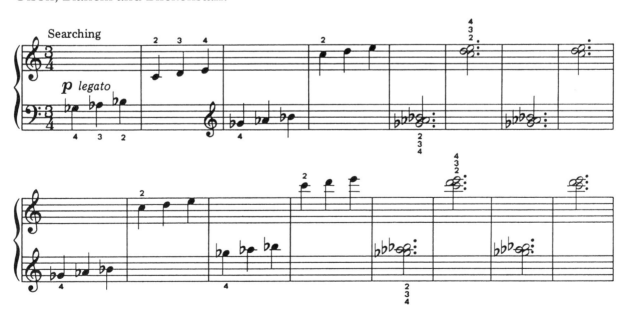

Example 103. "Two White Swans," from *Music Pathways,* Piano Discoveries Book B, Olson, Bianchi and Blickenstaff.

Both pieces look rather easy because the textures are very thin and patterned. There are no new rhythmic complexities, but each piece covers a wider range of the keyboard than the student is perhaps accustomed to experiencing. This basically will be the new complexity in addition to the pieces being in the whole-tone scale. The scale pattern, though, should be easy to read because much of the notation appears as single notes, except for a few harmonic intervals and some three-note tone clusters. The clusters, nevertheless, only appear after they have been presented first as single notes. Also, as an added feature, the whole-tone scale provides the student some experience with impressionistic sounds. Yet within all of the new and previously learned concepts, having to read and play over a wider range of the keyboard may be the only challenge. Students, consequently, will be able to absorb the challenge and reorganize their learning and performing gestalt, once again, at a slightly higher level of complexity.

New Aural Demands

Pieces like the next example offer the student an opportunity for controlling a melodic idea against an accompaniment pattern, similar to an Alberti bass figure used in many sonatinas and sonatas. Experiencing Alberti bass figures and other classical style characteristics in Stages IV through VI will make learning the style of these pieces at the intermediate level much simpler:

Example 104. "Intermezzo," from *Alfred's Basic Piano Library,* Lesson Book 3, Palmer, Manus and Lethco.

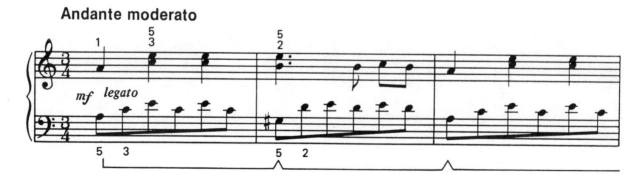

Although a student already will have experienced most of the items on the score, this particular texture—an accompaniment pattern against a melody containing a mixture of melodic and harmonic intervals—will still be demanding. In reference to the balance and clarity, the student should approach the concept of balancing the notes among each other as opposed to just playing the melody louder than the accompaniment, or in some cases, to just hearing a teacher inappropriately say, "Your left hand is too loud; play it softer." This may suggest to the student to ignore the sound of the left hand. Consequently, problems with getting a student to hear dynamics between the hands may be traced back to his early training with instructions, such as, "Play the left hand softer as it is the *right hand* that I want to hear." Perhaps this is the reason a large majority of students have trouble hearing what is happening aurally between the hands. One approach to solving problems with balance and clarity is to have the student work on a number of duets in a lyrical style, such as the following two examples:

Example 105. "Spanish Intermezzo," from *Alfred's Basic Piano Library,* Duet Book 3, Alexander.

Secondo

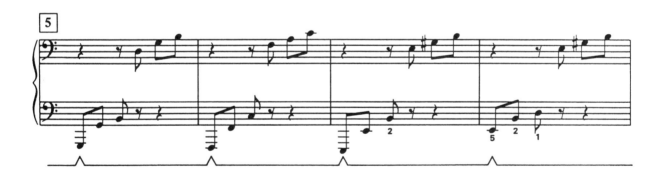

Primo

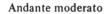

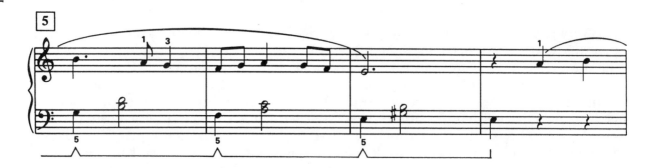

Example 106. "Hang Gliders," from *Alfred's Basic Piano Library*, Duet Book 3, Alexander.

Secondo

Primo

First, students will need to hear the balance, clarity and tonal control in their part, followed by hearing these items among all four hands. Some students, ironically, will control the situation aurally far better in duets than in solos. Perhaps the engaging sound between the two parts provides the student with an added incentive to listen and pre-hear more keenly. Too, students generally are captivated by making music with a partner. The duets from *Alfred's Basic Piano Library* are composed so that the student's parts sound very convincing when played just as solos. The student's parts are also designed to be easy to read, allowing for the primo and secondo parts to be played together practically at the time of assignment. The main thrust, therefore, can be one of making music as opposed to making corrections.

Some method books include pieces which acquaint the student with the entire keyboard very early on in a student's experience. For many, this places added demands on the student's ability to grasp the fundamentals of learning to read music. Students begin to approach the reading process from a visual–tactile standpoint only. The aural aspect of reading is neglected. Any transfer of learning becomes questionable. This is why pieces like "Drifting in Outer Space" and "Two White Swans" (Examples 102 and 103) should be assigned with special care. Assigning them before Stage IV can be problematic unless they are taught by rote. Retaining knowledge of the different positions on the keyboard and being confronted with so many accidentals is often too much to remember for most students during the first two or three years of study. Many students begin to have problems retaining what was learned from reading previous pieces, approaching each newly assigned piece with very little knowledge of what was gained from past experiences. As a result, teachers have begun to realize that concepts approached aurally and sequenced within a narrow range of the keyboard can be mastered much more easily than concepts that are presented over a wider range. As concepts become second nature, they can be presented gradually over the entire keyboard, especially through the use of 8vas. This will foster the transfer of learning. There should be more concern for the proper sequencing of the expansion of the keyboard range as opposed to how quickly it is presented. The following example illustrates this point:

Example 107. "Cheering up a Sad Clown," from *Circus Suite*, Rollin.

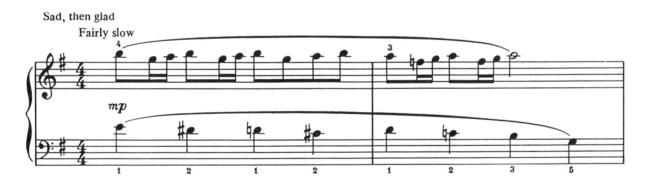

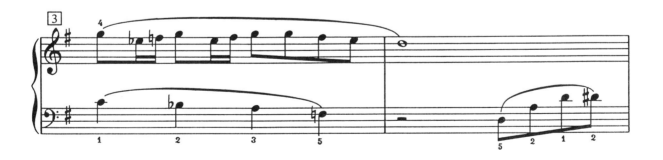

Throughout this piece, the setting includes numerous accidentals, a mixture of staccato and legato, contrasting articulation and a mixture of intervals. The setting, nonetheless, occurs in a rather narrow range of the keyboard. The emphasis of the piece is on the rise in the overall complexity rather than a thicker texture and a wider range of the keyboard. Although the piece will not be easy, the rise in complexity has not been complicated with being presented over a wide range of the keyboard. This brings to mind one of the top priorities to consider when assigning music to children: a rise in complexity, both notational and musical, should occur in comfortable settings before the student is faced with a similar type of complexity in other ranges of the keyboard. The same would be true with settings that contain tension-to-resolution harmonies on weak-to-strong beats. Students should first learn to treat tension-to-resolution appropriately on *strong-to-weak beats*, within the rhythmic structure, before they are introduced to the same musical phenomenon on *weak-to-strong beats*. When it is first introduced on weak-to-strong beats, the presentation should occur in a comfortable setting and preferably in one that doesn't change positions. (Tension-to-resolution occurs more and more commonly on weak-to-strong beats as the complexity of music rises. For instance, in the works of Johannes Brahms, points of tension quite regularly occur on weak beats and resolve on strong beats. This produces a dichotomy between strong-weak and loud-soft. The student is faced with playing dynamically loud on some of the weak beats and dynamically soft on the some of the strong beats. The student, consequently, should be comfortable with the concept in normal settings before it is attempted in the abnormal setting—weak-to-strong.)

With the next example, the basic demands will include perceiving, hearing and getting acquainted with playing inversions in a very straightforward setting:

Example 108. "Royal Procession," from *Bastien Piano Basics,* Piano 3, Bastien.

The rhythm is simple, as is the notational pattern which occurs against the chords and their inversions. The piece is in an easy key and it is practically void of articulation. The only aspect of the piece that may be difficult will be the inversions. The playing of the inversions should be guided by the ear, not by the eye looking at the keyboard to find the next set of notes. The inversions should be perceived and imaged aurally as units as opposed to the student having to think, "Let's see, I believe those notes are B (pause) D (pause) and uh (pause) G, which makes that a (pause) G chord." When this happens, the teacher will know that the recognition of triads and their inversions is still an abstract concept with that student. This indicates that the student needs more experience playing Stage III pieces with basic chord structures before continuing on with the literature of Stage IV.

Exploring New Tonalities

In Stage IV, students should continue to explore tonalities beyond three or four sharps and flats. The exploration should come now or the student will be plagued continually, at the more advanced levels of music, with just deciphering the notes in pieces in such keys as Db Major or C# Major. Compositions similar to the following example will offer that experience:

Example 109. "Jacob's Ladder," from *Bastien Piano Basics,* Piano 3, Bastien.

The textural setting is quite simple. There are no rhythmic complexities and the harmonic progression uses only primary chords. Subsequently, the student only has to comprehend the I-V7-I progression and what pitches belong together in the key of Db Major. The student hopefully experienced the tonal relationships in Db Major, early on, in the tetrachord form of the scale duets (Example 14).

136

In evaluating the difficulties in "Jacob's Ladder," one quickly sees that the melodic intervals are all simple with a majority being thirds. The student will only need to transfer the tonal relationships already learned and heard in other keys, such as D Major. After learning "Jacob's Ladder," the next example will further enhance the student's mastery of this key:

Example 110. "Prelude in Db Major," from *Bastien Piano Basics*, Piano 3, Bastien.

The student is experiencing the key of Db Major in two different settings, one using blocked harmonies and one illustrating the arpeggiated version. Other than the fact that one piece has blocked harmony and the other uses an arpeggiated version, the notes are similar in the two pieces. Most students will see and hear the blocked harmonic version more easily than the one-note-at-a-time arpeggiated version. The teacher, to some extent, will have to promote the student's hearing of the harmonic progressions, regardless of the version. When first attempting this piece, the arpeggiated figure should be blocked in order to enhance the student's grasp—both visually and aurally—of the harmonic aspect of the arpeggiated pattern. The blocking technique most definitely should be introduced at this time if it has not been done beforehand.

Contrasting Articulations

For many of the students, concepts will need to be experienced in many different pieces before they will be fully mastered. For instance, the next example, "Broken, but Busy," offers the student a chance to work on contrasting articulations in combination with the primary chords in F Major. This piece can be transposed into a number of other keys, thereby fostering the aural concept of tonal relationships within a key regardless of the changes in articulation:

Example 111. "Broken, but Busy," from *Alfred's Basic Piano Library*, Technic Book 3, Palmer, Manus and Lethco.

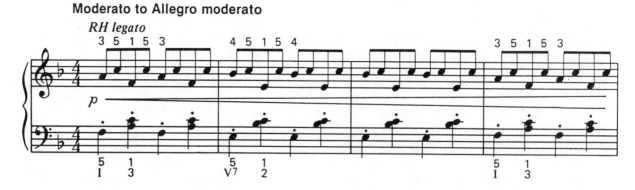

The triplet figure, introduced earlier in this stage, is another concept that should be encountered in numerous settings before a student can perceive and aurally imagine triplet figures without a struggle. The next example also includes the triplet figure, hands together, at the octave:

Example 112. "Triplet Rhythm Warm-ups," from *Bastien Piano Basics*, Technic 3, Bastien.

Expanding a student's basic foundation within a stage should normally occur before there is an expansion into unusual settings containing new complexities. In contrast to some beliefs, new musical complexities in thin-textured settings cause more problems for students than an increase in the number of notes in a familiar setting. That is to say that most students will continue to be comfortable with more notes—thicker textures—as long as the notes are couched in a familiar pattern, whereas a thin-textured score, displaying a series of unpatterned intervals, will be difficult to grasp. Thin-textured scores can be very deceiving. Even a few notes can be difficult to read if there is neither a logical pattern to the succession of intervals nor any feeling for a basic tonality.

Experiencing Unusual Textures

Some of the pieces with unusual textures, especially ones from supplementary books, include a number of complex ideas, such as: 1) the upbeat-to-downbeat problem; 2) the appearance of long notes occurring on weak beats; 3) the appearance of contrasting articulations combined with changes in texture: 4) the absence of any notes on downbeats; 5) thin, linear writing displaying stylistic characteristics; 6) melodies consisting of two-note slurs; and 7) thin-textured melodies containing a mixture of articulation.

Many students tend to read upbeats, staccato notes and the first note of two-note slurs all as downbeats regardless of where they occur in the measure. The eye may perceive an upbeat triplet-figure as a separate idea unrelated to the other notes within the strong-weak makeup of a measure. There may be a similar response to staccato notes, seeing and thinking of them as separate attacks and separate sounds. Many times two-note slurs are perceived as separate ideas unrelated to their role in a melody or phrase. The student thinks, "Let's see, a two-note slur marking means for me to play *Down-Up* and *Loud-Soft.* To add to the problem, the loud-soft is often played soft-loud without the student's realization. The student must learn to pre-hear the loud-soft rather than just learning to think it, and the pre-hearing must be done within the context of the measure and phrase, as opposed to pre-hearing it as an isolated figure.

All of these aspects of notation can become isolated concepts in the minds of the students, mentally conceiving them each time as new beginnings. A new beginning translates in a student's reading process as a new downbeat. This results in a hodgepodge of isolated ideas that fail to turn into a metered rhythmic grouping, the basic unit of phrasing. The listener becomes more aware of the individual components of the notation as opposed to hearing the phrase. Although unpatterned musical ideas do cause problems with one's musical control, this type of setting most definitely needs to be encountered by Stage IV or students will incur many difficulties as they progress into more advanced music. Some of the following examples may look simple because of the scarcity of notes. Yet the arrangement of the notation within each texture may make the pieces more difficult to learn than textures that contain many more notes. In deciphering the complexity of a score, the teacher must not only consider the density of the notation, but the arrangement of notation within the setting. For instance, many beginners as well as a large majority of more advanced students often have problems with upbeats. Perceived incorrectly, physical coordination and sound relationships will both be distorted. In perceiving the "Happy Morning," the student must be aware of the upbeat triplet figure throughout the piece:

Example 113. "Happy Morning," from *Guidelines for Developing Piano Performance*, Book 2, Olson.

If the first triplet is played as a downbeat, the phrasing will become confused throughout. How much easier the piece will be to learn if the student begins his "thinking and doing" on an imaginary downbeat rather than when the notation starts—on beat four of the opening partial measure. When the student waits until beat four, that beat will sound like a downbeat, immediately followed by another downbeat on beat one of the first full measure. Two consecutive downbeats will automatically disrupt the physical coordination and the tonal relationships. The musical motion needs to travel by the measure, involving one primary and one secondary pulse. Consequently, the mind, ear and the physical must be coordinated in the measure as one continuous circle. Without this circle, one will be more aware of the triplet figures and staccato notes than the phrase line. Thus, if the upbeat-to-downbeat and downbeat-to-upbeat concepts have not been learned, heard and felt before, now is the time to correct the problem.

As notational patterns become more varied, long note values begin to occur on weak beats. Take, for instance, this setting:

Example 114. "Small Brook," from *Guidelines for Developing Piano Performance*, Book 2, Olson.

The four eighth notes, beginning on a downbeat and leading to a half note on beat three, will often be played as four eighths on an upbeat leading to a half note on the downbeat. This incorrect perception disorganizes the rhythmic and aural aspects of the process as well as the physical grouping. Since the pulse pattern would include a primary pulse and a secondary pulse (may be also thought of as a measure pulse grouping), playing the half notes as downbeats completely throws the synthesis of rhythm, ear and technique "all out of sync."

Later in the piece, the textural setting changes from four eighth notes and a half note to four quarter notes per measure. This may also cause organizational problems. So often a textural change is perceived at a different tempo than the tempo used for the previous texture. In this case, perceiving the four quarter notes individually will result in four separate physical motions, producing four isolated sounds.

These are the two main perceptual problems in the "Small Brook." They both look quite simple to the eye, yet how a piece looks and how it should sound may differ entirely. A student must be taught to perceive music symbols holistically inside a metered-pulse pattern, regardless of how the combination of note values is placed upon the rhythmic structure. If the eyes organize perceptions by single pitches or by motives, the physical organization and the sound relationships, in turn, become incorrect. Similar problems may also occur with the next example:

Example 115. "Circle Dance," from *Guidelines for Developing Piano Performance*, Book 2, Olson.

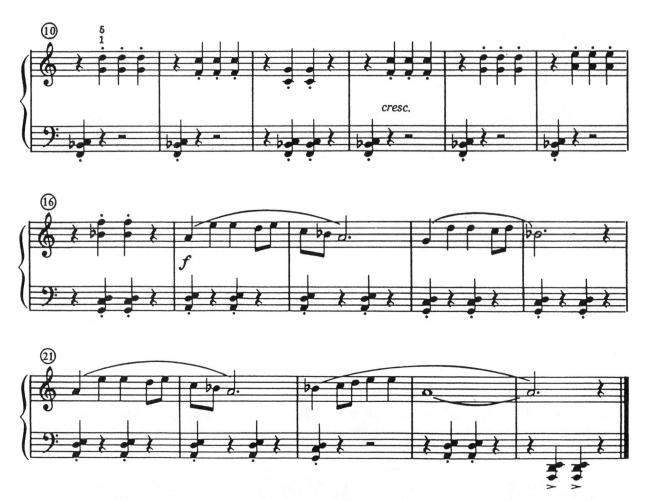

In "Circle Dance," the pulse pattern should be conceived by the measure or by a primary pulse on beat one and a secondary pulse on beat three. Attempting it in two primary pulses will make it more difficult because the real problem will be in keeping the perception, aural image and physical motions organized by the measure in spite of the contrasting articulations. Playing staccato chords on beats one and three, with a legato melody, will tend to pull the perception and aural image into two primary pulse-units, a situation that should be guarded against. Too, when the texture changes later in the piece to four quarter note chords per measure, the perception may disintegrate into four separate thoughts and aural images, here again producing four separate motions resulting in four isolated sounds.

Another problem often occurs in the third score, third measure, because there are no notes on beat one. Here, most students will delay their downbeat feeling to beat two because this is where notes begin to appear again. The delay in feeling the downbeat will disrupt the organization of the physical motions and the tonal relationships. Since there is an absence of any notes on beat one, the player must still feel the downbeat and follow through physically—outwardly or internally—with the downbeat feeling. Delaying the downbeat feeling to beat two will disrupt the circle of continuous musical motion.

The complexity of the texture in music lies not in the number of symbols on the page, but how these symbols are integrated in a setting for producing the musical message—the character and mood of the piece. Though the arrangement of the notation in the next piece is cumbersome, performing the composition musically in a convincing manner will be the basic problem:

Example 116. "Computer with a Problem," from *Seen and Heard*, Bittner.

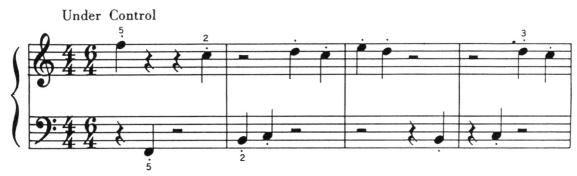

Here, there is an absence of any feeling for a specific tonality anywhere in the piece. There is no rhythmic variety— quarter notes prevail throughout, except for a change in meter from 4/4 to 6/4—nor is there any evidence of an intervallic pattern. Also, some measures begin with an absence of any notation on the downbeat. The 8vas will produce some keyboard mobility, but basically there is little in the notation that will promote a feeling for musical direction or phrase shape. This results in a musical texture called *pointillism* in which pitches are presented at random as opposed to being presented in some type of melodic succession. Although the setting is very unusual, it offers a wonderful opportunity for learning an interesting piece composed in a 20th century style.

In the 4/4 metered sections of "Computer With a Problem," should there be a measure pulse with a strong or primary feeling on beat one and a secondary feeling on beat three? Probably not because the pointillistic nature of the piece will need the middle of the measure, beat three, for an anchor, especially in the measures where there are no notes on the downbeat. Two primary pulses per measure would work better (♩ ♩). The same would be true for the 6/4 metered section (♩. ♩.). Interestingly simple and at the same time unusual, this composition presents an intriguing challenge in perceiving symbols in an abstract arrangement. Although the composition is very complex musically, it looks quite simple on the score. While different in design and slightly more complex, the following piece would be a similar challenge:

Example 117. "Popcorn Machine," from *Seen and Heard*, Bittner.

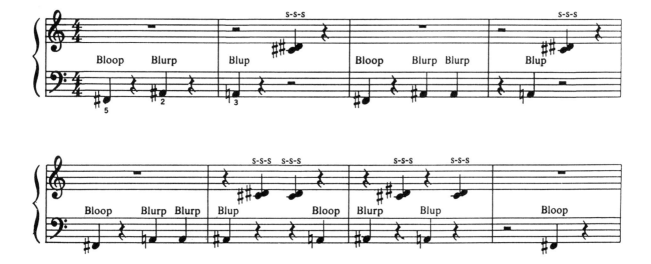

142

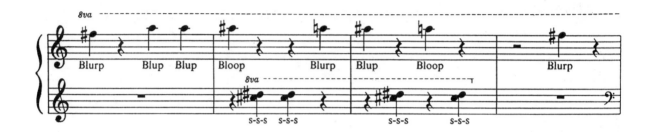

Musically, the full measure grouping, one primary and one secondary pulse, carries the musical motion more successfully, because it makes the syncopation more effective. However, the insertion of rests—some occurring on the downbeats—will cause the piece to be very exasperating for most students who attempt it by the measure, even for some intermediate level students. This makes it nearly impossible for most young students to think and play by the measure. The teacher, therefore, may have to be satisfied with the lesser choice, the two primary pulse groupings per measure. It would be easier if the piece could be played at a rather slow tempo, yet the piece would be much less convincing as the syncopations require a lively tempo.

Pop, Jazz and Blues

Students will need to acquire an inner sense of pulse before jazz rhythms in pop, jazz and blues compositions can be played convincingly, such as in the next five examples:

Example 118. "Four-Finger Blues," from *Patterns for Fun*, Book 1, Sheftel and Wills.

Example 119. "Subdominant Blues," from *Patterns for Fun*, Book 1, Sheftel and Wills.

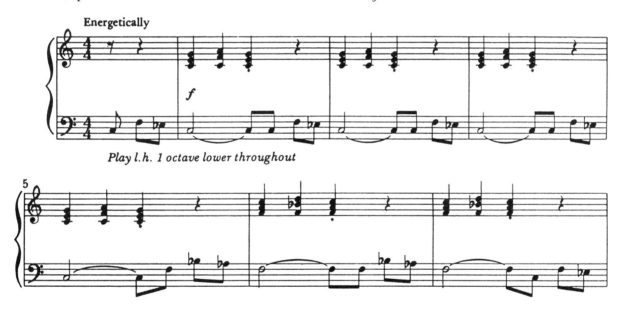

Example 120. "La Bamba," from *Alfred's Basic Adult*, All-Time Favorites, Level 2, arranged Palmer.

Example 121. "Broadway Boogie," from *Rock, Rhythm and Rag*, Book 3, Stecher, Horowitz and Gordon.

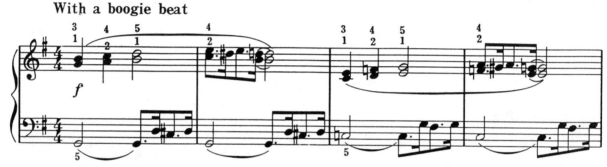

Example 122. "Sweet Beat Blues," from *Rock, Rhythm and Rag*, Book 3, Stecher, Horowitz and Gordon.

The syncopation, in the last three compositions, will nearly be impossible to execute properly unless there is a feeling for pulse—one that is intuitive or one that has been learned. Attempting to give dynamic emphasis to pitches on weak beats requires the perception of notes from the pulse standpoint. Without this, syncopation will sound academic or studied. Perception of notes in a rhythmic pulse is the key to why audiences love to hear jazz players or blues singers. Both performers have the uncanny ability to feel syncopation within a pulse or rhythmic swing. This same feeling should be developed during the elementary stages of piano playing because there are many examples of syncopation which occur not only in jazz or blues music but also in the music of most major composers, such as J. S. Bach and Frederic Chopin.

Tonal Relationships Under Long Pedals

During Stage IV, the student should be assigned some compositions that require controlling tonal relationships and phrase shapes under long pedals and in thin-textured settings as is found in the next example:

Example 123. "Greensleeves," from *Alfred's Basic Piano Library*, Lesson Book 3, arranged Palmer, Manus and Lethco.

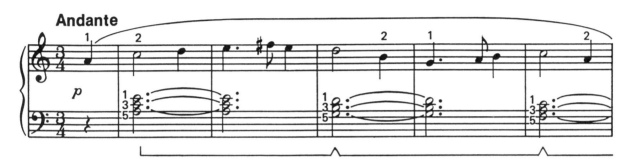

"Greensleeves" will be quite easy for Stage IV students to read, but pre-hearing the tonal relationships under long pedals will require careful concentration on the student's part. Although the markings suggest that the piece be played rather slowly, the pulse organization should happen in two-measure units. Using one-measure units will make it more difficult to pre-hear, because musically the smallest sub-phrase idea happens over a two-measure span. Playing slowly and using a larger pulse pattern—two measures—will not be easy for a young student. The teacher may have to be satisfied with one measure. (Many pieces at this stage contain musical ideas and pulse patterns that are identical in time span. On the other hand, in more advanced music, there will be examples of the smallest phrase idea being twice as long as the pulse pattern.)

More Complex Melodies and Pulse Groupings

Melodies that are made up of two-note slurs should be assigned only after single slurs have been mastered physically as well as aurally. As mentioned earlier, many students play *soft-loud* while they are saying *loud-soft*. They may say *down-up* but play the "up" three times louder than the down and show no outward expression that the sounds are reversed. According to placement in the measure and length of note value, there are some slurs that will need to sound soft-to-loud at the more advanced levels of literature. Most slurs, nevertheless, in the Stage IV music are placed in a context that suggest that they should be played dynamically loud-to-soft. The next example illustrates a melody that is composed of two-note slurs:

Example 124. "Sonatina in D Minor," Third Movement, from *Four Sonatinas in Varying Styles*, Olson.

At times, there will be examples of melodies made up of a combination of slurs which are cast in rather long pulse groupings. These type settings should be assigned only after the student has mastered very simple settings of slurs. The following example, much simpler that the previous one, includes a number of three-note slurs, but the overall texture is very simple and the pulse grouping only uses one measure:

Example 125. "Sonatina No. 3 in A Minor," First Movement, from *Beginning Sonatinas*, Olson.

Brightly

In attempting to discover the best pulse grouping for Example 124, try it several different ways. Always guide your decision by the following axiom: the faster the tempo, the larger the pulse pattern. The same is true with the opposite situation: the slower the tempo, the smaller the pulse pattern. Therefore, Example 124 played slowly would need a smaller pulse pattern—a *Learning Metric Unit*, two primary pulses. Talented students may be able to play it at a livelier tempo and use a larger pulse grouping—a *Performance Metric Unit*, one primary and one secondary pulse.

The larger pulse grouping will give the musical motion a wonderful feeling of leading to the next downbeat. At this tempo, the mind, ear, rhythm and physical all collaborate to help pull the musical motion on to the next downbeat, the next rallying point. The music, though, doesn't stop there, but it *goes through the rallying point* and on to the next circle of musical motion.

Students should learn this early on. Music is continuous and must never have a feeling of stopping on every downbeat. When it does, the listener detects the stopping in the tonal quality. "Sonatina in D Minor," played at a fast tempo, provides a very talented student with an exciting experience for feeling the lead-in to the next circle of musical motion. In other words, the measure grouping—*the Performance Metric Unit*—at tempo rhythm makes the musical motion sound quite convincing. The faster tempo and larger pulse pattern, however, may be very problematic for the slow or normal learner. For many students, the assignment of "Sonatina in D Minor" may need to be delayed until Stage V or VI.

As notational textures include more and more eighth note patterns, the more the line-within-a-line concept will appear, particularly in pieces which contain characteristics of the baroque style. Students with "excellent ears" will grasp the concept immediately, because they will hear "how the music goes." Others will need numerous experiences with settings similar to the next composition:

Example 126. "Stepping Down," from *Finger Progress*, Olson.

Here the simplicity of the left hand allows the student to concentrate on pre-hearing the line-within-a-line. A student's fingers won't "lock up" if they are directed by the ear as opposed to being directed by the eye. The simpler the setting, the easier it will be for the student's ear to operate. As a student progresses into pieces requiring more dexterity, the need for the ear to direct the physical becomes more and more imperative.

As has been demonstrated in this stage, a large portion of the rise in complexity has involved learning pieces that require the use of a wider range of the keyboard, faster tempos, interpretation of linearly designed textures, contrasting articulations and style characteristics. Subsequently, the all important basic foundation of reading, rhythm and range, as well as the importance of training the mind, body and ear to make music in a rhythm, continues to become more and more significant.

As the process for developing a system for learning and performing music unfolds, one better understands the need for those all important goals in piano study: teaching someone's mind to perceive symbols holistically in metered pulse patterns; turning those perceptions into aural images; and having those images direct the coordination of the physical in order to make the quality and quantity of sound desired. However, if a student's basic foundation of turning symbols into sound breaks down, all of these musical complexities will go for naught. The student will be struggling "to find the notes" and revert back to playing by the individual note value or motive. When this happens, the teacher will have to become the super diagnostician. Is the literature overwhelming the student, forcing a mental overload? Do many of the pieces involve too many unfamiliar settings? Check to discover what is causing the overload. The answer may be discovered in looking at the student's basic foundation. If the problem lies there, most of the student's literature curriculum should involve easier compositions which will allow the mind, body and ear to work in a rhythm so that synthesis control will return. When control begins to deteriorate, ease up on the challenge. Supplement the student's curriculum with less demanding complexities, or playing the piano will become frustrating rather than fun.

Chapter VIII

STAGE V

Most new concepts were introduced separately in the previous stages, then reiterated a number of times in other pieces before they appeared in combination with previously learned concepts. In Stage V, this will change. The previously learned concepts will appear immediately in juxtaposition with each other. As a result, the students will find more symbols to read at one time, raising the level of notational complexity. The musical complexity level, however, will tend to remain at the same level as Stage IV. Most of the notational patterns in Stage V will look familiar, but only if the student is perceiving them as they occur in one hand at a time. When looking at the patterns in both hands, the student will quickly see that the notation is now more complex. For example, playing a set of parallel triads in first inversion may not be difficult for a student. Yet when they appear opposite a melodic figure in triplets, the level of complexity rises considerably. Although much less complex, this type of diverse setting may be as difficult for an elementary level student as the octave passages opposite the triplet figures are for an advanced level student in the last movement of Beethoven's *Waldstein Sonata*, Op. 53.

Some of the diverse patterns in the Stage V compositions will be difficult for many students to play, especially when these patterns first begin to appear. A student, therefore, should have most of the reading concepts from the previous stages thoroughly mastered before attempting them juxtaposed against one another. If they are difficult to handle individually, the combination will play havoc with the student's rhythmic, aural and physical controls.

The main purpose of Stage V will be to prepare students for the style pieces in Stage VI and for the intermediate and advanced level compositions by the master composers. Although some style characteristics have appeared in the previous stages, especially in Stages II and IV, they were presented in easy notational settings. In Stage V, they will appear in much more complex settings. Students should gain some mastery of reading the more complex settings before the teacher involves the student with many new ideas on style. This will prevent the student from facing an increase in notational demands in combination with the demands brought about by the characteristics inherent in the different styles.

The Stage V literature will serve as a checkpoint for all previously learned concepts. The student's present level of learning may be evaluated from several perspectives. Is the student capable of reading Stage V pieces without encountering numerous problems with the symbols? Will the student attempt to recognize the symbols individually in a stop-and-start fashion, ignoring rhythmic groupings? Has the student already begun to delay practicing new assignments, and is the student prone to forgetting to bring the book containing the new assignments to the lesson? If most of the answers to these questions are yes, many of the Stage V literature assignments may need to be delayed.

The upcoming style pieces from Stage VI, especially baroque and classical ones, present many musical and stylistic problems of their own. With deciphering the score an added concern, the student will find the experience more problematic than satisfying. Betty may say, "Why do I have to work on these boring Bach dances?" Continuing on with the argument, Betty may relate that she thinks that all the pieces in the sonatina book are also uninteresting. Actually what Betty is telling the teacher is that it is going to take weeks "just to get the notes off the page." By then she may be bored and probably could care less whether the pieces are 20th century, classical style or otherwise. It is best, therefore, to have Betty first experience some basic teaching pieces from Stage V, which contain numerous combinations of previously learned reading patterns, before the style pieces of Stage V or VI are assigned.

Learning pieces that display a number of style characteristics requires not only perceiving the symbols, but turning those symbols into sounds that are characteristic of the style in which the pieces were written. For example, two- and three-note slurs, *portato* notes, tenuto markings and voicing of two lines in one hand should be perceived within the context of a style from the first attempts with a piece. This should occur by at least the later phase of Stage V or during the early phases of Stage VI. Perceiving within the context of a style prevents the student from getting a wrong aural and physical impression of a new piece. If it is a percussive Bartók work, the student's approach should be quite different than if it is a lyrical piece in the romantic style. The attacks, releases and character of each composition all should be considered within the context of a specific style.

Practicing Stage V and/or VI compositions without any consideration for style promotes a visual perception of the symbols as opposed to one involving the pre-hearing of musical ideas. This relates to ideas mentioned earlier concerning working mentally and physically on one track to learn the notes and having to create an entirely new track to learn "how it goes musically." Having a two-track approach results in practically no transfer of learning. The student will have to be taught the same aural concepts with every new piece, even from the same style period, the reason being that the student will fail to connect sound with how the symbols look. As the student progresses to the advanced level of literature, the teacher will still be reminding the student of the sound aspect of slurs, degrees of staccato and legato as well as balance and clarity.

Why is it that in competitions and recitals, the pieces in the classical and baroque styles usually are played less convincingly than those in the romantic and 20th-century styles? Most of the time the problem can be traced to an improper foundation for playing these styles. The two-note slurs, the *portato* notes and many of the staccato notes often sound out of context. The discrepancy in the student's basic foundation may make many sonatinas and some of the minuets from the *Notebook for Anna Magdalena* practically unapproachable unless they are taught entirely by imitation. The same will be true for most intermediate and advanced literature in the baroque and classical styles by the master composers.

Habits of how a student perceives and hears a score are so quickly ingrained in the mind that a system for learning and performing becomes very well developed by the late elementary level of study. These habits obviously can be both good and bad. The bad ones will need to be changed before the student approaches the intermediate level of literature or else the increase in notational complexity and style demands will be more than the student can handle. The student's mind will become overloaded with details. Progress will begin to slow and the child will become disenchanted even with the idea of taking lessons.

How much time should students spend with the Stage V pieces in reinforcing their foundation before advancing to the style pieces in Stage VI? There should be as much time as is needed for each individual. The situation will differ with each learner. The most gifted students may need very little time whereas other students may need to continue in this stage for the remainder of their musical experience. These usually will be students who will lack the ability or desire for learning the classics at the intermediate and advanced levels. The problem, nonetheless, may be due to lack of desire, poor practicing habits or musical background and/or little motivation to succeed in music rather than lack of talent.

Basic Objectives

Some of the overall objectives for learning and performing the literature from Stage V should include:

1. Continuing to keep the wrists synchronized with the rhythmic pulse grouping, although the notational patterns in the hands may be much more diverse than in previous stages
2. Continuing to coordinate the hands and fingers in spite of the figuration differences; for example, melodic lines occurring against Alberti bass patterns, alternating single and double notes and triplet figures juxtaposed against chromatic scalar passages
3. Continuing to create an aural image of the symbols, in both hands, regardless of contrasting articulation, voicing, diverse motivic patterns and divergent note values
4. Continuing to control perception, aural awareness and physical execution in a metered-pulse pattern even in complex style settings

As a rule, selections of music from this stage should include compositions which contain a mixture of patterns commonly found in the general texture of music in both major and minor keys, such as 1) the inversions of triads; 2) Alberti bass patterns built out of I-IV-V7 progressions; 3) scales, both diatonic and chromatic; 4) ostinato figures; 5) harmonic intervals of a third, sixth and octave; 6) triplet patterns; 7) an increased use of dotted eighth and sixteenth note combinations; 8) arpeggiated chord figures; and 9) a greater mixture of eighth and sixteenth notes within a melodic line.

Juxtaposition of Notational Complexities

Whereas musical examples in the earlier stages concentrated on the presentation of new concepts in easy settings, now the student needs to experience previously learned ideas in more complex settings. For instance, the next example displays a series of parallel triads in first inversion combined with a moving bass line with contrasting articulation:

Example 127. "The Hokey-Pokey," from *Alfred's Basic Piano Library*, Lesson Book 4, Palmer, Manus and Lethco.

This piece may be followed by the "Night Song," which is a similar setting yet slightly more complex. The first inversion triads are set in 6/8 meter against a broken chord figure:

Example 128. "Night Song," from *Alfred's Basic Piano Library*, Recital Book 4, Palmer, Manus and Lethco.

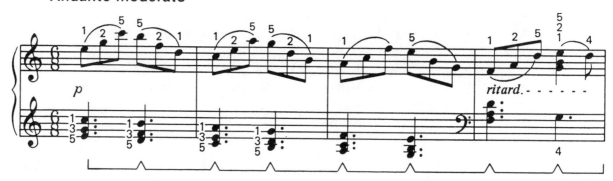

At first, the student may discover the latter example to be confusing, because playing two versions of the same chord simultaneously may be similar to students "patting their head and rubbing their stomach." Although 6/8 rhythm will not be new to the student, the combination of parallel triads in first inversion, combined with a broken triadic figure, probably will be. (Some students, though, may find the "Night Song" to be the easier of the two pieces because the notes in the left hand are identical to the right hand notes. The only difference is in the setting of the chords: one is blocked and one is a broken triadic figure.) The ease with which the student learns settings similar to "The Hokey-Pokey" and the "Night Song" will guide the teacher in assigning a much more complex piece, such as the next example. Even though the next composition, "The Glow-Worm," contains the previously experienced broken triadic figure in a triplet rhythmic pattern, there are many other factors that will make this setting much more difficult for most all students not only to read, but also to perform:

Example 129. "The Glow-Worm," from *Alfred's Basic Piano Library*, Recital Book 4, Lincke, adapted by Palmer, Manus and Lethco.

(mm. 17–19)

There are constant changes in the harmonic intervals in the "Glow-Worm" in addition to numerous position changes and continuous alternation of the broken triadic figure. In the right hand, the arpeggiated triplet figure remains in a closed position, but the constant changes in the harmonic intervals as well as the arpeggiated figures will require holistic perception of the patterns or the student will be, after several lessons, still "picking out the notes." Even though the triplet figures in measures 17–19 can be blocked in the beginning stages of learning, they will need to be played in an arpeggiated fashion at an Allegro moderato tempo in performance. This may cause the student to have physical problems with finger locking—having fingers remain energy-active long beyond the designated time value of the notes. Here, as in earlier problems with harmonic intervals, the physical problems will more or less disappear when the student begins to imagine aurally the triplet figures as opposed to just seeing the figures.

The next piece illustrates different arrangements of the triad, including inversions, a broken chord accompaniment and a broken triadic figure mixed with a scalar pattern:

Example 130. "Black Forest Polka," from *Alfred's Basic Piano Library*, Lesson Book 4, Palmer, Manus and Lethco.

(mm. 1–3)

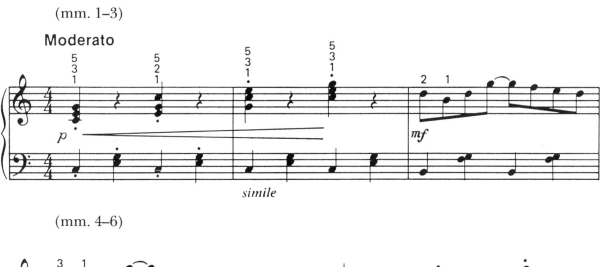

(mm. 4–6)

(mm. 10–13)

simile

Learning this piece will foster the recognition and aural awareness of triads as whole entities in several different positions and arrangements. Applying the blocking technique during practice sessions will enhance this recognition and aural awareness. The next four examples will also be helpful in learning to recognize and play triads in blocked and arpeggiated settings:

Example 131. "G Major Triad, All Positions," from *Alfred's Basic Piano Library*, Technic Book 4, Palmer, Manus and Lethco.

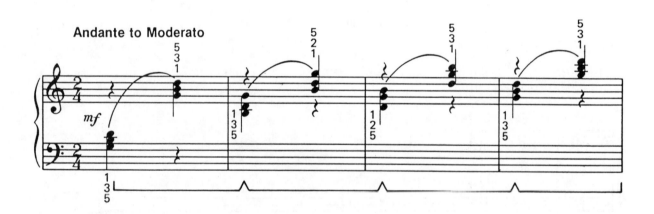

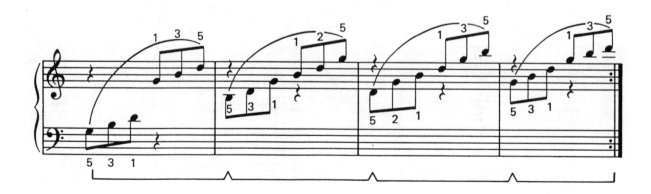

Example 132. "White Key Triads, All Positions," from *Alfred's Basic Piano Library*, Technic Book 4, Palmer, Manus and Lethco.

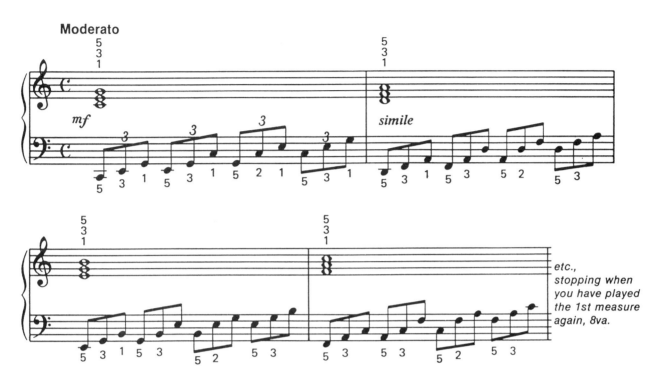

Example 133. "A Grand Finale," from *Alfred's Basic Piano Library*, Technic Book 4, Palmer, Manus and Lethco.

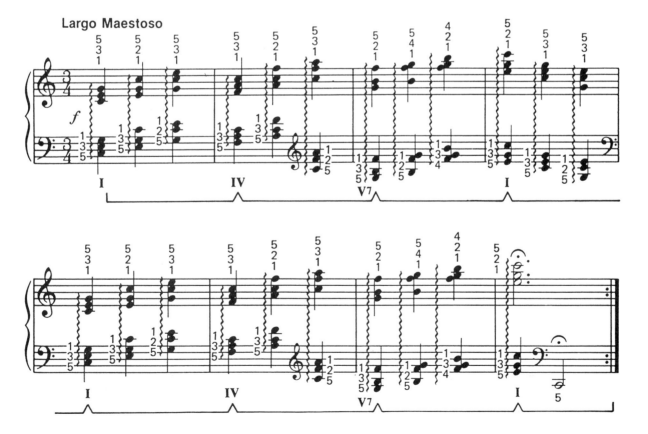

156

Example 134. "Virtuoso Triads, No. 1," from *Alfred's Basic Piano Library*, Technic Book 4, Palmer, Manus and Lethco.

Broadening the Tonality Foundation

Learning and playing pieces that make use of several sharps or flats should be a part of all students' Stage V experiences. This should be phased in gradually because without it the student will progress into more advanced literature being afraid of approaching a piece similar to the next example:

Example 135. "The Mill Wheel," from *Bastien Piano Basics*, Piano 4, Bastien.

In spite of the fact that this piece is in B Major with five sharps, the initial approach to reading it can be made easier by blocking the left hand into harmonic patterns, thus eliminating the search for one-note-at-a-time in the less familiar key. Even when using the blocking technique some students will be reluctant to practice a piece containing so many sharps. This is the stage, nevertheless, when the tonalities with several sharps should be presented. A majority of the pieces are still short in length and mostly patterned. The additional sharps, consequently, will produce only minimal difficulty for the student.

The Relationship Between a Rise in Complexity and Physical Coordination

As the complexity of the notation rises, some students in turn will experience a slight increase in problems with physical coordination, especially with wrists' synchronization. For example, syncopation on the third beat of a 3/4 metered measure may require an extra effort, because some students may attempt to play the syncopation as a downbeat feeling rather than an upbeat feeling, thus causing a disruption in their physical coordination. The downbeat will remain as the strong beat, but the weak beat—the third beat—will receive the dynamic emphasis. Successful treatment of syncopation on the third beat of a 3/4 meter must be perceived as a dynamic emphasis on an upbeat as opposed to a dynamic emphasis on a downbeat. Take, for instance, this next piece:

Example 136. "Etude No. 3," from *Piano Etudes*, Book 2, Bertini, compiled by Olson.

Upbeat Dynamic Emphasis (Syncopation)

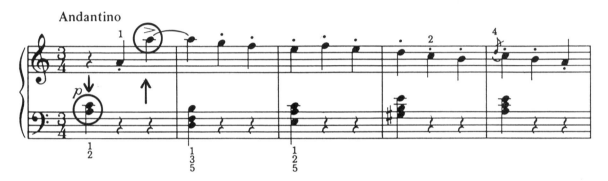

Downbeat Natural (Strong) Accent (Metric Strong but not dynamically loud)

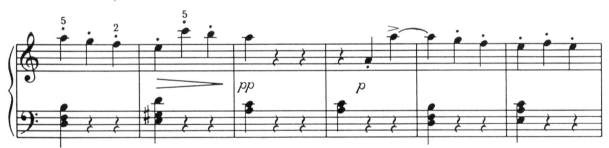

"Etude No. 3" is a perfect example of what has just been described. It is a setting that may lure the student into making a downbeat sound on a weak beat, resulting in a false re-barring of a measure, in turn, causing the physical to become disorganized. The complexity of the articulation and where it is placed upon the metric structure directly affect a student's physical coordination. Settings involving quick changes in articulation and dynamic accents on weak beats should be demonstrated and explained thoroughly to the student upon assignment. This will avoid confusion during the first week of practice.

In compositions similar to the next example, using words for the six eighth notes in each measure will help eliminate the separate perceptions, motions and sounds. Saying, Down-2-3, Up-2-3 should not indicate a large down motion or a high wrist up motion. It should serve only as a mental reminder that each group of six notes should be played within one overall motion. The first slur must come out of the staccato note motion, and the second staccato note and second two-note slur motion must be a continuation of the motion made for the first three notes in the measure. If the measures are metrically perceived and aurally imagined as one entity, the student will automatically make one overall motion per measure. It is only when each measure is perceived as four separate segments that the physical motion divides into four separate movements: one each for the staccato note, the two-note slur, the second staccato note and the second two-note slur. In other words, regardless of articulation, notational textures must be perceived as phrase concepts within a pulse grouping, not as individual pitches played as unrelated ideas. With this next example, incorrect physical motions can occur very quickly if the original perception of the symbols centers upon the details alone rather than upon the details within the pulse grouping:

Example 137. "Etude No. 7," from *Piano Etudes*, Book 2, Kabalevsky, compiled by Olson.

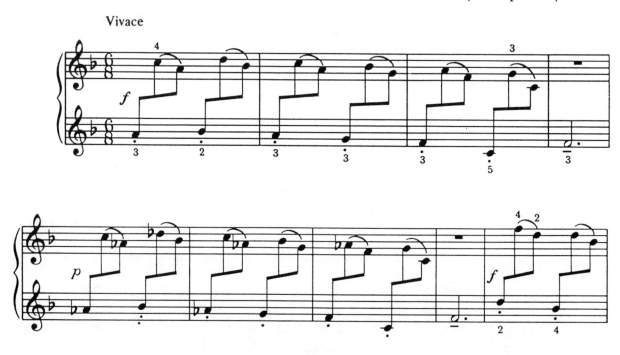

In the next etude, the patterns in both hands must be thought of and imagined aurally in a linear fashion or the piece will sound like chord-to-chord-to-chord-to-chord with no forward musical motion:

Example 138. "Etude No. 12," from *Piano Etudes*, Book 2, Biehl, compiled by Olson.

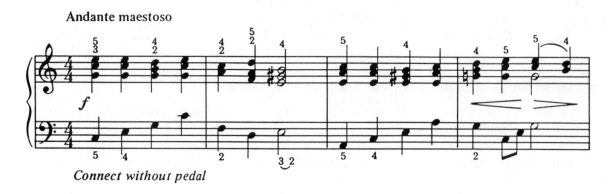

When using a half-note pulse pattern, both hands should be played in two grouped down-up motions per measure, especially at an Andante maestoso tempo. Yet at a faster tempo, the musical idea could be thought of by the measure, using one overall down-and-up-and motion. Using the one overall motion per measure, here again, is more of a mental suggestion rather than a physical one. Advising the student to stay "in the keys" is a must. Remaining in the keys versus leaving the keys (pulling weight out after each chord structure) will help promote the linear effect that is needed. When chord playing is perceived just as separate vertical structures, both musical motion and phrasing will be ignored. The same will be true for the following etude. Although most of the chords are arpeggiated, some students may still approach them strictly as vertical structures:

Example No 139. "Etude No. 9," from *Piano Etudes*, Book 2, Concone, compiled by Olson.

While the composer suggests that "Etude 12" be played without any pedal, the "Etude No. 9" markings include an indication for the pedal. The desired effect will be realized, though,

160

only if the pedal is controlled by the ear rather than by the foot. As is always the case, pedaling changes must be instigated by the mind and ear rather than just by the eye and foot.

Most intermediate level students have problems with pieces that require keen voicing and pedaling of chord structures. Perhaps that is due to the lack of experience with voicing and pedaling chords at the elementary level. After several pieces similar to "Etude No. 9" are learned, other slightly more difficult music should be introduced to the student, such as the following two examples:

Example 140. "Slumber Song," from *Piano All the Way*, Level 4, Gillock.

(mm. 1–4)

(mm. 9–12).

Example 141. "Intermezzo," from *Piano All the Way*, Level 4, Gillock.

(mm. 1–4)

(mm. 23–28)

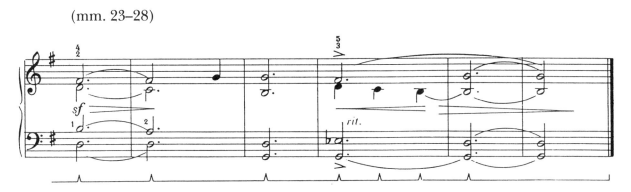

The voicing in the "Slumber Song" may be slightly easier to control than the voicing in the "Intermezzo." On the other hand, when examining the score more closely, one is drawn to the closed position of the score and the repeated chords in "Slumber Song," both of which will require sensitive tonal control. Once again, as a means of preventing additional problems with voicing and tonal control, the weight in the student's fingers and hands should not be lifted in and out of the keys after each chord is played. Constantly lifting the weight out of the keys after each chord makes the student "jab" every other chord. In the "Slumber Song," the student will be involved mainly with controlling the tone among the voices of the chords and melody except in the last score. This will be easier to control than the tone in the "Intermezzo," which involves the voicing of the lines within the chord structures in addition to the tonal control of the two voices in the right hand throughout the piece.

Careful pedaling will be needed in the performance of both pieces. Should the student follow the pedaling markings indicated by the composer? That decision will be up to the teacher. As a guide, the teacher may consider having the student make the pedaling decisions based upon that student's aural perception of how each piece should sound. For instance, one student may prefer to change the pedal in the "Slumber Song" after every two beats rather than after each beat as is indicated. Another student may decide that she likes the pedaling marked by the composer. In the "Intermezzo," the markings indicate pedal changes after each beat. Here again, the teacher may choose to include the student in the pedaling choices, particularly in places similar to measure one. The pitch G in the soprano voice on beat one resolves down to F# on beat two. Though the composer suggests a pedal change, let the student decide whether it is a more interesting sound to meld the dissonance and resolution under one pedal. This allows the student to participate actively in the interpretive process by being involved aurally with the decisions.

Syncopation and Other Complexities

The next two examples will be rather forbidding for some students unless they have already mastered the technique of playing syncopated rhythms as well as Alberti bass patterns. Approaching both ideas as new concepts in the same piece would be frustrating to say the least. The student would be facing a double challenge if he were expected to master a rhythmic concept at the same time a physical one is being presented. With the first example, the left hand part reveals an Alberti bass pattern set opposite a syncopated right hand part involving a mixture of single notes and chords:

162

Example 142. "He's Got the Whole World in His Hands," from *Alfred's Basic Piano Library*, Lesson Book 4, Spiritual, arranged by Palmer, Manus and Lethco.

With the second of these two examples, syncopation plays a major role in the makeup of the entire piece. The student will need to maintain a basic pulse throughout the piece or the syncopation will fail to be executed properly. As it appears in each hand, the syncopated melody with alternating articulation should be balanced convincingly against a basically chordal accompaniment that remains staccato. Most students will find the syncopation, particularly with the constantly changing articulation, to be a real challenge. This is because the syncopated notes can easily be treated mistakenly as long notes occurring on strong beats as opposed to long notes occurring on the weak beats. If this happens, the syncopated pitches will distort the recurring pulse grouping and negate any feeling for the syncopated rhythmic patterns. Despite the fact that this is a fun piece to play, the experience will definitely be a challenge:

Example 143. "New Orleans Carnival," from *Bastien Piano Basics*, Piano 4, Bastien.

(mm. 1–3)

Con spirito

(mm. 13–16)

Learning About Style

Music displaying classical style characteristics often is the most difficult for students to learn. Perhaps it is because the style demands that the musical ideas be presented in lengthy phrases in spite of the way the articulation sets up small motivic ideas. The music also calls for different degrees of staccato and legato as well as a convincing treatment of balance and clarity. Pedaling has to be used cautiously, and many times the music calls for a classical lyricism with some dramatic effects. The score often displays a number of important details of articulation which require very accurate execution. Here lies the problem: how can the teacher entice a young student to perceive and execute these many details and still make music? Some students prefer to omit working on pieces from the different style periods, especially the classical style, and opt for working on compositions that depict more contemporary pop sounds, thus requiring less work on details. With some students, this is not a bad choice.

By this point a student's musical education should be guided partially by that student's basic ability as well as his wishes and desires. The more classically oriented curriculum literature may not be the proper route for all students. The teacher, therefore, may need to design a curriculum for some students that is more oriented towards music that is less demanding, such as Book One, *A Splash of Color* and Books One and Two, *Just for You*, composed by Dennis Alexander (Alfred Publishing Co); and Books One and Two, *Something Special* by Randall Hartsell (Alfred Publishing Co.). Pieces from these books are easy to read, contain simple rhythmic ideas, have very few examples of contrasting articulation and are great fun to play. Interpretively, the phrasing is very straight forward, and most all of the important events that need musical attention occur on strong beats of the measure.

164

Consequently, many of the problems that are prevalent in music from the style periods—especially the baroque and classical—are eliminated. For instance, the next example is easy to read, has simple rhythmic ideas, no change in articulation and displays a broken-chord musical idea that moves by the measure:

Example 144. "Moonlit Shores," from *Something Special,* Book 2, Hartsell.

"A Touch of Gold" is somewhat similar. The pitches are easy to read and there are only a few different rhythmic ideas. The legato touch rules throughout the piece and the musical ideas move basically from downbeat-to-downbeat, all of which will make the piece enticing to the student:

Example 145. "A Touch of Gold," from *A Splash of Color,* Book 1, Alexander.

"The Last Dance" has a simple melodic line and a left hand pattern that can be *blocked* to help facilitate reading. It is in the key of C Major and has only one pedal change per measure:

Example 146. "The Last Dance," from *Just for You*, Book 2, Alexander.

"Tuesday's Child" will also be easy to read and phrase. The setting is in D Major with only three accidentals. There are a number of position changes in the left hand, but that can be handled easily by a Stage V student if the blocking technique is used for both reading and technical purposes. There are no changes in articulation as the complete composition should be played legato. The piece, however, as well as the previous three examples, does offer some challenge. The challenge, though, in this type of literature curriculum is a much less demanding one than the complexities found in literature that is more classically oriented.

166

Example 147. "Tuesday's Child," from *Just for You,* Book 2, Alexander.

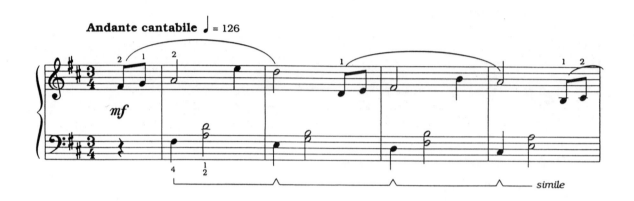

Classical Style Characteristics

There will be many students who will welcome the opportunity to work on pieces in the classical style because of the increased challenges. This is true, especially, if they have experienced many of the figurations beforehand that are inherent in the style. For example, an Alberti bass pattern opposite a melodic line will be troublesome for students, but it will be simpler to execute—with the proper balance and clarity—if it is first introduced in a setting with no changes in articulation similar to the following composition:

Example 148. "Lullaby," from *Alfred's Basic Piano Library*, Recital Book 4, American Folk Song, arranged by Palmer, Manus and Lethco.

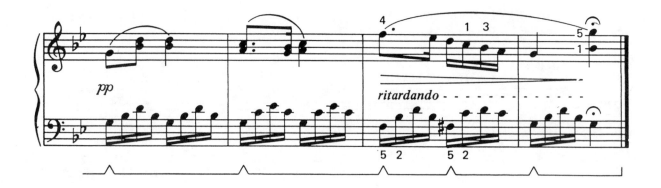

168

When first looking at the score of the "Lullaby," students immediately should recognize that the left hand Alberti bass patterns are built out of simple chords in G Minor and Bb Major. Although these figurations can be blocked at first, the student should continue perceiving the figurations as pitches belonging to chord structures even after they are played as written. Thus the student will be perceiving the pitches in the left hand as chord units and the pitches in the right hand as scalar patterns. In this way, the musical ideas can be considered early on, including the emotional reactions to cadential points, such as the major mediant leading to the dominant seventh, resolving into the minor tonic, measures 5–6. The language the teacher uses to describe these chord progressions may need to be simplified and adapted according to the student's theoretical knowledge. Understanding the musical significance of the chord progressions is more important than the complexity of the explanation. (The technical description is stated here only for the benefit of the teacher.)

The cross relationship, F and F# in measure 5, should be *heard* and reacted to emotionally as opposed to being *seen* only. Very similar to the texture of a sonatina, the "Lullaby" gives the student a chance to work on a sonatina-style composition without having to cope with any changes in articulations. The piece should be played with a legato touch throughout. The cadential points and other musical phenomena can be explained to the student in a very simplified language if the teacher deems it necessary. The main objective is getting the student to react emotionally to some musical events in a "classical-like" setting and to understand the reaction so that it can be transferred to other musical experiences.

To prevent physical problems in the "Lullaby," using words, such as *down-and-up-and*, will foster the synchronization of the wrists to the pulse grouping and prevent the "physical pumping" of each note. Since the tempo indication is marked, "Very slowly," there should be two strong-weak pulse groupings per measure, but the two should be perceived and aurally imagined hierarchically (the first one being slightly more important than the second one).

The following example also includes some figurations commonly found in classical style compositions, especially in sonatinas and sonatas:

Example 149. "Sonatina in C," from *Bastien Piano Basics*, Piano 4, Bastien.

169

In the "Sonatina in C," there are a number of figurations displayed that are common to classical style pieces, such as short motivic patterns (using a mixture of eighth and sixteenth notes) and long melodic scalar passages, all of which are usually cast in a thin texture. In some cases, the student may be more concerned with executing the short motivic patterns rather than showing any concern for how these patterns group to form phrase shapes. Concentration on the motivic aspect often involuntarily produces physical motions that delineate motivic rhythm rather than phrase rhythm. That is to say that the grouping of physical motions by motives will produce unwanted accents at the beginning and ending of the motivic ideas, which will disrupt the flow of the phrase rhythm. The problem, though, will be eliminated as soon as the student begins to perceive the motives within the larger context of the phrase rhythm. The correct perception should center upon the beginning and ending of the metric grouping—the pulse-unit—instead of the beginning and ending of the motives. The metric grouping will remain the same within the piece whereas the motivic grouping will change.

Romantic Style Characteristics

Many of today's students relate more easily to 20th-century pieces than they do to compositions containing romantic style characteristics. Yet, romantic style textures tend to foster more readily the teaching of musical phrasing, tonal control, pedaling, tonal and rhythmic nuance and the basic concept of tension and resolution in music. Most piano teachers, consequently, still approach the teaching of these aspects of musical playing with romantic style compositions. Contemporary style pieces, though, continue to gain popularity among students as their favorite style of music.

The next two examples will be excellent compositions for fostering the teaching of musical ideas and tonal concepts for any style playing:

170

Example 150. "Marshmallow Sundae," from *The Delicious Book*, Bergerac.

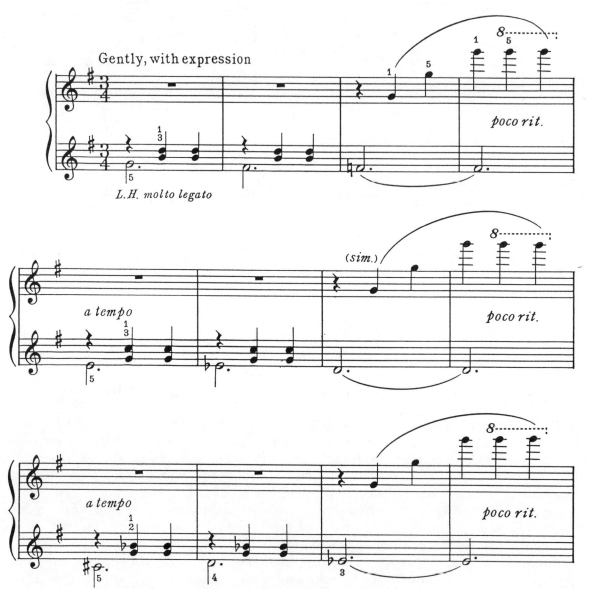

This composition not only offers experience with long phrase lines, balance and clarity, pedal control and a singing melody, but it also gives the student an opportunity to gauge rhythmic and tonal nuance in a piece that extends over a wide range of the keyboard. This is important, because by Stage V, students should learn some literature that spans several octaves of the keyboard. This is because pieces that cover a wide range of the keyboard are very prevalent in advanced romantic works by master composers, such as Chopin, Liszt and Schumann as well as in the music of many of the 20th-century Russian composers.

When one thinks of compositions in the romantic style, the Chopin *Nocturnes* often come to mind. These *Nocturnes* make many demands on the player, but they continue to remain very popular among pianists. Elementary level students as well as those at the inter- mediate level, therefore, should have as much experience as possible with compositions similar to the following:

Example 151. "Cinderella's Lament," from *Cinderella Suite*, Barrett.

Here, the long melodic note concept may be demonstrated and then described as a "fat" singing sound in comparison to a "lean" hit sound. Some students will relate to the concept very quickly while other students may have problems comprehending both the demonstration and the description. The teacher, therefore, should continue to demonstrate the singing quality, encompassing an exaggerated version of the desired sound followed by a sound that is directly opposite. Being unable to hear sound differences indicates that students are attempting to hear the differences through their mental processes without any aural involvement. Hearing or pre-hearing a full, singing-quality melodic sound is of paramount importance because the concept will need to be transferred to many other learning situations, especially ones in the romantic style.

In teaching a student how to produce a long singing melodic note, the *dying-tone* concept should be introduced. The student should understand that long note values begin to die away or decay immediately after they are played; therefore any short note values which directly follow must match the decayed sound. To the student, the teacher may say, "Teresa, always beware of short notes following long notes, because the short notes must match the decaying sound of the long notes." The teacher may continue with a comparison among playing the piano, violin or singing. With the violin, the continuation of bowing enables the sound to continue at the same dynamic level. A similar situation occurs when singing. A steady flow of air enables the singer to continue the sound level. At the piano, however, the sound begins to fade or decay immediately after it has been made, thus creating the built-in problem of the dying tone.

The concept of weight transfer or the rolling of weight from finger-to-finger should also be brought into focus in "Cinderella's Lament." This concept can be used in describing how to play the left hand accompaniment and the lead-in or upbeat eighth notes that occur several times in the melodic line. The weight transfer concept or rotation of weight from finger-to-finger can be used for explaining the difference in smooth legato playing versus "notey" or very articulated types of legato. (The smooth legato playing is used more commonly in romantic style playing and the articulated legato concept is more prevalent in specific types of baroque style pieces.)

These romantic style examples bring up the question of the basic purpose of assigning compositions. Should the teacher always be concerned with purpose when literature selections are made? Not always, but for most literature decisions, there most definitely needs to be a reason for assigning a composition or a type of music book. This is extremely important by Stage V. At this point, the student is preparing not only for the more complex style pieces in Stage VI but also for the intermediate and advanced level compositions.

Baroque Style Characteristics

Elementary level students in the past were assigned very few baroque style textures, because there were little available that was suitable for lesser advanced students. That is somewhat still true. There are, however, a number of compositions at the elementary level that make use of late baroque style characteristics as is evident in the next two examples:

Example 152. "Allegro Deciso," from *Kaleidoscope Solos*, Book 4, George.

Example 153. "Poet's Lament," from *Kaleidoscope Solos*, Book 3, George.

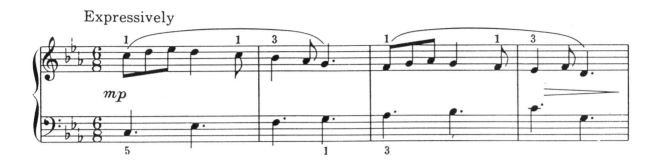

Two other excellent examples of pieces in the late baroque style, at this level, are as follows:

Example 154. "One Fine Day," from *Kaleidoscope Solos*, Book 3, George.

Example 155. "Important Errand," from *Kaleidoscope Solos*, Book 3, George.

These settings will be much easier for students than the minuets from the *First Lessons in Bach* (compiled and edited by Carroll/Palmer). For instance, the minuet from this collection that is included as Example 161 in Stage VI will be much simpler for students if they have already learned some late baroque or galant style pieces in easy settings, such as the four previous examples by Jon George. All four compositions fit very comfortably under the fingers. The melodic motion in each composition is centered in the right hand with the left hand outlining the harmonic motion.

20th-Century Style Characteristics

There are many examples of 20th-century style music in the teaching material for young children, some mildly dissonant and some rather austere. By Stage V, the less talented students and those who have not played any 20th-century style music may prefer the milder examples, such as the following two compositions:

Example 156. "Rhythmic Dance," from *Bartók: The First Book for Young Pianists*, edited Palmer.

Example 157. "The Bear," from *Everybody's Perfect Masterpieces,* Vol. 2, Rebikov.

Summary

From the many suggestions and guidelines outlined in this chapter, the teacher will be capable of deciphering which pieces will be most appropriate for individual students. To make those decisions, the teacher must evaluate the past work of each student. What are the strengths and weaknesses of William's past experience? How long should he continue playing core literature, jazz and blues compositions and mood music before he goes into compositions with textures displaying stylistic characteristics? Should Sally study a large array of music from this stage or should she go rather quickly to the Stage VI compositions? The teacher may surmise that Sally seems to grasp concepts with little need of them being reiterated in other compositions. With other students, the answers may be different. Alice may have many deficiencies which are beginning to surface. She may need to work, consequently, in Stage V compositions for some time before advancing on to the Stage VI literature. The teacher must make decisions based on each student's merits, practice habits and desire to learn.

Chapter IX

STAGE VI

Prologue

Stage VI involves learning and performing music that will prepare the student for intermediate level compositions composed in the different styles. Even though these compositions are composed in more complex settings, most of the pieces will use the stylistic characteristics previously experienced in the earlier stages. Stages I and III compositions emphasized concepts developing the student's basic foundation for reading, learning and making music. Stages II and IV concentrated more on adding musical complexities to the foundation, which in turn, challenged the student's learning process and performance control. Stage V presented the student with most all of the previous concepts and placed them in many different contexts and situations, combining contrasting ideas and raising the complexity level—musical, technical and notational. As students progress into the style pieces of Stage VI, those students with a solid foundation from the previous five stages should succeed with very few problems. There will be those, though, that may need additional work with less complicated music.

As a student approaches Stage VI, the teacher must discover if there are any discrepancies in the student's previous musical background. If there are, additional music from the previous stages may be assigned. This can include music that was found previously to be too demanding, which may have been books like the *Piano Etudes*, Book I from Stage III or the *Piano Etudes*, Book II from Stage V. Remember, literature and concepts from any of the stages must never be thought of as music just for that particular stage. The world of piano teaching encompasses many different kinds of learners. Whereas most of the recommended compositions at a given stage may be perfect selections for a large percentage of students, some of the music may be too difficult or too easy for others who are in that stage.

One of the most puzzling questions for all teachers at any advancement level is: "Which style of music should I teach first?" The question is difficult because the answer obviously will vary from student to student. Across the board, a majority of teachers find the romantic or 20th-century style compositions the easiest to teach and the classical style the most difficult. The best decision can be made only after the teacher carefully studies what attributes the student possesses in regard to learning music from the different styles. The student's reaction to the style pieces in Stage V should be a strong indicator.

The Baroque Style

When studying different styles of music, one quickly realizes how style changes occur on a very gradual scale. This may be explained to a young student from the standpoint of discussing changes in the style of clothes fashions, furniture or automobiles. It will be important to point out that popular styles from the past, for instance in furniture, are not necessarily discarded forever. The same is true with music. Numerous composers in the 20th century use baroque, classical and romantic stylistic characteristics in addition to contemporary compositional techniques.

The student should realize that composers from each of the style periods share a variety of musical textures, forms and compositional devices. For example, *Fortspinnung*—the spinning-out technique—is commonly found in music of the Baroque era, but that does not mean that all compositions in the baroque style display that technique. Too, much of the

178

music in the baroque style is basically contrapuntal in nature, but some compositions may display contrapuntal sections that alternate with homophonically conceived sections. The rhythmic texture is usually very homogeneous and the measures commonly group to form phrases, yet the phrases many times are asymmetrical. There often is more symmetry of sections than there is of the phrasing. (Symmetrical phrasing is more common to the classical style, e.g., 2 + 2 + 2 + 2.) The phrasing in baroque music normally is made up of motivic ideas as opposed to long melodic ideas. The harmonic and melodic or linear interest is commonly found to be well balanced. Although all baroque music is somewhat similar, it is by no means alike. For example, much of the music written during the late Baroque period begins to contain stylistic characteristics that are very common to the early classical style, which is sometimes identified as the *style galant*. Thus, an elementary level student needs to experience music depicting the stylistic characteristics from all parts of the Baroque era: the early, middle as well as the late years. Take for instance this next example:

Example 158. "Allegro Spiritoso," from *Artistry at the Piano*, Repertoire 3, George.

The teacher will quickly perceive and hear the energy of the spinning-out technique, the line-within-the-line concept in the treble clef, the bass line outlining the harmonic motion and the homogeneous rhythmic texture, all of which denotes the baroque style. The phrase structure, however, is symmetrical, thus revealing a trait more common to the classical style. This can be the time for the student to gain insights into style characteristics that bridge the gap between two different style eras. Rather than labeling the piece as being representative of a specific style, the teacher can guide the student into making the discovery himself. Considering the individual student's musical background, the following discussion may be instigated: "Does it sound like a classical sonatina? The phrases are symmetrical like those in classical style sonatinas, yet you may have observed that the basic compositional technique appears to encompass the spinning-out technique that we discussed recently in a baroque piece." Continuing on, the teacher may ask, "Do you think the composer prided himself in being able to combine compositional ideas from two different style periods?"

Learning about style through discovery techniques is much more meaningful and lasting than when the teacher simply gives out the information and asks the student if she understands. By discussing how the piece is made up of a mixture of compositional ideas from two style periods, the student will be able to grasp fully what is meant by late baroque or early classical labels. This information can be followed by ideas on types of articulation needed to depict the mood and character of the piece. In other words, demonstrating and explaining to the student that the piece needs an articulated legato sound to illustrate the character and mood of the spinning-out technique is a concept that will have some historical significance to the student.

The teacher will also want to discuss other aspects of the piece, such as a recommended pulse grouping and a performance tempo. The most logical choice for a pulse grouping would be the measure with a primary feeling on beat one and a secondary feeling on beat two. Although both voices must be heard, the energetic activity in the right hand dictates that it has the more important part. How can the perpetual motion be played to convince the listener of the style and mood of the piece? Through playing it very loudly? Not necessarily. An articulated-legato sound played with logical dynamic shape would be a better choice. How can you make the student understand what you mean by an articulated legato? By demonstrating for the student and perhaps by having the student tongue the sixteenths inside a pulse pattern, such as, la-la-la-la-la-la-la-la for each measure. The tonguing must not be thought of as individual attacks but as a group of sounds within a pulse grouping. With the more gifted students, the tonguing can be done dynamically also, relating directly to how each phrase should be shaped with regard to intensity. Another example of a similar texture would be the next piece:

Example 159. "Presto," from *Artistry at the Piano*, Repertoire 3, George.

Here again, the same type of practice procedures can be advocated. In the previous example, the spinning-out technique revolved around a scalar idea with a slight indication of a line-within-a-line. In the latter example, there is a more distinct line-within-a-line happening with only a few examples of strictly scalar writing. Both of these pieces, especially the "Presto," will be invaluable experience for the student when studying baroque works at the more advanced levels.

A number of other baroque style pieces can be learned easily if the setting is similar to the following example:

Example 160. "Prelude," from *Patterns for Piano*, George.

Energetically and distinctly

This piece and the baroque style pieces from Stage V will serve as excellent preparation for playing some of the dances from the *Notebook for Anna Magdalena Bach* as well as the optional dances from the *French Suites* of J. S. Bach.

The line-within-a-line concept, sometimes called a melodic-harmonic wedge, is present in most of the phrases of "Prelude." In the treble clef part, there is an implied moving voice and one voice—the repeated notes—that stays stationary. The melodic-harmonic wedge activity culminates generally into a one-voice scalar passage. In order to control the voices, the student should aurally imagine and maintain two kinds of conditions simultaneously in the right hand: one that executes the more important moving voice and one that controls the more subdued repeated-note voice. As the implied and repeated-note voices culminate into a one-voice scalar passage, the feeling of two conditions in the right hand will merge into one. If the moving voice and the repeated notes are played as one voice, the listener will fail to hear the line-within-a-line, thus the melodic-harmonic wedge.

Once again, the inherent perpetual-motion character of the previous example can best be achieved by having the student use an articulated legato. Since the composition is marked to be played "energetically and distinctly," a measure pulse should be used as the Performance Metric Unit.

Since they are much easier to read, compositions similar to the "Allegro Spiritoso," "Prelude" and "Presto" will be extremely helpful in preparing the student for pieces from the *First Lessons in Bach*, such as this next minuet:

Example No. 161. "Minuet," from *First Lessons in Bach*, edited and compiled by Carroll/Palmer.

Animato M.M. ♩.=69

The *Five Miniature Preludes and Fugues* of Alec Rowley offer the elementary level student a chance to learn some preludes and fugues in simple settings. Even though they are in miniature form, these pieces contain many of the characteristics found in the preludes and fugues of J. S. Bach from *The Well-Tempered Clavier.* Rowley has outlined such characteristics as the subject, answer, inverted subject, inverted answer and in some cases, examples of stretto and augmentation. The pieces are short and appear to be easy to read. But because of their contrapuntal design, they are more challenging to read and play than meets the eye. Most of the Stage VI students will be ready to meet the challenge and will find the next piece most interesting to play—that is if they have been successful with most of the music from the previous stages:

Example No. 162. "Miniature Fugue," from *Five Miniature Preludes and Fugues,* Rowley.

① Subject   ② Answer   ③ Subject inverted   ④ Answer inverted

182

The Romantic Style

As in the Baroque era, the master composers from the Romantic era used a variety of compositional techniques and musical forms. The character piece was one of the most popular forms for writing 19th-century piano pieces. These were short compositions, usually in a three-part form, expressing a definite mood or programmatic idea. There were a number of 19th-century composers who, in addition to composing very complex advanced works, wrote character pieces for young students. There also have been numerous 20th-century composers who have produced a wealth of romantic style compositions for students at the elementary and intermediate levels of study. A large majority of these pieces are very short, easy to read, thin-textured, simple in design and lyrical in nature. These pieces give students a wonderful opportunity for learning embryonic versions of the more complex 19th-century character pieces by the master composers, such as the nocturnes, waltzes and intermezzi.

Characteristically, 19th-century romantic style compositions display numerous examples of short-note values on weak beats leading to long note values on strong beats. This upbeat or lead-in characteristic is always handled more easily by the student if it has been introduced in non-complex settings. As is often said, "Learning a Chopin nocturne is by no means the place to learn how to play a Chopin nocturne!" In other words, most of the musical complexities found in the Chopin nocturnes or in any of the other character pieces by the 19th-century master composers should be first experienced by the student in very simple settings, such as in "Cinderella's Lament," Example No. 151, and as in these next three examples:

Example 163. "Waltzing," from *Happy Time*, Book I, Tansman.

Example 164. "Valse Triste," from *Piano All The Way*, Level 4, Gillock.

Example 165. "Navajo Legend," from *Kaleidoscope Solos*, Book 4, George.

In addition to the upbeat-to-downbeat idea, there are many other features common to compositions in the romantic style, such as homophonic texture; long, singing melodies; and repetitive accompaniment patterns. All of these characteristics will demand concern for:

1. Balance and clarity between the melody and accompaniment
2. Tonal and rhythmic nuance
3. Production of touches—attacks and releases—guided by aural images
4. Phrase shapes—influenced by melodic direction and harmonic progression, both real and implied
5. Aural control of pedaling

With Tansman's "Waltzing," there is a marvelous musical interplay between the two hands and an easily perceived rise and fall of the melodic line, both of which are supported by the implied harmonic progressions. Although the student may not be able to label all of the chords, blocking the left hand will enhance the possibility that the student will intuitively hear the fluctuating tensions and resolutions in the phrase lines. If the teacher's studio has two pianos, the teacher can help foster this intuition by playing the harmonic progressions at the second piano .

The same will be true with the "Navajo Legend." This piece is similar to the Tansman waltz, but much more difficult because of the rhythmic patterns consisting of a mixture of sixteenth and eighth notes. Although the "Navajo Legend" in performance will need the measure Performance Metric Unit—the whole note or one primary and one secondary pulse (♩ ♩)—some students may need to approach the piece first with two primary pulse-units (♩ ♩). This will provide the student with a foundation for understanding the note values on each quarter note beat and will also help establish where to place the notes on the difficult upbeat spot of the measure—beat four. The patterns using a mixture of sixteenth and eighth notes that occur on and lead into beat four must all have an upbeat feeling progressing to beat one. It will be difficult to perform these patterns with the proper tonal relationships unless the pitches are felt and imagined aurally each time they occur as lead-in notes to the next downbeat. The perceiving, hearing and executing should all begin on beat one of each measure and continue through to beat one of the next measure.

A majority of the elementary level compositions, including many of those in romantic style, unfold in four-measure phrases, culminating with a half cadence. In some settings, the cadence may be implied rather than being spelled out completely. There are some compositions, though, where the first four measures of an eight-measure phrase are directed toward a climactic point on beat one of measure five. This is followed by the second four measures being directed from the climactic point in measure five to a point of repose on beat one of measure eight as is illustrated in the next example:

Example 166. "Waltz," from *Artistry at the Piano*, Repertoire 4, George.

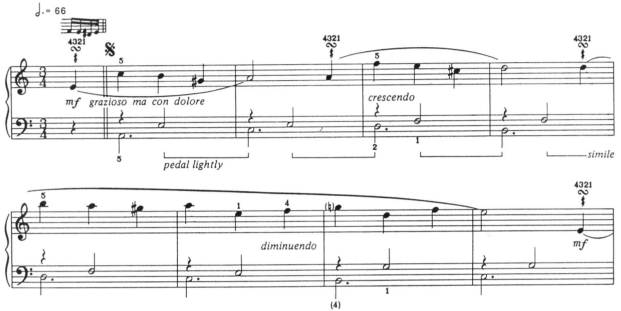

The 20th-Century Style

Piano music written by 20th-century composers gives the student a chance to learn a large variety of styles, forms, textures and moods. The wide array of compositions range from extremely mild contemporary sounds to contrapuntal textures in very dissonant harmonic language. Some of Dmitri Kabalevsky's and Aram Khachaturian's compositions for children are perhaps some of the best 20th-century music that is mildly dissonant, such as is evident in this next example:

Example 167. "Ivan Sings," from *Alfred's Basic Piano Library*, Recital Book 5, Khachaturian, arranged by Palmer, Manus and Lethco.

(mm. 1–7)

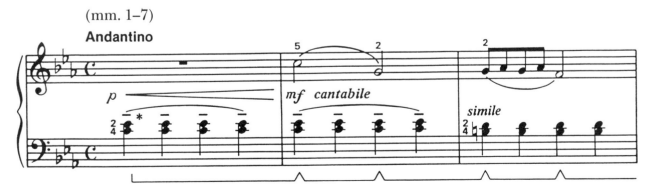

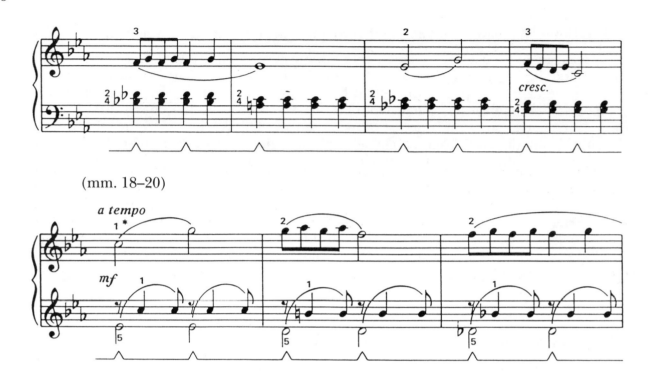

(mm. 18–20)

With "Ivan Sings," Khachaturian used no avant-garde compositional techniques nor did he include any striking dissonant sounds anywhere in the piece; therefore, it should be appealing to most students.

The next piece, with its unusual setting, can serve as a transition between the mildly dissonant 20th-century compositions and some of the more avant-garde selections:

Example 168. "Pagoda," from *Woodsprite and Waterbug Collection*, Beaty.

(mm. 1–4)

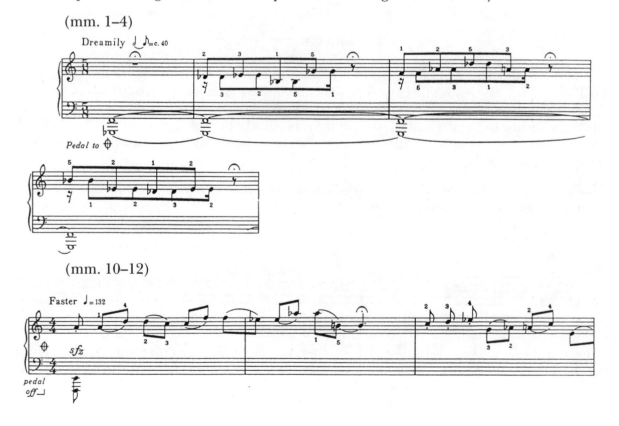

(mm. 10–12)

(mm. 13–15)

With the use of the fermatas, the first section (**A**) is cast in a 5/8 meter and offers experience playing musical ideas in a rather free rhythm. The use of the pedal throughout the first section (the first nine measures) automatically gives this section an experimental flavor. The second section (**B**) changes to a 4/4 meter with a much faster tempo and displays a melodic line built out of odd combinations of two-note slurs, ending in a glissando. The third section (**A¹**) is similar to the first section, suggesting a rounded-binary form. The piece concludes with a glissando played in each hand in contrary motion. Most students will approach these experimental sounds with great delight.

A new technique that students will also find most intriguing is the use of the forearm:

Example No. 169. "Big Mountain," from *Monsterpieces and Others*, Bolcom.

The suggested use of the forearm will be a pleasant surprise to the student. One may quickly detect a wide grin on the student's face as the teacher says, "Now with this piece, you get to play the left hand part with your arm." The student may respond with, "Hey, you must be kidding!" Although the novelty of using the forearm will be exciting, the technique may require some time for adjustment. Other aspects of the piece are quite normal. The piece is to be played very slowly. A singing tone is needed for the melodic idea and the left hand black- and white-key clusters are to be played very softly. The *una corda* and a "very heavy sustaining pedal" are suggested throughout. Young students often are more fond of playing these experimental pieces, similar to the "Big Mountain," than they are of playing lyrical pieces in the romantic style.

The next composition demonstrates another 20th-century popular idiom, that of using old compositional techniques in a new harmonic language:

Example No. 170. "Two Bassoons," from *New Pageants for Piano*, Book 3, Waxman.

Although the harmonic language most definitely reveals 20th-century sounds, the texture is basically contrapuntal, thus using 20th-century harmonic language in a baroque contrapuntal setting. In addition, there are several examples of the use of line-within-a-line, found commonly in music from the Baroque era. This piece will perhaps be more difficult for some students than the experimental pieces, mainly because of its contrapuntal texture and 20th-century harmonies.

The Impressionistic Style

For elementary level students, there is a scarcity of music available displaying impressionistic sounds, other than pieces written in the whole-tone scale, such as Examples 97, 102 and 103 from Stage IV. Impressionistic style pieces, nevertheless, do offer quality experiences in listening keenly to tonal relationships and pedaling; therefore, students will benefit greatly from as many experiences as possible with the style. The next example offers a wonderful opportunity for producing impressionistic sounds:

Example No. 171. "Reflet Dans L'eau," from *Artistry at the Piano,* Repertoire 2, George.

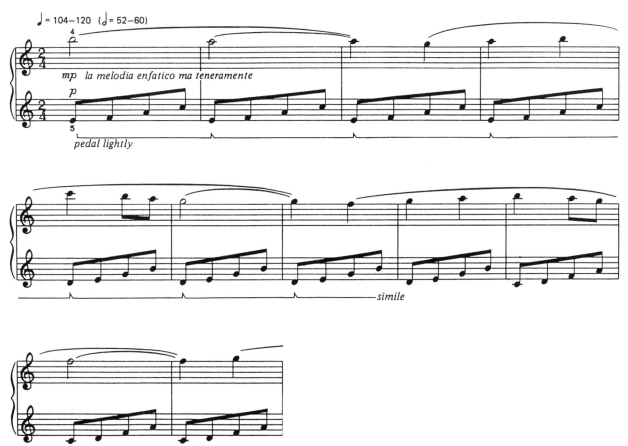

This piece requires a sophisticated use of the pedal as the composer suggests that the pedal be "neither fully engaged nor fully released." This may be the first time the student has had to consider how deeply to pedal. If the pedal is fully engaged, the shimmering effect of the left hand pattern will be more difficult to achieve. The composer asks for a light pedaling effect, one that is very shallow and easy to change without letting the listener become so aware of the change. The composer also wants the player to be conscious of the "singing" tonal quality in the melodic line and to be cognizant of how the long dissonant notes resolve into long consonant notes in the next measures. This occurs in each phrase to the point where the dissonant-to-consonant long-note concept finally resolves into one consonant note. Each time a group of measures resolves into a consonant note, it signifies the end of a phrase. This type of phrase ending is quite different from the normal *common practice period* cadential endings the student has experienced previously. The composer indicates the mood to be a "gentle, sparkling movement of a mountain brook." These suggestions, plus the notational setting, will require a student to rethink his process of how to make a piece musically convincing. This in turn will broaden the student's interpretive skills and demand the developing of aural control in a broader dimension.

The Classical Style

Compositions in the classical style are learned much more easily if the student has had a solid pianistic foundation as opposed to a student with a weak background and little desire to approach challenges. This is true in many ways because of the basic nature of the writing. As composers moved away from a more decorated, *Fortspinnung*, contrapuntal style of writing asymmetrical phrases to a thin-textured, less decorated, homophonic style of writing symmetrical phrases, keyboard players began experiencing many new problems. Some of these problems can be solved easily if the student becomes familiar with what was happening in the music world at that time. The discussion, adapted to each individual's level of musical understanding, might be similar to this:

"Stephen, let me explain about how this kind of music first came upon the scene. As the harpsichord began to lose favor, a new instrument began to emerge during the early part of the 18th century. The new instrument was known in the beginning as a *Fortepiano* or *Pianoforte*. Later, just like we shorten names in today's society, the name was shortened and became known as the *Piano*. Although he was not the only person working on creating a new instrument, a man named Cristofori, from Florence, Italy, was credited with its invention. It became more and more popular until it was considered the main domestic keyboard instrument in America and Europe by the end of the 18th century."

"In contrast to the harpsichord, the new instrument had the capacity of a wider range of dynamics from soft-to-loud, thus getting its name from the Italian word, *pianoforte* or *fortepiano*. With the development of the new instrument came the need for a new style of writing—the classical style. Obviously, the new style of writing was not only evident in keyboard music, but also in the compositions for other instruments. This was at the time the baroque style of writing was beginning to wane or become less popular and a new style was beginning to emerge. As with any style change, though, there were those who resisted the new ideas. Music began to take on the new look and was called *music in the style galant*. Part of the new look was the division of continuous melodic lines into smaller units, indicated by changes in articulation, such as two- and three-note slurs, and staccato, legato and *portato* markings. These appeared in thin-textured settings, using an abundance of only primary chords. It became more and more obvious that the old style was beginning to give way to the new, just like we begin to notice changes in clothes fashions on TV shows and in newspaper ads. The compositions written mainly during the transition time displayed characteristics from both the old and new styles. The textures were somewhat different but they revealed many commonalities. With these ideas in mind, let's investigate some music in that style."

With this kind of introduction, the student will become more interested in playing music in the classical style than if the music is simply thrust upon him without any explanation.

The general texture of pieces in the classical style often presents problems in all aspects of performance controls: mental, aural, rhythmic and physical. The texture commonly includes Alberti bass patterns, more than one voice to a hand, numerous scalar passages, and a variety of changes in articulation in addition to some ornamentation. In order to cope with this type of texture in intermediate level music, students will need much experience learning simpler versions of the style during their elementary level of study.

Carl Czerny's *The Young Pianist,* Opus 823, Book I, offers a wealth of material for these experiences, as is shown in the next four excerpts:

Example No. 172. "Number 9," from *The Young Pianist,* Opus 823, Book I, Czerny.

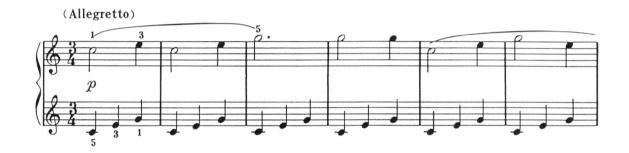

192

Example No. 173. "Number 19," from *The Young Pianist*, Opus 823, Book I, Czerny.

Example No. 174. "Number 26," from *The Young Pianist*, Opus 823, Book I, Czerny.

Example No. 175. "Number 27," from *The Young Pianist*, Opus 823, Book I, Czerny.

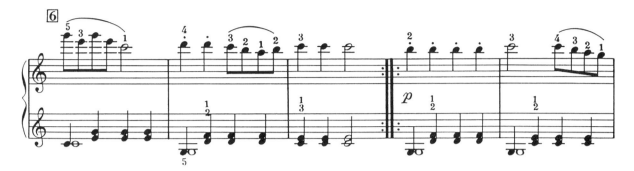

These excerpts as well as those throughout the volume gradually become more complex enabling the student first to experience the texture in very simple settings before a combination of complexities is presented. The complex "No. 27," for example, involves 1) voicing; 2) balance and clarity between the voices in the left hand in addition to balance and clarity between the melody and accompaniment; 3) frequent changes in articulation (staccato and legato); and 4) chord changes in the accompaniment pattern. Experiencing these complexities, sequentially, will prevent a student from becoming disenchanted with the style.

Many piano students learn to read classical style pieces note-by-note, followed by recognizing that some of the notes are marked legato, staccato and *portato*. The student later learns that there are degrees of staccato and legato in addition to learning that attacks and releases must be *heard* rather than just *seen*. This "piecemeal approach" or approach by isolation fosters many problems. Releases are frequently clipped, which result in numerous unwanted accents. Alberti bass patterns are commonly played louder than the melody. Voicing is sometimes ignored, allowing notes to be released in one voice that should have been held out full value. The pedal is depressed without any discretion as opposed to being used very selectively. The wrists tend to "pump out" each individual set of notes. As a result, the practicing of classical style pieces becomes completely unrelated to how the music should sound in performance. These problems can easily be avoided if the student experiences the concepts earlier in simpler settings. In addition to the compositions written during the classical era, there are a number of 20th-century composers writing teaching material in the classical style, as is illustrated in the following example:

Example No. 176. "Sonatina on Three French Folk Tunes," First Movement, from *Alfred's Basic Piano Library*, Lesson Book 5, Palmer, Manus and Lethco.

These experiences will prepare the student for working on the more advanced sonatinas, and later, the sonatas of Haydn, Mozart and Beethoven. As the student attempts the often played Clementi "Sonatina in C Major," she will be ready for the experience instead of finding it to be a time of great frustration. This particular Clementi sonatina does have its pitfalls, but they can be avoided if there has been proper preparation. The major problem lies in the student's inability to perceive and maintain a measure grouping with one primary pulse and one secondary pulse pattern. When the pulse concept is adhered to, the domination of motivic playing is avoided, such as making three downbeats, especially in measures 1, 2, 5, 6, 9 and 11. And this is just in the exposition! When this occurs, the student is perceiving and playing in a rhythm of articulation, not in a metric rhythm. She is perceiving note groupings according to how they are articulated, indicating that she is seeing the individual notes as opposed to hearing how the notes sound within a metered-pulse grouping. Students commonly group some of the pitches *according to directional changes* producing four separate pulse-units in places similar to measures 3 and 7:

Example 177. "Sonatina in C Major," Opus 36, No. 1, First Movement, from *Alfred's Basic Piano Library*, Lesson Book Level 5, Clementi, arranged Palmer, Manus and Lethco.

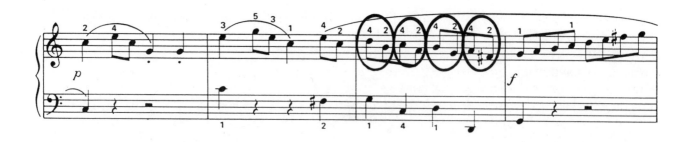

Another sonatina movement to study at this point is the third movement of the same composition. Both of these movements are in the sonata allegro form. (An explanation of this form should be given if it has not been done previously.) The opening movement uses most of the elements found in the form, except the codetta is missing. The third movement is a little more abbreviated with an absence of a real development section. In place of the development, a simple bridge-like passage develops the ideas from the first theme to a small degree. The bridge connects the first theme in the tonic to the second theme in the dominant, concluding with a modulation back to the tonic to begin the recapitulation.

Example No. 178. "Sonatina in C Major," Opus 36, No. 1, Third Movement, from *Alfred's Basic Piano Library*, Recital Book 5, Clementi, arranged Palmer, Manus and Lethco.

*Use the fingering above the notes the 1st time and the fingering below the 2nd time.

The sonata allegro form will be only one of the forms a student will encounter in the classical style. Many second movements will be in a simple three-part form and numerous third movements will be in the rondo form. In more advanced compositions, other forms of writing will be found, such as the variation form, the fantasia and fugal writing. Studying pieces in the sonata allegro form, though, will help enhance a student's chances of successfully learning and performing the other forms and types of music written in the classical style, as all of the music has many commonalities.

Epilogue

Studying to be an excellent piano teacher or an unusually fine performer can be "mind-boggling" if one considers the idea in its totality. Though when either is considered on a step-by-step basis, one realizes that neither is impossible. The secret is to organize a system or process for achieving these goals. In teaching and developing young children, one is aware that success comes more easily to those who have the most innate musical ability, optimal conditions, discipline and desire. Yet thousands of other students will achieve enormous successes in music with the proper training. This is where the teacher becomes important!

There should be an overall plan or system devised for instructing all students: the gifted, the slow learner and for the average student. This requires a flexible philosophy through which each student can be treated individually. Students perceive, think and produce as individuals; therefore, a system for teaching these students must be flexible enough to be adapted to each learner. This can be done as long as the teacher carefully considers music selections or the music curriculum best suited for each student. Every student must be challenged, yet not overwhelmed. This requires constant diagnosis of "where the student is at present and what challenges need to be approached next." Those early years of study set up the foundation for the entire system for learning and performing at the more advanced levels, making the teacher of young or beginning students the most important link in the entire chain of development.

INDEX

200